The Love Rematch

Also by KAY MARIE

The Love Match

The Love Rematch

Confessions

Confessions of a Virgin Sex Columnist!
Confessions of an Undercover Girlfriend!

To Catch a Thief

Hot Pursuit
Stolen Goods
Off the Grid

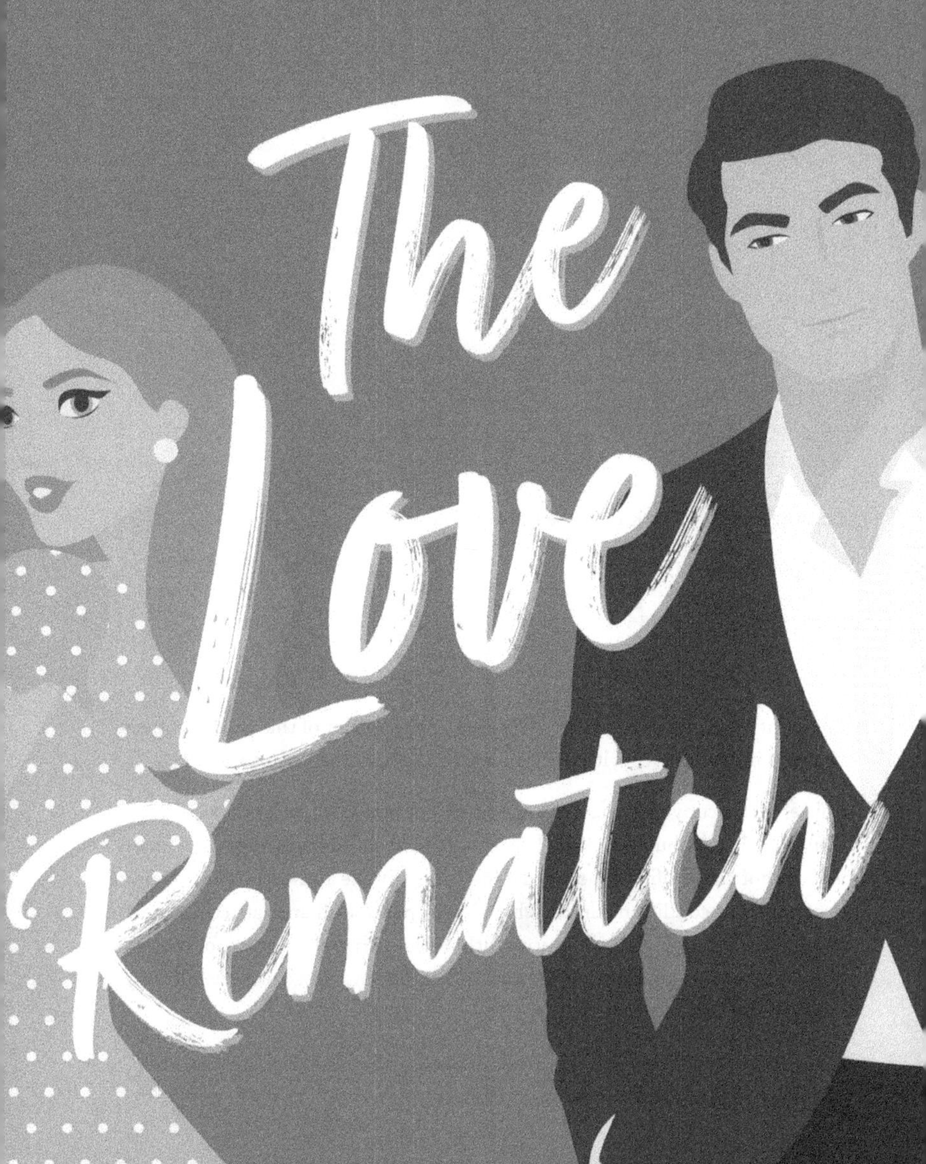

KAY MARIE
When the one that got away
becomes the one you can't escape...
The Love Rematch

*To my family for their unconditional love,
my friends for their overwhelming support,
and my fans for their incredible enthusiasm.
Thank you from the bottom of my heart.*

The Love Rematch

emily

"GET UP RIGHT NOW and turn on channel four."

Emily groans and pulls her vibrant floral duvet over her head. Bright colors are usually her thing, but right now, all she wants is darkness. What time is it? What day is it? And why on earth is her pillow yelling at her?

"Leave me alone," she grumbles.

"Em! Get up!"

"Sam?" She recognizes her twin sister's voice, but it can't be. Sam lives eight hundred miles away in New York City. "What are you doing in Georgia? How did you get into my apartment?"

"Good lord, if I was in Georgia, don't you think I'd be strangling you right about now? I called on the phone. You answered. So get your ass out of bed and turn on channel four before you miss it."

"Miss what?" Emily feels for her phone on the mattress. She doesn't even remember taking it off the nightstand.

"Miss Mom."

"Mom?"

"On channel four."

"On channel four?"

"Em!"

"I'm going. I'm going."

Taking the Band-Aid approach, Emily throws off her covers in one dramatic swoop. *Cold. Cold. Cold.* She rolls from her bed and half falls into the closet to snatch her hot-pink robe. A morning person, she is not. Especially pre-coffee. It's almost inhumane that her sister called this early. Can't Sam sense this pounding headache? Aren't they supposed to have twin telepathy or something?

Emily stayed up way too late the night before getting caught up on orders for Emily Ann Designs, her small—but growing!—jewelry label focusing on fiercely feminine designs, her own personal mantra. After all, knights in shining armor are overrated. All a woman needs to take on the world is a pair of killer earrings and a ring with enough carats to cut—the girlier, the better. But working all day at her mother's flower shop, plus most weekends during the always insane wedding season, leaves little time for her own business. About once every two weeks she has to pull an all-nighter creating, packaging, and shipping her Etsy orders. Not that she's complaining, of course. The more orders she gets, the more money she can save, and hopefully, the sooner she'll be able to branch out full-time. Besides, her late nights are the perfect excuse to binge-watch old seasons of *The Love Match*.

Yes, that's right.

The Love Match.

Sure, the dating show is an overly manufactured fairy tale

that ends in heartbreak nine times out of ten, but she loves love. And seeing as she's a struggling entrepreneur with no time to breathe let alone date, it's the closest she's coming to romance anytime soon.

No regrets.

Besides, there's something morbidly fascinating about watching the lead kick suitors off one by one with the particularly brutal yet catchy send-off, *I'm sorry, but you're not my perfect match.* At least in the real world, people offer an excuse. *It's not you, it's me. We want different things in life. I'm in love with someone else.* Whatever it is, it's something. But simply telling someone to their face, *Sorry, but you're not it?* Utterly savage.

"Hello? Em?" Sam's tone hardens. "Did you stop to make coffee?"

Emily pauses with her finger poised over her Keurig. "Maybe..."

"There's no time! Turn on channel four!"

"All right, all right."

She presses the button anyway and winces at the telltale hiss. Sam snorts through the phone, but doesn't say anything as the sound of voices fills the room. Emily clicks a few times until channel four blinks to life, and there in the crowd gathered outside the New York City studio is her mother, Tina Peters. She's wearing a salmon cable-knit sweater, dark-wash jeans, a tan leather belt, and an adorable puffy white vest Emily fully intends to steal, but it's the sight of the colorful beaded headband that brings a smile to her face. The piece is an Emily Ann original. Her mother is nothing if not her number-one fan.

"I can't believe Mom's on *Wake Up, America!*"

"Em—"

"This is her dream!"

"Em—"

"Did you know she was going?"

"Em!"

"What? How cool is— *Oh my god.*"

"There it is."

"What is she holding?"

"You have eyes."

"WHAT IS SHE HOLDING?"

Emily's mouth drops open in horror as the camera angle shifts and brings her mother even closer into focus, thereby enlarging the puzzle-piece-shaped monstrosity in her arms. Glitter. Ribbons. Gemstones. The poster is a three-year-old's wildest dream. It practically screams *Bedazzlers Anonymous.* And smack-dab in the center is Emily's face along with the phrase *Emily Ann needs a man! #EmsthePerfectMatch* written in iridescent silver Sharpie. Every time her mother breathes, the words catch the light with a mocking twinkle.

"Oh my god, Sam."

"I know."

"Did she tell you she was doing this?"

"Obviously not."

"It's like a freaking billboard. How did you not— Wait. Is that a photo of *you*?" Emily studies the auburn waves and honey-tinted irises staring at her from the center of the poster. It's the same heart-shaped face, plump lips, and doe eyes she sees in the mirror every morning, yet not. "DID YOU GIVE HER THE PHOTO?"

"Stop yelling at me. No."

"Sam."

"Do you really think I would have woken you up to watch this if I had supplied the photo? I value my life, thank you very much."

"What about Dad? Where's Dad?" Emily scans the crowd for a glimpse of her father, Callum Peters, his bright red hair usually easy to spot.

"He got boxed out a few minutes ago," Sam explains. "Middle-aged women are vicious. If you look two back and one over, you can see the top of his Falcons hat."

"That traitor."

"Come on. We both know Mom wears the pants in— Oh no."

"What are they doing? Sam, they're walking over to her. What are they doing? Sam. Sam!"

"I, um, I…"

The phone goes silent as the two hosts of *Wake Up, America!* stop next to their mother.

"That's quite a sign," Eden Edwards says with a perfectly rehearsed chuckle before turning her multimillion-dollar smile to the camera, as if letting the rest of the country in on the joke.

Quite a sign, Emily thinks. *QUITE A SIGN!*

"Thank you," her mother says into the offered microphone. To every other viewer, she probably looks like a sweet middle-aged woman. But Emily has seen that self-satisfied smirk one too many times. Her mom is practically diabolical when it comes to meddling. Emily blames her job. Spending so much time designing floral arrangements for engaged couples in love has left her with an almost unholy desire to see her own daughters married off. And unfortunately for her, neither Emily nor Sam is very obliging. "This is my daughter Emily. Isn't she beautiful?"

Actually, that's your daughter Sam, Emily silently corrects. *You know, the one whose life you're not currently blasting to smithereens!*

"She is," Eden comments sweetly.

For a brief, shining moment, Emily thinks that's the end of it—her mother's one gleaming taste of morning-show spotlight—until the co-host, Matthew Starhan, starts reading the poster aloud. His voice is crisp and clear in the microphone.

"*Emily Ann needs a man.* Hey, that rhymes! *Emily Ann needs a man. Emily Ann needs a man!*" He proceeds to do a little mock cheer with imaginary pom-poms, and the entire crowd joins in. Damn that perfectly charming former NFL player. Damn him straight to hell! "*Emily Ann needs a man. Emily Ann needs a man.* I like that."

Her mother leans toward the microphone, obviously pleased with herself. "It took me a while to come up with."

Emily growls at her television screen. "Is this really happening, Sam? Or am I still asleep in my bed, having a horrible, horrible nightmare that the co-host of a show watched by millions of people every morning just started a chant about my nonexistent love life?"

"No." Sam doesn't even have the decency to stifle her snort. "This is really happening."

"I'm going to kill you. No, first I'm going to kill Mom. And then I'm going to kill you."

"Quiet. I want to listen. It isn't every day your sister gets absolutely massacred on live TV."

"Sam—"

"Shh!"

"Hashtag Em's the perfect match," Matthew continues reading. "Like the show? *The Love Match*?"

"Yes," her mother says as a positively gleeful twinkle lights her eyes. She's about to go in for the kill. "I'm trying to nominate my daughter to be the new lead."

"Well, I have to admire your tenacity, but last season's runner-up, Ashleigh Bromberger, is the new lead. We had her on our show last month."

"Oh, she *was* the lead..." Her mother trails off with a mysterious air, and both hosts lean in with curious expressions. "But I have it on good authority that she won't be the lead for long."

"Really?" Eden jokes, then glances quickly off screen as if to check how long before the next commercial break.

But Matthew's all in. That little gossip. "What have you heard?"

"That she and Brad had a little too much fun in the dream suite, and her little souvenir is starting to show. So, I highly doubt thirty men will want to compete for her heart. But my Emily, on the other hand—"

Chaos erupts, drowning her mother out. Every single woman in the audience starts talking at once—and Emily suspects every single viewer at home has too, as her sister says into the phone, "Holy shit, is that true?"

Sam's a lowly analyst at an investment banking firm with hardly enough time to wipe her butt, let alone watch television, but *The Love Match* has a hold on all the women in the Peters family.

Emily momentarily forgets about her mortification playing out on live TV. "Oh my god, is it? I *knew* they had a weird vibe on 'After the Final Puzzle Piece', but a baby?"

"I think this is a *Love Match* first."

"And Mom had the scoop!"

"How?!" they blurt in unison.

"Um, uh, we need to—yeah, commercial break!" Eden Edwards says into the camera, but not fast enough.

In a show of herculean strength, their mother snatches the microphone from an unsuspecting Matthew's hand. "You can find her on Instagram, at EmilyAnnDesigns! Emily Ann needs a man! Hashtag Em's the perfect ma—"

The screen switches to a car ad.

Emily shuts the TV off. "What just happened?"

"Our mother is either a marketing genius or completely insane, and I'm not sure which."

"Marketing genius?"

"She got your Instagram handle on live television, tied it to a massive scandal, and assigned you a hashtag. Genius. On the other hand...she's certifiable. And I say that with love."

Emily plops onto her vintage mustard couch, hugs a colorful pom-pom pillow to her chest, and buries her face between her knees in an attempt to calm her racing pulse. Sam's right. That could have been great publicity, which she sorely needs if she's ever going to make her dream career a reality. And yet...

Emily's heart sinks. "Sam."

"What?"

"I…"

She sits up and runs her palm over the velvet cushion, watching the yellow hue shift as the fibers catch different angles of the light. It's the reason she fell in love with this couch in the first place. It reminded her of the vanity stool she used to sit on for hours in her grandmother's house, trying on all her costume jewelry. Emily had been meticulous, combing through clip-ons and faux pearls, each design holding a secret meaning, each presenting a different message to the world. Entire mornings went by while she looked in the mirror, deciding who she wanted to be that day.

Sam had never understood.

Emily can picture her sister now, flitting in and out of the reflection with a scarf thrown dramatically around her neck and a brush before her lips like a microphone while she belted out Lady Gaga without a care in the world. But that was Sam. Loud. Boisterous. Born to be the center of attention. Emily had always been different—the quiet twin, the introspective one. They were like two sides of the same coin.

"Why me?" she finally whispers into the phone. "I mean, I know I still live in our hometown, and sure, when I have a moment to stop and think about it and actually breathe, I might be a bit lonely. I haven't gone on a date in I don't even know how long. But I'm focusing on trying to build my business. Mom knows that. I mean, am I really this…pathetic? I know she worries, especially about me, after everything, but surely I'm not in such desperate territory that Mom had to do, well, *that*? And what about you! You're—"

"I'm what?"

Emily rolls her eyes at the snark in her sister's tone and

flattens her palm against the cushion with a sigh. "You're alone, too."

"I went on a date last night, thank you very much."

"And what happened?"

"I got mine and then I sent him home."

Despite herself, Emily smiles.

"Em?"

"Yeah."

"Don't take it personally. Mom's just...Mom. She wants what's best for us. And honestly, if she had thought of a witty catchphrase that rhymed with *Samantha*, it would have been my name on that board—along with my photo. You know the woman is wedding-crazed."

Emily snorts and relaxes into the plush velvet. Her sister has a way of making everything seem better. "Can she really not tell us apart?"

"We both know I'm more photogenic."

"We're identical."

"Not to the camera." Sam's grin is somehow audible.

Emily rolls her eyes, ready to retort before her phone buzzes. "Wait, I—"

It buzzes again.

And again.

And again.

The vibrations continue as she switches her sister's call to speaker and frowns down at the screen. Messages pour in, one after another after another. Some of the names belong to people she hasn't spoken to in a decade.

"Sam. Something's happening."

"Oh shit."

"What shit?"

"Shit shit."

"Shit shit what?"

Buzz. Buzz. Buzz. Emily doesn't know whether to throw her phone across the room or unlock it.

"Shit. Shit. Shit."

"Sam!"

"Don't go on Twitter."

Emily immediately opens Twitter. "Shit!"

"You're trending."

"I'm trending."

"Don't click—"

Too late, Emily thinks as she scans the feed for *#EmsthePerfectMatch.*

EMILY ANN NEEDS A MAN! How about thirty? DO IT! #EmsthePerfectMatch

Wow—she has the BEST mom in the world!!! I wish my mom would start a national scandal for me!! #EmsthePerfectMatch

Mortified. Mortified. Mortified. I have actual secondhand trauma for this girl. Yikes. #EmsthePerfectMatch for a lifetime of therapy.

I KNEW ASHLEIGH WAS PREGNANT! #EmsthePerfectMatch

This chick has got to be the biggest loser in America. Do you really want to watch an entire season of this mess?? How desperate can you get? #EmsthePerfectMatch #NOT

She closes the app...and opens Instagram.

"Oh my god, Sam. I have a thousand missed notifications. Wait—fifteen hundred. No, two thousand."

The number climbs higher and higher and higher.

What is happening?

Emily closes Instagram and opens her Etsy shop. Fifty new orders have been placed in the last five minutes. Some of her items are sold out!

What in the actual hell is happening?

"Em. I think this is really happening. I mean, this might *really* be happening. Listen to this. *I stalked her on Instagram—she's definitely* Love Match *material! Wow, her earrings are to die for! Did anyone else see the bangles in her shop? Love! Emily Ann does need a man! Beautiful and talented. How is she single?*"

"I just saw one that said I'm the most pathetic person on the planet. Don't believe everything you read."

"Well—what about this? Ashleigh Bromberger released a statement. She's pregnant."

Emily gasps.

Sam continues, talking in a way that makes it clear she's skimming while she speaks. "She didn't know how to tell people so she'd been keeping it to herself. Yada yada. But she's really pregnant. And she's off the show."

"So? They'll find another girl from last season."

"What if they don't? What if they find you instead?"

"Sam..."

Emily's voice is small. The bright pops of color in her living room normally provide a cheerful source of comfort, but right now, they're garish. The rainbow pillows mock. The floral paintings stare. The gold lamps jeer. Warmth creeps up her neck as her breath quickens. She applies pressure to her temples with her free hand, while in the back of her mind, Matthew Starhan and a horde of middle-aged women are still chanting, *Emily Ann needs a man. Emily Ann needs a man.*

"I can't do this, Sam," she whispers.

"Why not? Think of what it would do for your brand, for your business! Exposure to millions of people? You'll never get another opportunity like this."

"I know, I know. But I just— I just can't."

Sam pauses on the other end of the line. Her steady breathing is the only sign she's still there, until her voice cuts through the bullshit. "Is this about Jake?"

Even after all these years, the sound of his name strikes like a bullet straight to Emily's heart. "No."

"It is." Sam scoffs. "It's about Jake. It's *always* about Jake. I can't believe you right now."

"It's not about him. It's about— You *know* what it's about."

"Keep telling yourself that," Sam derides.

"I'm being—"

"Listen to me. He left you. He left you without taking a single glance back. Don't even think about throwing away this opportunity because you're still holding on to some dream you had back in high school."

"That's not—"

"If they call you, if they approach you about doing the show, you need to say yes, if for no other reason than it will give you thirty great chances to finally get over your ex."

"Would you listen to me for a second?" Emily snaps. No one can comfort her quite like her sister, and no one can annoy her so much either. She takes a deep breath. Calm. Collected. Unbothered. "I'm not *under* him."

"But you want to be," Sam states, not like an accusation

but like a fact. The words land heavily, an anchor in her gut. "And therein lies the problem."

The phone goes dead. Emily stares at the blank screen, denial a plug in her throat.

It's not about that, she wants to scream. *It's not!*

But is it?

Her phone lights up with another incoming message, saving her from answering. Then another. And another.

Buzz. Buzz. Buzz.

She stuffs it between the couch cushions.

Her butt vibrates.

Buzz. Buzz. Buzz.

She throws the stupid thing at her hot-pink armchair. It ricochets off the polka-dot pillow and lands on the floor with a *thud.*

Buzz. Buzz. Buzz.

"Damn it!" Emily screams and stomps across the room. With a triumphant shriek, she turns the damn thing off. But in her head, she still hears it, like a gnat she can't escape.

Buzz. Buzz. Buzz.

CHAPTER TWO

THE MASSIVE SCREEN at the end of the conference table flickers to life, revealing the vast blue of the Pacific Ocean and…a protruding hairy navel. Jake winces and drops his head into his palm. The creator and executive producer of *The Love Match*, Nick Weiss, is a lawsuit waiting to happen. He's a genius in the realm of reality television, which almost by necessity means he's also the personification of athlete's foot as a person—disgusting, embarrassing, known to cause burning, and obnoxiously hard to remove. Jake's been trying to escape the man for nearly four years to no avail.

"Damn computer." Nick's deep voice fills the room. The camera angle shifts, dropping to a precariously knotted towel before scanning all the way up Nick's bare, unfit chest to settle on his face, which is puffed with filler, frozen from Botox, and fake-tanned enough to be a cautionary tale.

Jake almost prefers the hairy navel.

"I assume you all saw the update from Little Miss Knocked-Up this morning?" Nick says as he settles into his pool lounger. He does seventy-five percent of his business from the deck of his thirty-million-dollar Malibu mansion. That asshole. "And if you haven't, then what the hell are you doing here?"

Everyone around the table nods and Jake hastily joins in. He flew in on the red-eye this morning after two weeks of shooting intro footage for the male suitors, then came straight to the office—he barely knows what his name is, let alone what Nick's talking about. But *fake it till you make it* is practically gospel in this town.

"Good," Nick says, then leans so close Jake can almost smell his putrid, eggy breath through the screen. "What the FUCK are we going to do?"

"It's not that bad," Trish Levithan, their other executive producer, says with a tired voice. They have a nickname for her on set—the Ice Queen. Partially due to her white-blonde hair always pulled back into a severe bun plus her sharp, inscrutable features, and partially due to her heartless, albeit brilliant, ability to break even the toughest contestant into a sniveling mess of emotions. If there's anyone allowed to be exhausted by Nick, it's her. The two of them have been together since the first season of *The Love Match*, in more ways than one if the rumors are true.

And they are.

Last season, Jake caught the two of them going at it like bunnies behind the mansion. He thought it was a rogue contestant and took a camera crew out there. If he were as cutthroat as some of his coworkers, he would have sold the footage to TMZ for a pretty penny, but Hollywood hasn't completely broken his moral code...yet. Still, he didn't say no when they offered him the promotion. Meet *The Love Match*'s newest field producer. That title is the only reason he's in this room right now, along with a handful of other senior crew.

To his left is Nina Chen, his co-field producer and the rebellious counterpart to Jake's all-American pretty boy. He has dark brown waves, baby blues, and the build of a natural-born athlete, though in reality he avoided all sports until he moved to California and began surfing. While Nina has half of her stick-straight black hair buzzed to the scalp, a dark strip of liner across her monolid eyes, an endless supply of leather jackets, and a pair of well-worn biker boots to provide an extra few inches to her meager height. She's intimidating, but with an open smile that cajoles everyone into believing she's their best friend. It's a lethal combo that's made her incredible at this job, which she's already held for six long years and twelve successful seasons.

Next to Nina sits Fred Jones, their director. He's a former weight lifter who could double as their bodyguard, but behind his bulging muscles, he's the sweetest person in the entire crew. A jar of homemade chin-chin rests in the center of the table, a gift his wife often supplies during filming. It's amazing what those little Nigerian fried cookies do for morale.

Across from Nina and Fred are Craig Bolander and Eva Chase, the story producers who compile the raw footage into workable episodic storylines. They don't get out much, and they look it. Both a little pale, both a little pudgy, both a little '90s film geek in their attire. Eva's a quintessential mousy brunette, and Craig's balding with glasses.

And at the far side of the table sit the suits. Two network

execs and a lawyer. Or is it two lawyers and a network exec? Honestly, Jake has a hard time keeping them straight. But he does know one thing—their presence spells disaster.

What the hell did I miss?

"Not that bad?" Nick retorts, cutting Trish off. "Not that bad! We have thirty suitors headed to set next week, an entire show to produce in the next two months, and no female lead! How much worse can it get?"

"Well," Nina offers, "we—"

"That was rhetorical."

"It was bound to get out eventually." Trish steps in. "We've been working on a plan—"

"Yeah, well, that plan just took a big, steaming shit on all of our faces. Say goodbye to an on-air pregnancy test, followed by a surprise visit from Brad and a romantic proposal under the stars. We've lost control of the storyline—and I fucking *hate* losing control of the storyline! Now the whole goddamn world knows she's pregnant, and anything we do will look like a hack job. She's off the show—I don't even want to mention her name. I mean, for fuck's sake! We only learned about the pregnancy last week at her medical exam. How the hell did this random woman from bumfuck USA figure it out?"

The vein in the middle of Nick's forehead pulses, an effect made all the more terrifying by the fact that nothing else on the upper part of his face can move.

Random woman? Jake wonders.

"Is one of you the leak?"

"Don't be ridiculous," Trish says.

"Maybe you got a little loose with that sidepiece you've been banging at the gym," Nick continues, though as far as

Jake knows, Nick's the only person in the meeting who has any side-anythings. "And she told her friend, who told her friend, who told her mom, who told her knitting club, who told the whole fucking world?"

In a shocking display of emotion, Trish sighs and closes her eyes.

"None of us said anything," Nina cuts in, while everyone else hastily concurs.

Again, Jake finds himself agreeing to something with less than a hundred percent honesty. Two nights ago, when his mom melted down on the phone—something about grandbabies and always being alone and a bunch of other things Jake blocked out—he caved and gave her the one sliver of information that would make the tirade stop. A bit of juicy gossip about her favorite show. But his mom knows better than to say anything to anyone else.

Doesn't she?

"There was that reddit post a few days ago," Fred says, ever the peacekeeper. "Someone got a photo of Ashleigh at the beach and her bikini left little to the imagination."

Thank you, Fred.

"We quickly shut it down with some comments about body-shaming," Nina adds. "It didn't gain much traction, but if mommy dearest saw it..."

Mommy dearest?

Jake's lost again.

"That's all well and good," one of the suits intervenes. "But we have a bigger problem—the new season starts filming in a week. It's too expensive to adjust the schedule, and this franchise is too big to risk missing a season. We need a new lead, yesterday, and we have permission from the higher-ups to make it happen."

"Oh, well, if you have their permission," Nick comments under his breath, but right into the microphone so everyone can hear. He's the creator of the show, and like most rich people in Hollywood, he doesn't like being reminded that there are people even more powerful than him. For the most part, the network gives Nick free rein, but with a mounting disaster like this? Jake isn't surprised they're stepping in.

"We sent a list to the president last week, as soon as we found out about Ashleigh's pregnancy," Trish says. "The two runners-up, Tiffany and Lauren, have already been announced for the new season of *The Love Match in Mexico*, so they're out. And we had to paint Sarah as the villain because of that fight between her and Ashleigh, so she's out. But we've still got other Laurynne, teacher Jen, and virgin Mandy as options. The virgin thing might be a little stale, but she did poll well, better than Laurynne after that whole group date fiasco."

Oh god.

Jake stifles his snort. Four of the girls decided to turn a group date photoshoot at the beach into a skinny-dipping session. It could have played well if they hadn't gone full mean girl, calling Mandy a *prude*, a *killjoy*, and worse yet, a *priss* in their interviews. The conservative viewers backed Mandy for sticking to her morals, and the feminine viewers scorned the girls for the name-calling. It was television gold— and though the public would never know it, karma had done its job. All four girls ended up getting sand stuck in a truly unfortunate place from the rough surf. They complained about the burning for days, and one girl even got sent home because her infection needed medical attention.

Ah, the joys of reality television.

"We don't want any of them," the suit says.

Trish balks. "But—"

"We want *her*."

"*Her* her?" Trish asks.

"*Wake Up, America!*, her?" Nick slams his fists on the table and his camera nearly topples. "So desperate she needs her mom to find her a boyfriend, her? Hasn't been tested by the viewership or undergone any psych evaluations, her?"

The suit shrugs. "That's who they want."

Jake briefly wonders if he can pull out his phone and open Twitter without anyone noticing. What a day to accidentally fall asleep in the cab!

"She's trending number one across the country. She's got the look, and more importantly, she's got a story. The mom angle has never been done before. We haven't had an unaffiliated lead since season one. The higher-ups want to take the momentum and run. The producers at *Wake Up, America!* already agreed to bring the mom back for a segment next week to pimp the new season. We'll be pushing our two best shows at once. It'll be big for ratings. And—"

"They don't give a shit what any of us think?" Nick fires.

The suit shoots a tired look in his direction. "No."

"Well, fuck me."

"No, thank you," Nina mutters under her breath.

Jake fights a grin.

"Pull up her photo," Trish says, tone inscrutable.

Nick's fuming face cuts to half the size as Fred splits the

screen. A blurred image fills the blank space, becoming clearer and clearer by the second, until—

"FUCK!"

Every head in the room swivels toward Jake, as if his coworkers have only just remembered he's there.

Trish speaks into the silence. "Something you want to share?"

"I, uh… I—" His brain short-circuits. Actually, scratch that. His brain implodes, blown apart by the nuclear explosion that is the first sight of her face in seven years. His gaze goes straight to her lips, plump and bow-shaped. Those lips still haunt his dreams. Hell—those lips still haunt his entire goddamn life. No other woman's can measure up. And when he closes his eyes, they're there, laughing, smiling…slightly parted and shaped in the perfect O as her nails dig into his back.

Fuck.

"Jake? Earth to Jake?"

He keeps staring, and staring, and staring.

It's not her.

Jake narrows his eyes, studying the slope of her Cupid's bow and the curls at the corners of her mouth. He doesn't know how he's always been able to tell them apart when no one else ever could, except to say that for him, there's only ever been one Emily Peters, and this isn't her.

He takes his first breath in what feels like hours.

It's Sam.

It's not her. It's Sam.

"Jake!"

He snaps back to life. "Yeah?"

"What the hell happened?" Nina asks.

"Sorry, I—" His gaze drops to his Apple watch and he lifts his wrist. "I got a message from home I wasn't expecting, but I'll deal with it later. I'm good."

"You sure?" Trish asks.

"Yeah, I'm sure."

She stares at him for a moment too long. They all do, silently questioning if he's really ready to be in this room.

He is.

Focus, asshole. Focus. It's just Sam. She hates you, but what else is new. You can deal with her for six weeks. To keep this job, to prove your worth, you'll do whatever it takes.

He's been waiting for an opportunity like this ever since he stepped foot in this town. Longer, if he's being honest. Ever since he saw *Finding Nemo* at five years old and realized what a father-son relationship was supposed to be. Ever since he got lost in superheroes, Jedi warriors, and suave spies proving again and again that good triumphed over evil. Ever since he discovered outcasts, geeks, and other damaged characters like him struggling to find their place in the world. Movies had always been his escape, his lifeline. And after so long, he's finally landed a position with some sort of weight, some sort of meaning—a stepping stone to something more.

He's not about to fuck it up over Sam.

"Nina, what's her story?" Trish finally asks. Jake breathes a little freer when the boss shifts her gaze to his counterpart.

"I wasn't able to find much yet, but she grew up in Georgia," Nina says. Hearing the name of that state makes his stomach flip. "Then she lived in New York City for a bit. She's got what appears to be an identical twin sister—don't even say it, Nick—and they run some sort of jewelry or fashion accessory line together. I need to look into it more. Her father is a local police chief, which will go over well with our conservative viewership, and you all know her mother, who I believe owns a flower shop. That's about it. No dark secrets I could find—yet."

"There are no dark secrets," one of the suits says. "We ran a background check this morning. Here's what we found."

The man slides a folder across the table to Trish, who starts mumbling as she shifts through it.

Jake tunes them out. He already knows more about Samantha Peters than he needs to, and he's not particularly interested in learning anything more. Her photo, her memory, her name—they've already brought too much to the surface, and some things are better left buried.

Why is this happening?

His mind races.

Pieces form, twist, start to fit together. His coworkers keep mentioning her mom. And *Wake Up, America!* And her mom. And—

You have GOT to be kidding me.

Jake sucks in a breath.

His mom.

His mom is the reason this is happening.

I'm the leak.

I'm the fucking leak!

Nick's theory wasn't that far off. Jake told his mother about Ashleigh's pregnancy. And she told Mrs. Peters—probably during a garden-club meeting. And Mrs. Peters then proceeded to tell the entire world.

Did they co-conspire to get Sam on the show?

Is his own mother working against him?

What the hell, Mom!

"I said, are you good with that, Jake?"

He blinks twice, unable to figure out what he's missed, and goes with the safe bet. "Of course, Trish."

"Good. You'll continue handling the men. Nina, you'll start working on her profile, wardrobe, and storyline. Fred, see if we can adjust one or two of the dates to focus on her fashion design background."

Jake frowns.

Sam...and a fashion design background?

That doesn't—

She's not—

"Charles." Trish turns to one of the suits. "Tell the network we're on board with the plan, and have Legal send over the paperwork. Nick, stop pouting."

"I'm not—"

"And I'll track down our new lead," Trish continues over his protest. Then she glances at the screen and folds her arms. "Get ready, Emily Peters. I'm about to change your life."

Jake flinches so hard he may as well have been shot.

Everyone else stands.

Everyone else moves.

He sits there bleeding out and numb.

Nina is the last to leave the table. She tosses him a confused look when she finally stands. As she starts to step out of reach, he grabs her forearm. "What name did Trish say?"

"Honestly, Jake." She tries to shake him off. "Pull yourself together."

He tightens his grip. "What name?"

"Emily Peters. The same name that's been trending on Twitter for about six hours, and I suggest you commit it to memory because you'll be hearing it a lot for the next six weeks if this girl isn't a total idiot and accepts the platinum-encrusted spoon we're about to hand-feed her with. I don't know what family emergency you've got going on, and I'm sorry if it's overwhelming, but you're in the big leagues now, Jake. If you can't keep up, Trish and Nick won't hesitate to replace you with someone who can. And I say that as your friend, okay? Now, let me go."

He drops her arm as if it's on fire. "Sorry, yeah. Sorry."

Nina pats his back on her way out. The second the door closes, he rips his phone out of his pocket and opens Twitter.

#EmsthePerfectMatch

#EmilyAnnNeedsaMan

#EmilysMom

#EmilyAnnSUCKS

#NOTmyperfectmatch

#EmilyforPresident

Jake throws his phone across the room. For a second time that morning, he screams, "FUCK!"

emily

WHO IS *this sultry woman and how the heck did she get here?* Emily asks, looking in the mirror. She's unable to recognize herself beneath the camera-ready makeup and the elaborate updo, unable to find the soul hiding behind those dramatic smoky eyes.

It's like a twisted version of the game she used to play at her grandmother's vanity, trying on all different sorts of jewelry, acting out different characters in her mind. Back then, she knew exactly who she was. It was the outward message she wasn't sure how to convey. Now, the woman reflected before her seems confident, alluring, and ready to take on the world. Inside, though, she's a jumbled mess of nerves—no clue how she's supposed to act, what she's supposed to say, or if she'll be able to get through the next six weeks with her sanity intact.

Because it happened.

She's the new lead of *The Love Match*.

She's here, somewhere off the coast of California, in the

guest cottage of the official mansion, about to start filming. And still, for the life of her, she can't quite figure out how.

The past week was a blur. Not even twelve hours after her mother's mortifying fifteen minutes of fame, the call came in. Someone named Trish Levithan saying she was about to change Emily's world. If not for Sam's voice in the back of her mind, she would have said no. She wanted to say no. Instead, in a horrible bout of word vomit, she said yes.

Why. Why. Why.

The next day, she was on a flight to California to begin what's been the quickest seven days of her life. There was a physical examination, a psychological evaluation, a makeover, a wardrobe consultation, a manicure, a pedicure, and about a thousand questionnaires. Plus she had interviews on no less than five podcasts, meetings with reporters, and even a small segment for *Wake Up, America!* with her mom—her performance as a grateful, not-at-all-mad, and doting daughter could have earned her an Oscar.

She's been poked, prodded, hardly given a single moment to herself. Yet still, somehow, whenever she's had a spare second to think, there's only been one thing on her mind.

Or one person, rather.

Jake.

Emily groans and closes her eyes, unable to look at her reflection without seeing her sister's mocking expression staring back. Sam's accusation plays on repeat in the back of her mind.

It's about Jake. It's always about Jake.

It isn't.

It's not.

But, UGH, right now it is. Because Los Angeles is the city he left her for. Being here and knowing he's close has her on edge. Being around cameras again, on sets with equipment and crew, hearing the way these people talk, it's brought her right back to high school, his lens always trained on her face, his lips moving passionately, speaking a mile a minute about this upcoming director or that new indie film. Even now, Emily can't stop her thoughts from shifting to him.

Has he seen all this media frenzy?

Will he be watching?

What will he think?

She tells herself it doesn't matter—that's he's in the past and she's moved on. Still, the hairs at the back of her neck rise, as if he's standing right there, so close she can feel his warm breath on her skin. In two hours, she's going to meet thirty very single and very attractive men who will be fighting for her on national television, yet all she's doing is obsessing over the one man who decided he didn't want her.

God, I hate myself.

"So what do you think?" Nina, her new handler, asks, pulling Emily back into the present. The makeup artist left a few minutes ago, leaving the two of them alone. Despite the headset draped around her neck and the clipboard at her side, all of Nina's focus is securely on Emily. It's overwhelming. The producer points to the dress rack. "The black one, the navy one, the nude one, or the red one?"

"I, um..." Emily licks her lips. This is the first outfit millions of people across the United States will see her wearing. It's what they'll base all their first impressions on. It's going to set the stage for the entire season. Most importantly, it's the last decision she has left to make before all of this becomes real—which means it's her last chance to stall.

"It's just a dress," Nina comments softly.

Emily nods.

They both know it's not just a dress. But she appreciates the warmth in the producer's tone, and the attempt at friendly affection, even if she isn't sure she can trust it.

"Okay," Nina says, trying a different angle. She pads across the room in her worn biker boots and slips off her leather jacket, then lifts the black dress. The satin skirt pools against the ivory rug as she holds the thin spaghetti straps to her shoulders. "It's black. It's elegant. It's maybe a bit boring, but sophistication never goes out of style. Square neck. Princess cut. You're a confident, classy woman."

Emily frowns, unsure.

Nina reaches for the navy gown. It's too short to hit the floor, even on the producer's smaller frame, and hangs in asymmetrical lines. "Navy usually says *schoolteacher*, but the one shoulder and the asymmetrical skirt give this some edge. It's slinky. A little blingy. You're a mystery. You're keeping secrets. The viewers should stay on their toes, and the men too."

Emily swallows and shifts her feet.

It hits a little too close to home.

"No?" Nina puts it back and grabs the red one. Even on the hanger, the plunging neckline and precariously high slit clearly leave little to the imagination. "Sex kitten. Bombshell. A redhead who isn't afraid to wear red? You're bold and daring and ready to give the men the challenge they've been waiting for."

There's no way she's wearing that. "Pass."

"I figured." Nina hangs the red dress back up and lowers her voice. "Between you and me, that was my least favorite option. Red never goes over well on the first night, but Nick insisted, so..." She rolls her eyes and then smiles when her gaze settles on the final dress. "The last option is this beauty."

Nina lifts the nude dress from the rack. It glistens in the light. Every inch is studded with crystals, giving off an old-Hollywood vibe Emily is unable to resist. As part of her contract, she made the network agree to let her style her own accessories, and the second she sees it, she already knows what earrings she would choose—two studs made from chaotic nests of gold wire with cubic zirconia teardrops hanging below each one. They aren't available in her shop. They're a pair she made for herself, the first pieces she was able to design after everything went down with Jake, but it doesn't even matter. She'll have the rest of the season to promote her brand.

"High neck," Nina continues. "Low back. It's your classic *business in the front, party in the rear*. The nude color will immediately give all the men dirty thoughts, but the cut is conservative enough not to alienate the viewers. It's my personal favorite. It says, *Yes, my mother shamed the entire country into helping me find a boyfriend, but no, she didn't need to. I'm here and I'm hot and you all better watch out. I'm keeping my cards close, and oh, by the way, I have a great ass*, which"—Nina glances pointedly south—"you do."

Emily forces a laugh. "Thanks."

"So, which will it be?"

She stares at the rack, seeing the dresses, yet not really seeing them. Her indecision isn't about an outfit. She already knows which dress to choose. It's about the people who will see her in that dress, all ten million of them, judging her, dissecting her every comment, wondering how she's single and what's wrong with her and what exactly she's hiding. People with secrets aren't supposed to go on reality television —isn't that what everyone says? And yet...

Emily swallows.

How is this my life?

"I think I want...air."

Emily shoves away from the vanity, throws the nearest window open, and sticks her head outside.

Breathe. Just breathe.

I can do this.

Think about my business. Think about my dreams. Think about Emily Ann Designs in every mall across America. Hell, in Europe too. The globe! That can be real. All I need to do is stick it out for six weeks. Six measly weeks! And, added bonus, I get to make out with thirty hot men.

Everything will be fine.

Everything will be amazing.

The fresh, salty air is helping. She's on the other side of the country, but it almost smells like home. Not the lowcountry marshes or the misty morning dew, but the beach. Waves crash against a distant shore, their steady drum calming. She closes her eyes.

One. Two. Three.

One. Two. Three.

One. Two—

"I need to get the guys into their limos." A deep voice interrupts her momentary reprieve. "Do we have an arrival order yet from Trish?"

Emily's eyes fly open. Any sense of calm evaporates. She knows that voice. She'll never forget that voice. The last time she heard it, his arms were wrapped around her, his body enveloped her, his warmth seeped into her bones.

I'm here, Em.

I'm here and I won't let go.

They were the last words he told her before vanishing in the middle of the night, never to be seen again.

Until now.

I've got to be hallucinating. Right?

It's not the first time. This city has been playing tricks on her mind. At the airport, she nearly toppled onto the baggage claim carousel thinking she saw him. Then at the hotel, she actually toppled into a bellhop thinking she saw him. And at the studio, she slammed directly into a glass door thinking she saw him.

This is just like that.

It has to be.

Unless...she never hallucinated him. And all those times he'd really been there. And now, he's really here.

No. No. No. No.

She stares at the lawn lit by bright floodlights. He's too short. He's too tall. He's blond. He's—

Jake.

Oh god, it's him. It's really him. She's not hallucinating. Or if she is, she's damn impressed by herself. He seems so real.

Different than she remembers—broader, even from this distance, suaver somehow, more debonair in his navy suit with his brown hair falling in a slight wave across his brow—but still Jake. A grown-up version of him. A version she never could have come up with on her own.

"What are you looking at?"

Emily screams and grabs her chest. Heads turn. She drops to the ground before Jake can catch her gawking from the window.

"Emily?"

She yanks Nina down beside her, digging her fingers into the other woman's forearm with what must be painful force. Nina gently extricates herself and looks at Emily as if she's an alien newly arrived from planet crazy.

"You're freakishly strong," the producer grumbles, rubbing her skin. "What are we doing on the floor?"

"Shh," Emily demands. "There's a contestant out there."

"I promise you there's not."

"There is. I just saw him. He's got a suit on."

"Hold on." Nina crawls onto her knees and peeks over the sill. She snorts, then turns back to Emily. "That's Jake. Don't mind him. He got promoted this season and is now under the false impression that he's somebody important. I told him the suit makes him look like a jackass, but what do I know? I'm just more experienced, more qualified, and more senior than he is, so naturally, he ignored me." She rolls her eyes. "Men."

Emily's chest constricts. She's still stuck on hearing his name out loud. On hearing it confirmed. "Um, you said Jake?"

"Have you guys not met yet? He's the field producer in

charge of the guys. I'm surprised he hasn't introduced himself. Hold on. I'll—"

"No!" Emily jerks Nina down again.

The producer flops to the ground, this time with a glare as she snatches her arm back. "Seriously, what do they feed you in Georgia?"

Emily shrugs. "Peaches?"

"Well—"

"Nina. You there?"

Emily freezes as his voice comes through her handler's headset. If they weren't so close, she wouldn't have heard. But she does.

"I'm getting the suitors into the limos now. What's your status?"

Nina snaps her headphones on and murmurs into the microphone. "I need a minute."

Emily can't hear Jake anymore, but she doesn't have to. The damage is done. Nina's words sink in. He's a field producer. He works for the show. He's in charge of the men. Her men. Her thirty second chances.

"I need to talk to my sister," Emily blurts.

"One sec," Nina says into the microphone, then lowers the headphones. "What?"

"I—" Emily gasps for air. All of a sudden, she can hardly breathe. Her skin is on fire. Her head feels as though it might explode. "I need to talk to my sister!"

Understanding dawns in Nina's dark brown eyes. It's obviously not the first panic attack she's seen on this set. "We're too close to filming," she says gently. "It's okay to be nervous. I get it. But I promise, nothing is—"

Emily grabs her by the shirt and tugs, a woman possessed. Nina almost looks impressed. "I need to talk to Sam. Now."

"Your phone is already in the vault."

"Then give me yours. I have her number memorized."

"It's not—"

"Please." Emily's voice cracks. They both hear it. Nina's face softens, while Emily hardens her expression in a pathetic attempt to maintain her composure. "Please. I won't ask again, I promise. I just need to talk to my sister alone for five minutes before this whole thing begins. I just need to hear her voice."

Calculations spin in Nina's gaze. Emotional pleas clearly won't be the way to win her over in the future, but right now it works. Probably because the show hasn't even started and the last thing Nina needs is a loose cannon for a lead, but Emily will take it. As soon as Nina slips the phone from her pocket, Emily grabs it and starts dialing. The producer leaves the room. And while Emily is smart enough to know Nina's probably eavesdropping outside with one ear against the door, she's not smart enough to care.

The call rings.

Pick up. Pick up. Pick—

"Hello?"

"Sam, it's me," Emily whispers and collapses against the wall. Hairpins dig painfully into her scalp, but she's too strung out to notice. She pulls her knees to her chest, clutching the phone for dear life with one hand and cupping the other around her lips as if somehow that will magically make her impossible to overhear. "He's here."

There's a pause. "Who?"

For the love of god! "Who do you think?"

"Santa?"

"Sam!"

"You're the one who made me guess."

"Jake," she whisper-screams into the receiver. "Jake is here."

"WHAT?"

"I know!"

"HE'S THERE?"

"I know!"

"What a little weasel! He must've seen you were going to be on the show. Did the producers bring him on? Is he one of the suitors? Is he trying to win you back? Is he—"

"No, Sam, he—"

"Oh my god. I'm booking a flight to California right now. They want a show? I'll give them a show! I'll rip his fucking balls off for pulling a stunt like this. I'll feed them to my neighbor's Yorkie—that little mongrel is absolutely vicious when she wants to be. I'll—"

"Sam."

"God, I can't believe him!"

"Sam!"

"What?"

"He's not *on* the show."

"He's not? Then what—"

"He's a producer," Emily says, tripping over the word. "He's producing the show."

"A producer." Sam repeats the word as if it's in a foreign language. "So he's not there to win you back?"

Emily's heart flips. "No."

"He's there to…set you up?"

"I—" Her face twists, and she imagines her twin's expression is probably the same. "I guess? I hadn't really— I didn't—"

"Ha!" A barking laugh comes through the line. It devolves into an uproarious fit of giggles.

"Sam." Emily is not amused. "Sam!"

Her sister pauses her laughter long enough to string a complete sentence together. "Don't you see how amazing this is?"

"No," she deadpans. "I don't."

"Emily." Sam's voice sobers. "Think about it for one minute. Jake left you. Jake broke your heart. And if he works for the show, then he obviously knew you were the new lead, and he didn't even warn you. Either he thinks his being there isn't a big deal, or he's still a little chickenshit, but no matter what, you have an opportunity here. You're about to spend six weeks with thirty guys fighting for your attention, and your ex-boyfriend has to film every glorious moment of it. So you can keep doing what you're doing, which sounds a lot like freaking out in a coat closet somewhere, or you can show him what he's been missing. You can make him hurt, Em. You can get your revenge."

"Revenge."

The word rolls across her tongue, tangy and sweet. She savors it, like a sour candy that's shocking at first, then tastier and tastier with each passing second.

"Revenge," Sam repeats. The word emerges like the sun bursting over the horizon of a brand-new day. "Do it, Em. Make him hurt." Voices filter in through the background. Her sister must still be at the office, dropping everything when Emily needs her, like always. "I've got to go. I love you."

"I love you, too."

Emily hangs up, and though she won't be able to speak to her sister for another six weeks, Sam's voice lingers.

Revenge.

Revenge.

Revenge.

Emily turns to the dress rack again. Her gaze lands on the nude gown covered in crystals. She traces the edge of the seam and imagines the collar circling her neck, the cut dipping all the way to her butt crack, and the earrings she designed dangling from her lobes. She remembers what her producer said.

I'm here and I'm hot and you all better watch out.

She pictures Jake's response.

And she gets dressed.

A LINE of limos fills the driveway—five cars, six men each, all under his charge. Bow ties are in place. First lines are finalized. Gimmicks abound. All that's missing is a girl.

The girl.

Emily.

Jake swallows. He doesn't know what to do with his hands. He puts them in his pockets—too casual. He crosses his arms—too abrasive. He clutches his clipboard—too scared. He's been dreading this moment for a week, losing his nerve to cross paths with her at every opportunity and backing out at the last minute. Hell, he jumped into the janitor's closet at the studio to avoid meeting her face-to-face in the lobby. He's a coward and he knows it. He owes her more than this. He should have called her the second she signed the contract. He should have gone to her hotel room to explain. He should have at the very least sent her an email. But now, it's too late. She's almost here. He can't run anymore. He can't delay. And he can't figure out what to do with his goddamn hands!

"Jake."

"What?" he snaps and turns to Fred, who is sitting behind a camera, glaring at him instead of watching the mansion door. Jake takes a deep breath. "Sorry. What do you need, Fred?"

"For you to relax," the director says. "I'm having anxiety just looking at you. It's messing with my first-night mojo. I need to feel the romance, the ambience, the spark of new love, not your slow descent into neurotic hell."

"Sorry." Jake drops his arms to his sides, then crosses them, then lifts one hand to his chin.

"Jake."

"I know. I know. It's just—" He runs his fingers through his hair and accidentally dislodges his headset. It falls to the floor with an embarrassingly loud crash. Jake hastens to get it back in place. "It's my first night as field producer. I need this to go right. I need this to be perfect."

He's only half talking about the job, but Fred doesn't seem to notice.

"Come here."

Jake obliges and crosses the distance between them. He's careful to keep his head turned toward the limos, trying to delay the inevitable for a few minutes longer.

"Look here." Fred motions toward the camera.

Jake takes a deep breath and puts his eye to the lens, a spot that usually feels like home. Instead, his pulse climbs. His palms sweat. On the other side of that camera, a fountain twinkles, candles flicker, blooming roses sway gently in the ocean breeze. What the camera doesn't show is the massive fan providing said breeze, or the dead bushes piled up in the corner that needed to be replaced two days ago, or the spotlights scattered around the driveway. Television versus reality. Mundane versus magical. Jake knows this—he knows all the tricks. He doesn't need to see any more, doesn't want to look any closer.

He can't turn away.

His eyes train on the heavy wooden door barely visible through breaks in the foliage. A countdown starts in the back of his mind.

Tick.

Tick.

Tick.

"You may be new at this," Fred says, unaware of Jake's mounting panic, "but I'm not. Romance is my calling, Jake. It's in my blood. Even if you have thirty of the most undesirable men in America in those limos, I'll turn them all into Prince Charming. I've got this. *You've* got this. Calm down."

A sweeping motion catches his eye, the one he's been dreading, the one he's been waiting for—a slow-motion car crash he can't escape.

There's a sparkle.

Then a gleam.

Liquid starlight shifts through crimson petals, until—

Boom.

Emily emerges from the garden like Venus from the sea. The spotlights catch the crystal studs along every inch of her dress, illuminating her like some sort of fever dream. He's delirious, woozy. Though he's imagined this moment a million different ways, she's more beautiful than he thought possible, more disarming, more striking, more...everything. His gaze goes straight to her mouth as she pulls her plump lower lip between her teeth, a nervous habit he remembers far too well. Her hair is swept up, revealing the graceful arch of her neck. She turns to look over her shoulder, and he chokes on his own breath as the soft skin of her back is revealed. He can't help but follow the line of her spine, down, down, down, his imagination taking him the rest of the way, and he groans in physical pain.

She spins as if she heard.

Her golden eyes look directly into the lens, a mix of nerves and determination. They gleam with something he can't quite place.

Suddenly, he's back in time.

It was the first day of school, senior year. Jake leaned against the lockers, fiddling with his camcorder, while his best friend, Nate, droned on about how that year everything was going to be different, how it was finally their time. He put his eye to the viewfinder and tuned out the hum of voices, the minutiae, the noise. His world calmed. He zeroed in on the small details the camera allowed him to see—a subtle touch, a nervous fiddle, a broken smile. He swept his focus across the hall and searched for something interesting, something new, something—

Wait.

He backtracked, stopped, and waited for the crowd to part

again. Then he hit record. Zoomed so close, all he could see were two golden eyes as bright as the sun. They held no shadows, no darkness. They glittered with a vibrancy Jake had never felt, but he did then. A prickle sparked in his chest like a warm ray shining directly on his heart. He zoomed out, needing to see more. A button nose appeared, then a smattering of freckles across a rosy cheek, and perfect Cupid's-bow lips. Then—

"Dude." Nate elbowed Jake in the side, ruining the shot. "Twins."

He tried to shake his friend off, but it was too late. He'd lost her. Jake dropped the camera and glared at Nate, who was still looking down the hall.

"Dude," he said again, this time grabbing Jake's forearm and shaking it. "Redheaded twins!"

Jake looked to the side.

Everything stopped.

Like a perfect shot in a film, the sort that didn't exist in real life, a cloud parted outside, sending a single beam of light through the window. It landed directly on her face as she ducked her head, covered her mouth, and laughed softly into her fingers. The yellow polka dots on her dress shifted with her mirth. Auburn waves fell over her shoulders as they shook, partly shrouding her features. He was distantly aware of the twin two steps ahead, drawing everyone else's attention with her sweeping gestures, but he couldn't look away from the first girl. Her introversion had him intrigued. What would it take to see behind that secretive smile? Like a fly that had already flown too close to the trap, he was stuck in the tape, unable to do anything but wait for the inevitable doom.

Gone.

That's what he was.

Gone before he ever even arrived.

"Cut," Fred calls, and Jake returns to the present. He pulls himself away from the camera and stumbles back on unsteady feet before tripping over some wires. A strong hand grabs his forearm to steady him, then pats his back in friendly camaraderie. Fred returns to his chair. "I wasn't rolling," he says into his mic. "We've got to film the entrance again."

"Hold on, Fred," Nina shouts across the courtyard, forgoing the comms. "I want to make a few introductions first, get Emily acquainted with the crew before we officially start the show. It's been a hectic week and she hasn't gotten a chance to meet everyone yet."

"Just tell me when," he calls back as he fiddles with the buttons, making adjustments.

"Jake!" Nina says upon seeing him at Fred's side. "Come here."

Emily's head whips around.

They stare at each other for a heartbeat, a glance he feels all the way in his toes. She doesn't look surprised. Her lips purse, and even though it's been seven years, he knows exactly what's going on inside her head.

She's pissed.

"Jake!"

He marches over on autopilot. The funeral procession blares in the back of his mind. Emily doesn't take her eyes off of him. They're like lasers, digging into his skin. He wants to look away, but he can't. On some level, he loves the burn.

"Jake, this is Emily," Nina says, oblivious to the fact that the woman by her side is tattooed on his heart.

He's spent the last seven years trying to erase her and never realized until this very moment, standing close enough to smell the citrus on her skin, that not a single goddamn trick worked.

"For future reference, it'd be a good idea to introduce yourself to the lead *before* the first night of filming," Nina continues, then turns to Emily. "And Emily, this buffoon in a suit is Jackson Moore, aka Jake."

Emily arches a brow. It doesn't take much to decipher the look in her eyes. *Jackson Moore? Is that who you are now?*

He straightens his spine and proudly draws his shoulders back. *Yes.*

Jacob William Henry III died the night he crawled out of her bed, got into his pickup truck, and drove until there was no road left to drive on. Thirty-six hours passed in a blur of gas stations and tears. The first thing he did when he woke up to the view of the Pacific Ocean with hardly any memory of how he'd gotten there was change his name. The boy she knows is gone.

"Nice to meet you," Jake says, his voice cold, too hard to recognize.

Emily flinches. Hurt flashes over her eyes, but she catches herself at the last moment and drops her gaze to his outstretched hand. A silent beat passes before she slides her fingers between his. They're warm and soft and everything he tried not to let himself remember. It's over too soon. She abruptly jerks her hand away. When her arm drops to her side, she flexes her fingers as if they've been burned.

He doesn't want to notice, but he does.

Emily catches him watching and shoves her hands behind her back.

"Nice to meet you, too," she says, her voice a bit too sickly sweet. It resonates with an undercurrent he can't quite place.

"Jake here is in charge of all the suitors," Nina says before leaning in and dropping her voice conspiringly. It's a move he's seen her use before, to make the lead comfortable, to get past their guard. "I know we can't give too much away, but what do you think? Anyone with husband material in those limos?"

Bile stings his tongue. He forces out a gruff reply. "Sure."

"That's convincing." Nina rolls her eyes and hooks her arm through Emily's. "Don't mind him. Come on, let's go find you a glass of champagne to cut the first-night jitters."

Guiding Emily away, Nina glances subtly over her shoulder with a frown. Her gaze is hard, the best-friend mask gone and the producer back in full force.

Get your shit together, she silently commands.

He wants to—he does.

But as Emily walks away, he traces the line of her spine one more time and a prickle forms at the base of his neck, making his shoulders writhe. She grabs a flute off a tray and downs the bubbling liquid in one quick shoot. Her gaze finds his over the rim of the empty glass before she squares her shoulders and looks away.

The undercurrent in the air clicks into place.

He finally understands her hidden message.

Game on.

Jake looks to the limos, where the thirty men under his

charge are tucked away. In six weeks, one of them is going to get down on one knee and propose. He's responsible for making it happen. His job, his future, his entire career hangs on finding the former love of his life a fiancé.

Game on, he repeats, mentally securing his defenses. *Game fucking on.*

emily

THE WAIT for the first limo might be the longest ten minutes of Emily's life. Jake stands directly in front of her with his jaw set and his head resolutely turned toward the end of the driveway as he mumbles into his headset. She tries not to stare, but every time she looks away, her gaze lands on one of the gigantic cameras zeroed in on her, and her heart leaps into her throat. What are people going to think when they see her? Will they hate her? Love her? Does she look too nervous? Too rigid? Too poised?

"Don't look directly into the lens," Nina gently prompts for the fifth time.

Emily jolts and stares ahead. She studies the cobblestone pathway, the lush California foliage, the dark asphalt glistening with the slightest shimmer beneath all these spotlights. But her focus inevitably drifts back to those polished loafers, up those long legs, to those tapered hips visible below his navy suit jacket, which pulls tight across his wide shoulders. She remembers what it felt like to run her hands through his silky brunet hair, to have his deep blue eyes intensely focused on her. He had been tall and thin with more bones than muscle the last time his weight had settled between her hips, and part of her wonders what he feels like now with his biceps so clearly straining against the fabric, no longer a boy but a man.

He looks at her then, as if he can hear the thoughts racing through her mind.

Emily doesn't look away.

Jackson Moore.

Is that who he is now, with the tailored suit and the detached voice? She misses the awkward teenager with mussed-up hair and a worn Star Wars T-shirt. When *he* looked at her, she came alive.

Right now, all she feels is cold.

Two headlights flash in the space between them. Jake breaks eye contact first, and Emily follows. A limo approaches. Her heart pounds. She shifts her feet and relaxes her arms. Loose gravel crunches as the tires slow. When they come to a stop, Jake walks over and reaches for the door. He pauses with his fingers latched around the handle.

Oh god.

Oh god.

Oh god.

"Just breathe," Nina whispers from the side. "Smile."

She tries to twist her face into some semblance of excitement, but she can feel Jake watching her from the corner of his eye and she seizes up. She's not sure she can do this with him here, indifferently watching her every move, as if nothing that happened between them mattered when it did.

It still does.

"Do you have to fart?" Nina asks, the question carrying loudly across the silent anticipation. "Because you can fart if you have to. We're all on your side. We'll edit it out later."

Emily feels her cheeks go red. She laughs—from nerves, from awkwardness, from maybe having to fart? The tension in the air breaks and suddenly the door swings open. Before she has time to regain her composure or look at Jake or think about the fact that millions of people will soon watch this moment unfold, a man in a slate-gray suit tumbles from the limousine.

Literally tumbles.

Emily gasps and takes half a step forward before she realizes it's on purpose. His head tucks before it slams against the pavement and he rolls smoothly to his feet with a confident grin.

"Gotcha," the man says as he straightens his lapels and smooths his deep black hair.

She laughs and puts her hand to her racing heart. "I guess you did."

"And I plan to keep you," he murmurs in a deep, gravelly voice that makes her stomach clench. Two of the brightest green eyes she's ever seen pin her in place, and a dimple puckers his cheek. He takes her hand and lifts it to his mouth, like something out of a movie. "My name is Ethan, and I can't wait to talk to you more inside."

He presses his lips gently to her skin, then as quickly as he came, he's gone, dropping her hand and walking toward the mansion, more apparition than man.

But his kiss lingers.

Emily clasps her hand to her chest and laughs softly. She watches the empty spot where he stood a moment ago, overwhelmed, a little awed, mostly just confused at how this is even her life. Maybe the next six weeks won't be so bad after all.

"Cut!" the director yells.

She flinches.

Right. This is for TV. This isn't real.

"Emily, you were perfect," Fred says in a kind voice. "But Ethan, get back here. I'm going to need at least two more takes of that entrance to make sure we get the angle right coming out of the limo."

Ethan reemerges and offers her a wink as he's ushered back toward the limo by the assistants, not given a moment to say a word to her even if he wanted to. She can't help how her gaze follows him, then flicks a little to the side, landing on Jake. His eyes are practically molten. If looks could kill, Ethan would be six feet under.

Maybe he's not so unaffected after all, she thinks with a satisfied smirk.

Ethan climbs back into the limo and Jake slams the door shut with so much force, everyone jumps.

"Lay off the Wheaties," Fred jokes as he rearranges a camera.

"Sorry." Jake's voice is gruff, annoyed.

Emily's grin deepens. Sam was right. Revenge *is* sweet.

Jake turns to look at her with a scowl, but before their eyes meet, Nina is there. She offers her a sip of water through a straw. Over the producer's shoulder, Ethan takes another diving spill from the limo, this time with a camera about five inches from his face.

"You did great," Nina murmurs in a low voice, as if it's a secret and the two of them are in cahoots. "Don't mind the reshoots. The first take is the only one that matters for you. We want your genuine reactions for the show. The rest is to give our editors options. What'd you think of the first guy? He's hot, right?"

"I guess." Emily shrugs. "I hardly know him."

"He looks like Henry Cavill and Colin Farrell's love child. What else do you need to know?"

His full name? His life dream? His Starbucks order? She offers Nina a wry grin. "His shoe size?"

The producer snorts. "Save that one for the interview room."

"We're ready," Fred calls.

Nina backs away slowly, holding Emily's gaze. "One down, twenty-nine more to go. You got this."

She turns to the limo, straightens her shoulders, and pointedly ignores Jake for the next four hours—which is the ungodly amount of time it takes for them to film all thirty arrivals. When the last guy walks through the door, Emily is exhausted. Their names and faces are mostly a blur. All she remembers are the gimmicks. Big Ben, who came dressed as a clocktower asking her not to run away at midnight. Cowboy Cooper, who rode in on an actual horse. Floatie Frank, who decided to show up in a full scuba suit with a pink flamingo around his waist for some unknown reason. Was he a marine biologist? She can't remember. Then there was Sexy Pierre, the Frenchman whose accent actually made her knees go weak even though for all she knew he'd whispered the French word for *moist* in her ear. Oh, then someone threw a football at her face—thank god she grew up in the South and spent enough time on the high school sidelines to be ready for *that*. And then there was the yo-yo guy, the pink suit, the real estate broker with the smarmy smile, and the man who brought her a milkshake. It was strawberry—*blegh*. His name went in one ear and out the other after she caught Jake chuckling softly to himself while she pretended to enjoy the drink. It was a sweet gesture, and she hadn't wanted to make anyone feel bad, but, god, she loathed strawberry ice cream. Of course, it was Jake's favorite. She'd had half a mind to chuck it at his head.

Freaking Jake.

Always there. Always watching. Always in the back of her mind. She can't escape him. Thirty seconds with a new man, then Jake. Then thirty seconds with someone else, then back to Jake. *Jake. Jake. Jake.*

"How are you holding up?" Nina asks.

Emily flinches. "Good."

"Good." Nina grins. "Because we have about twelve more hours to go."

"Twelve?" Emily groans and slumps back into the folding chair the assistants had provided while they set up her entrance into the house for the cocktail party.

"Night one is a beast," Nina says sympathetically. "But it's all downhill from here. You cut ten guys tonight, then five at the next ceremony, and just like that, you'll be halfway through the suitors."

She makes it sound so...formulaic. Which it is, Emily knows, but now having met all thirty men, she already feels guilty for what the next few weeks will bring.

"Nina." Jake's voice comes softly through the comm around her producer's neck.

Emily stiffens as if electrocuted. Thirty men wait for her on the other side of the wall, and not a single one of them has caused the same heart-stopping reaction elicited by the whisper of his voice.

She needs that to change.

It's *going* to change.

"Yeah," Nina says into her mic.

"Ready when you are."

"I'm ready," Emily blurts and jumps out of the chair, desperate to get away from his voice, from his memory, from him. The second her heels *click* on stone, her poor toes scream in protest and she whimpers. She can already feel the blisters forming. "Ow, ow, ow."

"Your feet?" Nina asks.

Emily nods.

"Leave it to me," her producer says, giving her a slight push toward the door. "I'll find some slippers and Jake can tell one of the guys to make a Cinderella moment out of it. That'll play well with the viewers. In the meantime, remember what I told you. A little speech, and then enjoy. Some of the early guys have been drinking steadily for the past four hours while waiting for you, so don't be surprised if there's at least one person completely bombed in there. Happens every year. Just try to get to know as many of them as you can before the puzzle ceremony, which'll be in about, oh, nine-ish hours."

Good god. It might as well be nine years.

I'll never make it.

"Oh, and I almost forgot," Nina continues, either unaware of or choosing to ignore Emily's groan. "If you need a break or want to be rescued or have to speak to me for any reason, our safe word is *platypus*."

"Platypus?" Her face twists.

"Yeah, *platypus*, because they look all cute and cuddly, but they're actually venomous loners who don't like to be touched, and what woman can't relate to that, right?" Nina winks and nudges Emily with her elbow. "Good luck."

Emily swallows as Nina backs out of the shot. An assistant comes to remove the folding chair, and the host of *The Love Match*, Keith Holson, emerges from the garden. It's still surreal to see American's dad, here in the flesh. He's shorter and shinier than she ever imagined he would be, his light brown hair coiffed and his gray suit perfectly tailored. They already filmed two quick scenes together by the limos, but still, butterflies flutter as he approaches. She can't help it. She's a superfan of *The Love Match* and even though she's somehow now the star, the fangirl inside won't quit. *Keith Holson* is here. *Keith Holson* is taking her hand. *Keith Holson* is squeezing her fingers encouragingly and telling her that tonight is the start of her epic love story.

Somehow, she believes him.

At least, the first time. By takes four and five of the same prepared speech, the mystique has worn off a little, but she keeps the smile on her face. The butterflies switch to a nervous swarm as two production assistants dramatically throw the double front doors wide open, revealing a sea of handsome men waiting in the foyer. Emily sashays forward and takes a deep breath, giving herself an internal pep talk, then opens her mouth to begin her speech and—

"Cut!" Fred calls.

She deflates.

Those same two assistants usher her back through the door. Fans are moved into new locations. Lights are shuffled around. The doors are thrown dramatically open one more time, and—

"Cut!"

One more time. Then the cameras move inside, and she walks through the door a few more times until the lighting is perfect. It takes nearly half an hour to walk five feet into the mansion, and she can't help but wonder if it's a sign of things to come.

Why did this show always seem so real? So romantic?

Because it is, she tells herself, trying to ignore how manufactured it feels behind the scenes. *My conversations with these men will be real. My moments with them will be real.*

Nina gives her the go-ahead, and Emily snatches a glass of champagne from the offered tray, determined to make tonight count. For once, Jake is nowhere to be seen. It leaves her feeling lighter, freer, like a bird untethered and ready to fly.

"I can't believe I'm here," Emily starts, sticking to the script she and Nina prepared the night before. "I can't believe my mom bullied the entire country into helping me find a boyfriend." Some of the men laugh. Others cringe. She plows on, silently cursing Nina for convincing her to include that line. "I want you all to know how honored I am to have the opportunity to meet you. I've been a huge fan of the show since the first season, and I never imagined I would actually be here, feeling like Cinderella after she snuck into the ball, but it's all real. I don't have to run home at midnight. I get to stay, spend time with all of you, travel the world with some of you, and hopefully, by the end of this, fall in love. I really, truly believe my future husband is in this room, so—"

Movement catches her eye—a navy suit in the doorway.

The hairs on the back of her neck rise.

He's watching her. She knows he is.

It takes all her willpower not to look, to keep her focus on the men as she lifts her glass high into the air. "I guess all that's left to say is 'Thanks, Mom!' Cheers!"

Clink!

Thirty-one champagne glasses meet, the bubbles catching the light as laughter fills the air. Beaming smiles fix on her. Sexy, attractive, smart, eligible men surround her on all sides, and her hope swells like a rising tide.

This is her time.

Emily downs her drink and dives in.

jake

THIS IS FUCKING TORTURE.

Jake crosses his arms and leans against the doorframe, trying to appear casual when in reality his fingers dig so deep into his skin they practically draw blood. His every muscle spasms with the effort to keep still, to not charge across the room and rip every one of these assholes away from her. She's so much better than them, so much better than this show, so much better than him. He doesn't understand what she's doing here, how she's single, or why that douchebag is lifting his hand to her face and brushing back a strand of her hair.

What's his name? Ben M.? Ben K.?

Ben who-the-fuck-cares lets his fingers linger on the spot beneath her earlobe, then strokes her skin. His head tilts. His chin dips.

He's going for it. Jake sees red. *He's actually going for it. On the first fucking night!*

The suitor's face inches closer, the world moving in slow motion. Jake's not usually one for misogynistic tendencies, but all he wants to do is run over there, grab that jerk's hand from her neck, and smash his face into the floor. He knows —*he knows*—violence is never the answer. But god, he wants to anyway.

And the poor guy hasn't even done anything yet.

I need to get out of here, Jake thinks, pushing off the wall. Emily hasn't glanced his way once in nearly seven hours. It's as if he doesn't exist, which was fine in theory, when she lived all the way across the country and he could shove any and all thoughts of her into the forgotten corners of his mind. But it's different with her here, talking to every other man in earshot. She's so close and yet so fucking far away. It's driving him insane.

"I'm going to go check in with Trish," he mutters to an assistant as he storms down the hall in search of his EP. He finds her in the video village, frowning into a set of monitors as the camera zooms in on Emily ducking away from the incoming kiss.

Jake grins.

"God." Trish sighs and presses her fingers to her temples. "This is a complete disaster."

"Trish?" he asks cautiously.

She turns to him sharply. "What are you doing here?"

"I came to check in." He steps into the room, already feeling better with a little distance—*little* being the operative word, seeing as Emily's face is on about a dozen different television screens. Her doe eyes stare at him. But the air is fresher somehow. He can finally take a breath, unlike his boss.

"Good." She refocuses on the screens. "Because if I hear

the phrase *that's so nice* one more time, I might blow my brains out."

"What do you mean?"

"Emily—she's so..." Trish waves her hand through the air, searching for the word, then scoffs. "I can't even think of a word. That's how dull she is."

"Really?"

Jake fills the spot next to his boss, putting his producer hat on for what feels like the first time that night, and stares at the screens, trying to see what the viewers see instead of the girl he's loved for the better part of a decade. She's always been on the quieter side, with a serene sort of confidence, but that was what Jake loved about her. Sam was the loud one, the boisterous one, the attention seeker. When Emily smiled, it felt as if it were just for him, a secret he was lucky enough to be let in on, making him feel special, chosen in a way he'd never been before. Sam was the more obvious leading lady— the bold star of an action film or a mainstream rom-com, the typical blockbuster hit. But Emily was the type of character he preferred—a headliner at the Sundance Film Festival, the sort of film that spends hours peeling back the layers but leaves the audience walking away with more questions than answers. He could have filmed her for hours. Hell, he did. And still, he always wanted more.

But *The Love Match* isn't a show built on nuance. There's no time to waste on layers. They have ten episodes to get through thirty men. Ten episodes to build an epic love story. Everyone is an archetype, fitting neatly into a comfortable set of preconceived notions. On these cameras, Emily doesn't come off as an introspective woman with mysteries to uncover. She comes off shy, reserved, maybe a bit stuck up. She's too polite to be entertaining, but even worse, she's too demure—not with the men, but with the camera. This show only works when the lead bares her soul right from the start. The men should have to fight to learn about her, but the audience should already know. They should be like her diary, accepting all her secrets, all her hopes and dreams. Right now, she's giving them a blank page.

It's not the Emily he knows.

And though he wants to blame the cameras, he can't. Not entirely. Even in her introversion, Emily always had a spark. Her energy was infectious, making him feel light. In her presence, he came out of the shadows and stepped into the sun.

What happened?

He's afraid he already knows the answer.

"What did Nina say?" Jake asks, his gaze still on Emily.

"She's trying, but they're too fresh. The trust hasn't been built. It's why we haven't gone with an unaffiliated lead in ages, because they're more open to producing if they see us as friends. Emily isn't there yet. She's still unsure. If Nina presses too hard, it might work against us."

"You want me to stir something up?"

"You mean do I want you to do your job?" Trish turns to him, an eyebrow raised. "Yes. That'd be nice for a change."

The jab stings, mostly because he knows it's true. "You're right. I've been distracted tonight, but it won't happen again."

"I need more than a drunken idiot falling into the pool."

"Understood."

"More than a jealous asshole pumping his chest."

"Understood."

"I need something promo-worthy."

"Give me ten minutes."

"Five."

Jake is already out the door. This is exactly what he needed. He's reinvigorated. Electricity shoots down his veins like a double shot of espresso. Screw romance. This is where he thrives—on giving an asshole just enough rope to hang himself in front of ten million viewers. And Jake knows the perfect guy.

He finds Margarita Gonzalez, one of his production assistants, in the hall. She's in jeans and a slightly worn UCLA hoodie with her dark curly hair twisted into a topknot bun. A pair of black glasses frame her light brown eyes, and her cherry-red lips are pursed in concentration.

"Rita!"

She flinches when he calls her name, and corrects her slouch. "Yeah?"

"Have you heard anything good from Chet tonight?"

"Define *good*."

"Something that will make America cheer when Emily sends his ass home."

Rita grins. "In that case, yes. Yes, I have."

The man is a walking steroid, more muscles than brains. His biceps are so overinflated they might burst. He's a practical advertisement for toxic masculinity with the way he bench pressed Emily during their one-on-one time and then demanded a plate of cold cuts upon his entrance to the mansion. Jake spent five hours with him shooting B-roll footage, and it had been five hours of his life he would never get back, but even he was surprised by Rita's next words.

"We have him on camera calling Emily a *hot piece of ass* who he wouldn't mind *bending over the couch*."

Jake's fingers curl into fists. "He actually said that?"

"That's not even the best part." Rita smiles. "He must've thought the mics turn off in the bathroom, or that we wouldn't use the audio, because he gave himself a little pep talk in the mirror and it's..." She trails off and lifts her fingers to her lips. *Chef's kiss.*

"Excellent."

Jake's wheels spin. He speaks into his comm. "Nina, can you keep Emily and Cooper in the same room for the next five minutes? I'm working on something."

"Care to tell me what?"

"Where's the fun in that?"

He smirks as her sigh comes audibly through the comm. Thirty seconds later, he's found his way to Chet, who is, surprise surprise, eating a plain beef patty while he flexes in the hall mirror.

What a fucking asshole.

This is going to be sweet.

"Chet, my man," Jake says, putting on his best bro-voice. "How's your night going?"

"Good." He meets Jake's eyes through the mirror, unable to turn from his own reflection, and prattles on for a solid minute before Jake finds an opening to intervene.

"I heard from Nina you're one of Emily's favorites so far."

"Bro." Chet pumps his chest. "Obviously."

"But you could stand out even more, if you want to. You know, really make an impression."

"I'm listening."

"I've got some information, but obviously I can't barge in and tell Emily myself. You, on the other hand…"

At that, Chet finally turns around to look Jake in the eye.

"What do you say?" Jake reels him in. "Want to help me get one of these assholes eliminated?"

Chet grins.

Gotcha.

About thirty seconds later, Chet disappears through the door and Jake presses the button on the side of his mic. "I want all cameras on Chet, right now. Fred, do you copy?"

"Copy."

"Nina, is Cooper still near Emily?"

"Yes."

"Trish?"

"Yes, Jake?"

"You're about to get your promo."

Jake retakes his spot in the doorway, no longer feigning a casual pose as he rests his shoulder on the frame and fights to keep the Cheshire cat grin off his face.

"Hey, Cooper," Chet calls across the room.

The cowboy turns, red hair visible under the rim of his hat, crystal-green eyes curious. He's in well-worn jeans, a white shirt, and a black jacket, the sleeves rolled up to his elbows. His skin is the sort of tan one only gets from working outside. And when he opens his mouth, Jake knows that Midwestern drawl will be the final nail in Chet's coffin. The guy is so full of himself he doesn't even realize he's facing off against the living, breathing

American version of that Scottish heartthrob from *Outlander*. It's no surprise whose side the female viewers will take.

Well, no surprise to Jake.

"Yes?" Cooper says with caution.

"I have a question for you."

"Shoot."

Emily looks over from her spot on the couch. Chet notices her watching and stands even prouder. Jake feels not even an ounce of guilt for what's about to happen. Sure, he might have given Chet the shovel, but the asshole is going to bury himself.

And it will be great fucking TV.

"How old are you?"

"Twenty-eight." Cooper scrunches his brows, trying to follow where this is going.

Chet smirks, cocky as ever and confident he's about to deliver a killing blow. "Don't you think that's a little old to still be living with your parents?"

Cooper recoils, then releases a surprised laugh, deep and rich, sure to make about a million panties drop the second it airs. "You don't want to do this, Chet. Trust me."

Funny enough, Jake knows Cooper is coming from a good place. He spent six hours shooting footage with the guy on his ranch. He's as nice as they come, honest and hard-working, the true American cowboy stereotype to a T.

But it's also the exact wrong thing to say to someone like Chet. The underlying challenge to his manhood won't go unanswered.

Sure enough, Chet leans in. "Oh, I think I do."

"I'm trying to keep you from embarrassing yourself."

"Embarrassing myself?" Chet laughs in his face. "The twenty-eight-year-old who still lives at home wants to keep me from embarrassing myself?"

His voice is rising.

Everyone turns to look.

Come on, Em. Come on, Jake thinks.

She pulls her lower lip between her teeth, hesitating.

Show them who you really are.

"Tell me, Cooper. Do you open with that line on the first date, or do you wait to introduce them in the morning?"

"I'm serious, man. Drop it."

"No, really. I want to know. Does your mom surprise you both with breakfast-in-bed?"

"Don't bring my mom into this."

"Too close to home? You a bit kinky like that?"

Cooper stands taller. His attitude visibly changes with that last insult—it went too far. And finally—*finally!*—Emily steps between them.

"I think you've had a bit too much to drink, Chet," she says, her back to Cooper, clearly trusting him more. "Why don't you go outside and get some air."

Jake rolls his eyes. *Too diplomatic. Come on.*

"I don't want air," he snaps, too far into the argument to remember why he's even here. It's not about Emily anymore. It never was with him. It's a dick-size competition, and he's too un-self-aware to realize he already lost. "I want an answer. Unless, of course, Cooper can't give me one, because he's never brought someone home..."

Ah, yes. The virgin insinuation, Jake thinks. *Chet's really checking all the douchebag boxes tonight.*

"Well, I think it's sweet that he lives at home," Emily says, giving Cooper a soft smile that makes Jake's stomach twist.

Focus.

Focus.

"Maybe you're the kinky one then," Chet mutters.

Emily turns back to him slowly, one of her brows rising in a look that literally chills Jake's blood. "Excuse me?"

"You heard me."

Cooper moves to intervene, and for a second, Jake fears everything he set up will be for naught. Then Emily puts her hand out, holding the cowboy back. Her eyes burn like molten amber. The crystals on her dress catch the light as she steps forward, the click of her heels loud in the sudden silence. She doesn't stop until she's inches from Chet, her face arched up to make her seem taller, her shoulders proud. Quiet she may be. A pushover she is not. Her lips curl like a lioness's on the hunt as she opens her mouth.

"Get out."

"What?" Chet scoffs.

"You heard me," she says, repeating his words against him. "I know what you're probably thinking. I know what everyone is saying about me online. That I'm pathetic. That I'm a loser. What kind of desperate do I need to be for my mother to practically beg America to put me on this show? But I'll let you in on a little secret, Chet. Something I figured out a long time ago. Something I hope every woman watching already knows. I will never be so pathetic, so desperate, or so lonely that I'll settle for someone like you. Someone who belittles other people to make themselves feel bigger. So yes, get out. Get out of this room. Get out of this mansion. And get out of my life. Because I'd rather end up alone than end up with you."

Beautiful, Jake thinks. The moment. The delivery. The girl. Simply stunning on all accounts, especially when she whips around and stomps across the room, leaving Chet gobsmacked, his mouth bobbing comically like a fish's, his brain just as empty. Jake doesn't think it can get any better, and then she pauses to glance back over her shoulder. The moment extends for an extra beat, the effect so perfect he's sure Fred is losing his mind behind the camera. She's a director's dream right now, and she always has been.

"Oh, in case I'm not being clear, Chet," she sneers, practically spitting his name—which, really, is how a name like *Chet* is meant to be said, anyway. "You are *not* my perfect match. Goodbye."

"And scene," Jake murmurs softly.

It's just enough righteous fury to gain the viewers' support. Any more and she risks coming off as a shrew. Unfair, yes. But that's reality television.

Nina must have the same thought because she starts flailing her arms to catch Emily's attention, then ushers her toward an open door, completing the dramatic exit. Chet stands like a stunned idiot, watching her go. Cooper takes the opportunity to step up next to him. He pats the other man on the back.

"I tried to tell you," he murmurs, but these mics pick up everything. *God bless modern technology*, Jake silently commends, fighting a grin as the cowboy continues. "Oh, and by the way, that home you're so worried about? It sits on about two hundred thousand acres. I live in my own three-bedroom house on my family's ranch, and I can assure you, the ladies I bring home don't mind it one bit."

Then he follows Emily out the door, snatching the pair of silk slippers Nina left on the console as he goes.

Chet is practically purple by the time he storms over to Jake.

"What the fuck, man?" he seethes. "You set me up! You said you wanted me to get one of these assholes eliminated—"

"And you did."

Chet stops cold, as if his own stupidity has literally smacked him in the face. Jake steps to the side, anticipating the security guard who has marched down the hall to escort the bastard out. He can't help but laugh under his breath as Chet gets hauled from the mansion, kicking and screaming, every second captured for millions to see. The so-called tough guys never go quietly.

"Well done, Jake," his boss says over the comms, her voice laced with unbridled approval.

His grin widens and he drops his head back against the door, soaking in the victory. "Thanks, Trish."

He rolls his face to the side, unable to keep from looking toward the spot where Emily disappeared, his longing too strong to ignore. It's part of him. A living, breathing thing beneath his skin. But the doorway isn't empty like he expected.

She's there.

She's watching him.

She knows exactly what he did.

For the first time since the limos, Emily meets his gaze. Jake doesn't even care that there's not an ounce of love in those eyes, just fury. He'd rather have her rage than have nothing at all.

emily

EXHAUSTED DOESN'T EVEN BEGIN to cover how Emily is feeling as she walks into her bedroom, strips off her dress, and blindly grabs an old T-shirt from the drawer. She's too tired to turn on the light, too tired to scrub off her makeup, too tired to even think of bothering with a pair of pajama pants. It takes all her energy to stumble over to the bed and faceplant on the comforter—to hell with the sheets. A balmy evening breeze blows in through the windows she left open earlier, and it's perfection on her overheated skin. After sixteen hours of filming, the equivalent of thirty first dates, and an excruciatingly drawn-out puzzle ceremony where she sent ten men home, all she wants is silence. And darkness. And, well, a slice of cake wouldn't hurt, but she'll settle for ten hours of uninterrupted sleep.

Before her head even finds the pillow, her eyes are closed.

Her brain shuts down.

Ocean waves lull her to sleep, then—

Thump!

Emily jerks awake.

"It's me."

His voice sends a shiver down her spine, cooling and stoking her panic at the same time. The pounding of her heart intensifies as he steps closer, silhouette barely visible against the moonlit sky. His hand finds hers in the dark, warm and large and solid. She jerks away. Her fingers burn where they touched.

"What the hell, Jake?"

"Shh," he urges and retakes her hand.

This time, she lets him drag her to her feet, her curiosity getting the best of her. As they enter the bathroom, her foot catches on the frame and she stumbles forward. His arm comes around her waist. Suddenly, she's flush against his chest, a spot she's been a thousand times before but never quite like this. It's like hearing an old favorite song on the radio and only just realizing what every dirty lyric actually means. Familiar, yet alarmingly new. He smells the same, like an ocean breeze with the hint of cedar musk. Everything else is different—the ripples across his abdomen, the breadth of his chest, the muscles flexed beneath her hands. Sturdy fingers grip her hips, no longer awkward but assured. He takes a sharp inhale, pushing his hard body that much farther into hers. Warm breath washes over her forehead and she glances up. She can't see his mouth, but she can sense it there, hovering out of reach. In the dark, he feels more like a dream than anything real.

They stay like that for a breath.

Two.

His arm shifts. She doesn't know where his hand is going, if she should move away, if she should stop him, if she should—

Click.

The light blinks on and the spell should break, but it doesn't. He's got stubble where there never was before. His hair is perfectly coiffed, not in the shaggy disarray she remembers. But his eyes are exactly the same, deep blue and stormy, the ocean right before a hurricane, dangerous and powerful, a force strong enough to bowl her over, yet she doesn't move.

She can't.

"Jake."

It comes out breathier than she meant, not at all reprimanding. He presses a finger to her lips. His gaze follows, as if involuntarily. A beat passes while he stares, transfixed. Then he bends his finger, tugging gently on her bottom lip until her mouth parts. A puff of warm air escapes as all the breath leaves her lungs. It brushes over his skin and a feral gleam lights his gaze. Before she can make sense of it, he tears himself away. She's left by the door, struggling to breathe as he turns on the faucet, then the shower. The spray thunders, finally drowning out the frantic beating of her heart. By the time he spins back around, she's recovered enough to cross her arms and scowl.

He, on the other hand, looks as if he got sucker punched. He rakes his gaze down her body with a strangled groan and stumbles back, half falling into the glass shower door as he shields his eyes. His voice is pained when he finally blurts, "Jesus Christ, Em."

"What?" She shrugs and glances down. It takes the sight of her bare legs to remember she's wearing nothing but an old *The Breakfast Club* T-shirt and a thong.

Oh, right.

Offense is the best defense. She juts out her hip, trying not to care that it makes her left butt cheek all the more visible. "*You* snuck into *my* bedroom, remember? What did you think I'd be wearing?"

"Not...*that*," he sputters, staring to one side, then the other, then up at the ceiling. Basically, anywhere and everywhere except her left butt cheek. "What happened to your flannels? Those—" He waves his hand through the air, as if trying to catch up with his own brain. "You know, those pink ones with the rainbows on them?"

Yes. She knows exactly what flannels he's talking about. They're in the other room, still packed in her suitcase, not that she'll give him the satisfaction. "I'm not seventeen anymore, Jake."

"Yeah," he says gruffly, finally looking at her. "I know."

"And you lost the right to come traipsing through my bedroom window a long time ago."

"I know. I—" He pauses, frowns. "Wait. Is that my shirt?"

Shit. Her shoulders writhe. She was *really* hoping he wouldn't notice that. *Shit. Shit. Shit.* Sam's voice filters through her brain. *Revenge. Stay on the offensive. Revenge.*

"What if it is?" she retorts, gripping the hem and lifting it a few inches higher. She's not entirely sure who is in control of her body right now but not exactly mad either. "You want it back?"

"Jesus, Emily. No." He covers his eyes and whacks his head on the wall in his haste to turn away. "Ow." Then he slams his elbow into the glass door so hard it rings. "Fuck." Finally, he snatches a towel off the wall and throws it in her general direction. "Would you cover yourself up? I can't think with you standing there like that."

She rolls her eyes and picks the towel up off the floor. A memory comes unbidden as she wraps the cloth around her waist. It was the night she found out she was accepted to the Fashion Institute of Technology in New York. Sam and Jake were the only two people who even knew she applied, and when she texted him, the response was immediate.

We're celebrating. I'll be over in 10.

She showed Sam her phone, and her sister immediately pulled a miniskirt from the closet and pushed Emily toward the window.

"I'll handle Mom and Dad. Go!"

She'd never snuck out of the house before, never gone to any parties, never broken any rules. That was Sam's MO. Emily was the good girl. She was happier spending the night with her sketchbook than watching her sister flirt with any number of imbecile boys not worth the dirt on her shoe. At least, she had been until Jake. He made her want more—more for her life, more for her future, more for her heart. And when his pickup truck drove by, headlights off, not stopping until he reached the neighbor's house, she had this feeling as if everything was going to be different. As if all her life she'd been half-asleep, and now suddenly, she was alive.

His camera was rolling before she even opened the door.

"Emily Ann Peters, I'd like the first official interview before you're a huge fashion megastar. When you arrive in New York next fall, what's the first thing you're going to do?"

She rolled her eyes and hopped into the passenger seat, then stuck out her tongue. "Call my boyfriend, of course."

"Good answer. What next?"

"Hmm…" She settled her head back and lifted her feet onto the dash, grinning when she noticed his focus go right to her legs. The miniskirt had been a good call. "Real answer?"

"Real answer."

"I'm going to go sit in Bryant Park with a slice of dollar pizza and my sketchbook and dream."

He put the camera down and slid his hand behind her neck to tease her hair with his fingers. The gentle massage shot lightning down her spine. It sounded cliché but his eyes were glowing as he took her in, happiness and pride a force within his gaze. They hadn't been dating for very long, but it didn't matter. When he looked at her like that, she could see their entire future mapped out in perfect color. She'd go to New York to study fashion. He'd go to Los Angeles to make movies. They'd talk on the phone every day. They'd visit as much as possible. They'd find a way to make it work. Their dreams might have been pulling them in opposite directions, but their hearts were tied, bound, smushed together somewhere in the middle, inseparable.

"Congrats, Em."

She ducked her head, embarrassed. He trailed his fingers down her arm, barely touching her, yet somehow the path felt drawn by fire. Then he took her hand, lifted it to his lips, and started the engine. He didn't let go until they reached their destination. At this time of night, the beach parking lot was barren, so Jake didn't try to hide anything. As they got out, he pulled a bottle of champagne and two plastic cups from his back seat. She giggled nervously.

"Where'd you get that?"

"My mom." He shrugged. "You planning to report me?"

"If my dad knew I was here, we'd have much bigger problems than underage drinking." She snorted. "But, um…"

He sensed her hesitation. "What?"

"Nothing. It's just, um, you know I don't usually drink, and—"

"Em." He put the bottle on the ground. "I'm not trying to make something happen tonight. All I want to do is celebrate with you."

"I know, Jake. I know."

"Listen." He cupped her face and stroked her cheekbone with his wide thumb. The gentle scrape of rough skin left her tingling. "Nothing is going to happen tonight, or any night when you have a drink. Okay? I don't want to be someone you wake up in the morning and regret. I'd never forgive myself."

"You promise?"

"I promise." He waited a moment to make sure she believed him, then grinned and stepped closer. "But seeing as we haven't even opened the bottle yet…"

He put his arms on either side of her, caging her against the truck, then captured her mouth in his. She couldn't say how much time passed. Nothing mattered outside of her hands on his back, and his hands in her hair. At some point, she lifted her leg around his waist to urge him closer. His fingers found her thigh, then slid up, up, up, under the hem of her skirt and to the edge of her panties, before—

"Jesus, Em." He pulled away panting. "You're going to kill me."

She tried to tug him back. "Jake."

"No. No…" The second *no* sounded more for his benefit. He held his hands up while backing away and grabbed the bottle. "We have celebrating to do. Come on."

They went to the beach, and while yes, they made out on the towel a few more times, he was true to his word. She got drunk, and he got drunk off her getting drunk. They splashed in the surf. They stared at the stars. They sang and talked and he took a few more videos, until finally, a torrential downpour forced them back to the truck. She was shivering and soaked. He grabbed an extra T-shirt from the back seat before averting his eyes—though she did catch him taking a peek in the rearview mirror while her back was turned. He simply grinned as she playfully shoved him around. Then he dropped her off at home and waited until she crawled back through her window before driving away—a perfect gentleman.

She slept in his shirt every night for a week, the smell of the salt and sand and him too inviting to resist. He never asked for it back, so she never gave it back. Then he left, and she shoved it into the far reaches of her closet with all the other things that reminded her of him that she couldn't bear to look at anymore.

When she came home from New York, she threw most of those things away—most, but not all. The shirt reminded her of him, yes. But more importantly, it reminded her of a night when anything seemed possible, and that felt better than all the hurt his memory might have caused. She washed it twenty times in a row to get any lingering bits of his smell out, damned if she was going to give up her favorite shirt and the memory of one of her favorite nights because she got dumped. Plus, all that washing only made it softer and more comfortable.

Take that, Jake, she thinks as she finishes cinching the towel around her waist and looks up. There's a question in his downturned eyes, his pouted lips, his furrowed brow. The memory of that night plays as clearly in his gaze as it did in her mind, and there's no doubt as to what he's asking.

Do you regret me?

No.

Even after everything, her answer is no, which leaves her all the more annoyed. She crosses her arms, hiding the silhouette of the famous John Bender fist pump, one of Jake's favorite movie endings. He made her watch it about a hundred times, and each time, she died a little inside when Claire parted with her diamond earring—a perfect brilliant-cut solitaire stud. And she gave it up...for a boy.

Screw symbolism. Relationships come and go, but jewelry is forever.

The left side of Jake's mouth lifts in a half grin. "You're thinking about the earring, aren't you?"

"No."

"You are. It's written all over your face."

"I'm not."

"You *are*."

"Okay, I am. Sue me." She throws her hands in the air. "It's a really stupid ending. What girl would break up a gorgeous diamond set like that—for a guy she spent nine hours with in detention? It's so clearly written by a man."

Jake sighs and crosses his arms, leaning against the tiles. "It's sweet."

"It's idiotic."

"It's romantic."

"It's blasphemous."

"Are you serious right now?" He pushes off the wall, incensed.

She puts her hands on her hips, not backing down. "I don't joke about jewelry."

"It's not about the earring."

"That's easy to say as someone who's never owned a diamond in his life."

"Come on, Em. You know why she does it."

She should stop. She knows she should. And yet... "Why?"

"To show Bender she cares." He stares at her hard, those blue eyes freezing her in place. "Even if they never speak again, even if everything goes right back to the way it was when they start school on Monday morning, they had a connection. They shared a moment. And to her, that moment had more value than the most precious thing she owned."

He pauses to swallow. His arm lifts. His gaze drops. Emily's follows, watching in slow motion as he lifts his hand, stretches forward, and presses his pointer finger to her skin, caressing her forearm. It's barely even a touch, yet her stomach flips.

"He didn't matter to anyone else in the world," Jake whispers softly. "But he mattered to her. And she wanted him to know that."

His eyes find hers.

Are we still talking about a movie?

Emily's heart lurches.

She looks away, licks her lips, and steps back. "What do you want, Jake?"

"I needed to talk to you, and your room is the only place on this whole property that doesn't have a hidden camera, or a mic, or a nosy production assistant looking to get ahead."

Suddenly, the shower and the faucets make sense. White noise. Cover. An uncomfortable tickle scratches down her spine, and she shifts her weight. All the exhaustion from the day piles on, along with the realization that he didn't come here for her. He came for him. To clear his conscience. To get something off his chest. She's the dirty little secret, the body in the closet, the past he wants to keep hidden.

Well, fuck that.

"If you came here to say something, then say it."

"I'm sorry."

She snorts and arches a brow. "There's a long list of things you might be apologizing for, Jake. I'm afraid you're going to have to be a bit more specific."

"I should have called."

"Which time?"

He runs a hand through his hair, a frustrated sigh escaping. Emily is pissed off to find disgruntlement only makes him more attractive. The mussed-up waves. The clenched jaw. The sliver of exposed skin she can't keep her gaze from dropping to as his shirt lifts, revealing hard, tanned flesh. There's a challenge in his eyes, as if he's daring her to revisit the past. Beneath it, there's pain. No one else ever seemed to realize when he was hurting—not his mom, not his friends, not his teachers—but she always knew. He could never hide from her, and he can't now. History sizzles between them, a pot boiling over with everything left unspoken.

Emily looks away first.

"I'm sorry I didn't call to let you know I work for the show," he clarifies softly. "I should have given you the heads-up before you signed the contract."

"Why didn't you?"

"I don't know."

"Sam said you were being, and I quote, *a little chickenshit.*"

He snorts and rolls his eyes. "Of course she did."

"Is that the truth?"

"Yes." He says it too quickly, as if it's an out he's more than willing to take. Anger curdles in her gut. Dishonesty is the one thing she can't handle from him.

"Why are you really here, Jake?" Surprise lifts his brows. "And don't pretend it's about an apology, because we both know you've never been big on those. Are you afraid I'm going to out you to the crew? Don't worry. If you want to be Jackson Moore, be him. I won't tell them who you really are."

"No." He shakes his head and stands full upright. "Em, that's not—"

"Are you worried about your job? I won't interfere. Do all the producing you need to do and don't worry about me. Bring on the ex-girlfriends. Bring on the fights. Bring on the drama. I understand this is a television show and I'm under no delusions that I'm actually going to meet my husband out here."

Her stomach twists on the word.

His face pales. "Em—"

"*Emily*," she corrects, squaring her shoulders. "You're not the only one who's changed."

"I can see that."

"Good."

He crosses his arms, rising to the challenge. "Don't trust Nina."

"I don't."

"I'm just saying, she's a producer. It's her job to become your friend, to blur the lines, to get you to tell her things you wouldn't tell anyone else."

"I already said I don't trust her."

"Or Trish."

"Noted."

"Or any of the assistants."

"Wow. Your coworkers sound wonderful."

"Or the guys," he plows on. "They all have their ulterior motives."

Emily arches a brow. "Are you really in a position to give me dating advice?"

"I don't want you to get hurt."

"Since when?"

"That's not fair."

"Why not?"

"*Emily.*"

He says her name like a plea, each letter dragging like the edges of a serrated knife getting caught in the mounting tension. They're toe to toe, breathing heavily into the silence. Their chests eb and flow like a tide, together, apart, together, apart. Her neck arches up. His bends down. This close, she can almost taste the words he won't say.

Before, she was the one who looked away.

Now, she needs to know.

"Say it," she demands.

"What?"

"Whatever it is you came here to say, Jake. Stop pretending it was to warn me about the toxic world of reality TV. Or do you really think I'm such a naive idiot, I didn't do any research before handing myself over to your show?"

His jaw clenches.

"Say it."

One second passes.

Two.

The room is hot. Steam billows from the shower, making his shirt mold to his skin. She's half tempted to reach out and throttle the answer out of him, but in the thick vapors swirling around them like a veil from the outside world, she doesn't trust herself. The heart he broke? Still a malfunctioning disaster. But her body can't seem to remember that and she leans a little bit closer. The muscles in his neck relax. His Adam's apple lowers and lifts slowly, his skin glistening with a sweaty sheen.

"Why did you leave New York?"

Emily jerks back as if slapped. The room spins.

"I saw it in your file," he continues. "You were there for less than a year. You postponed your acceptance to FIT, and then withdrew without even taking a class. Why? What possible reason could you have had for doing that? For abandoning your dream?"

She reaches a hand to the wall to steady herself, completely unprepared for the onslaught of fear and pain that courses through her, all consuming. He sees her reaction, he must, but he doesn't stop. If anything, his voice becomes more demanding, laced through with the sort of hurt he's always tried so hard to hide, as if her choice betrayed everything they once stood for.

"And don't give me some bullshit answer like you weren't cut out for it. You were made for that school, for that city. What the hell happened?"

He's right.

She was made for it.

The few hours she spent there were a stolen slice of the life she could have had. She'd allowed herself one morning to walk the halls, pretend to be an incoming student, and sit in on some of the classes she would never be able to take. One morning to breathe in the energy of so many passionate creatives. One morning to imagine what it could have been like to be just another dreamer in a city overflowing with them. And then she walked to the main office, withdrew her acceptance, and flew home.

She ran from New York.

She's been running ever since.

And she isn't about to stop now.

"Get out, Jake."

He blinks at her dark tone, all the frustration in his face seeping away, replaced by uncertainty. He's gone too far, and he knows it, but it's obvious he doesn't understand why. Her throat burns. The pressure on her chest grows, no longer pushing inward from his presence, but outward, a bomb ready to explode, all her secrets and all her control slowly unraveling. He lifts his hand and lets it hover, as if unsure he's allowed to close the space between them.

He's not.

"Get the fuck out," she says again, this time presenting her back so he won't see the tears gathering in her eyes. "I don't owe you any answers."

"You're right," he says softly. "You don't."

It takes everything for her to keep her voice even, to keep the heave rattling up her lungs at bay. "You wanted to pretend we were strangers earlier. Let's be strangers. Don't talk to me unless it's about the show. Don't look at me unless it's through a camera. And don't crawl into my bedroom in the middle of the night to dole out unsolicited advice."

"Okay."

In the fogged-up mirror, she watches him roll his shoulders and resettle into this new arrangement, a phantom from another life ready to meld back into the shadows. But she knows him well enough to know he's not quite done. And she knows herself well enough to know that if she opens her mouth to stop him, she'll lose all tenuous grip on her emotions—and deep down, she wants to know what a goodbye sounds like from him. If this can help make up for the one she never got before.

He's careful not to touch her as he squeezes by and walks out the door, but it's almost worse that way, every point of her body acutely aware of his tantalizingly close warmth, and the sudden cold as he slips into the dark. He gets as far as the window before he stops, the way she knew he would. Emily doesn't turn to meet the gaze she can feel roving up her legs, along her spine, over her profile.

"America will love you, if you give them the chance."

The floorboards creak as he climbs onto the sill.

"Give them that chance, Em. Let them in, and they'll fall. Trust me. It's impossible not to."

CHAPTER EIGHT

STRANGERS, Jake thinks as he arrives on location the next day. *I can do this. I don't know her. We're strangers.*

Security leads his team through the underground hallways of SoFi Stadium into the heart of the football field. Seventy thousand empty seats surround them. Light floods in through the glass canopy overhead. And plastered across the jumbotron in eighty million high-definition pixels is Emily, mocking him with that perfect smile.

I can't fucking do this.

Strangers don't go into cardiac arrest at the sight of one another.

Strangers don't sleep in one another's old T-shirts.

Strangers don't lie awake in a cold sweat all night picturing one another naked.

Okay, two of those things might only apply to Jake—but one is entirely Emily's fault. *Why the hell does she still have that shirt anyway?*

The image is burned in his brain. Emily's ass. The sliver of her flat stomach as she tugged on the edge of *his* shirt. The barely there strip of cream fabric across her hipbone. Her ass, again, because really it's a perfect ass, and the moment his gaze landed on her exposed left cheek, his brain jumped back to a time when he was allowed to cross that distance, dig his fingers into her soft flesh, and lay claim.

I sound like a fucking barbarian.

He feels like a fucking barbarian, like some sort of starved, feral cat. He's jealous of a T-shirt for god's sake! He thought he got her out of his mind after he left Georgia, but it had all been a giant lie, a trick his heart played on him. Thoughts of her had been festering under the surface, out of sight, out of mind, growing and growing. Now with her suddenly back in his life, they've become one of those horrible, ingrown pimples that he knows is there but he can't figure out how to pop, so it just gets redder and redder, more painful and more obvious. He may as well have a sign on his face that reads: *I love her. I'll always love her. And we will never EVER be strangers.*

Her mom can bedazzle it for him.

"Jake."

He turns to find Nina. "Yeah?"

"Let's talk logistics."

Together, they divide the twenty remaining suitors into two teams—selected for optimal drama, with every brimming feud from the first night in mind. The assistants are already conducting the pre-group-date interviews, each carefully determined question meant to bring prior arguments up to the forefront. Between the competition for Emily, the very loosely regulated "tag" football, and the fact that most of the men were clearly selected for brawn over brains, some shit is definitely about to go down. And Fred will surely capture every glorious moment of it. There's only one problem as Jake sees it.

"You'll never get Emily into a cheerleading outfit."

Nina frowns. "What do you mean?"

"She just…" He bites his tongue and shrugs. "She doesn't seem the type."

"Well, it's a good thing I'm her handler then, and not you, because she's already dressed and waiting for my signal, which I'll be giving in about five seconds." She clicks on her mic. "Fred, you all set? Jake and I are good to go. If you give the okay, I'll send Emily out."

"Ready Freddy," he replies.

They both roll their eyes. Nina smiles. Jake would normally join her in the joke, but he can't. His gaze is glued to the tunnel where Emily is set to make her grand entrance. A knot about the size of Georgia clumps in his throat. A lot of people in this country live and breathe football. To them, the sight of a cheerleader might be a wet dream. And Jake doesn't have anything against those people. He really doesn't. But to see Emily like that? To see her become one of them? It's an absolute nightmare.

It's going to break him a little.

It's going to take one of the few good memories he has left and twist it into something unrecognizable.

Jake closes his eyes. Simple as that, he's back in his senior year.

It was homecoming night. School started about four weeks before, and though Nate had declared him Emily's official stalker, he had yet to gain enough courage to talk to her. Because look at her. She was gorgeous. She was funny. She was charming. She was one half of the most popular duo in school simply because they were new and interesting and every guy was hoping to date one or two or preferably both at the same time. What the hell could he offer? A screwed-up life story and dreams he would probably never achieve?

Instead, he was doing what he normally did and was using the camera as a cover to scan the crowd for her. Officially, he was there to take video footage for the yearbook committee. No, he didn't have that much school spirit, but any excuse to get behind the lens was an escape he'd take. Besides, his mother would have been hurt if he hadn't come. They were honoring his father that night. Whoop-de-fucking-doo. The bastard didn't deserve Jake's spit, let alone a plaque in the school trophy case. But he'd won them four state championships about a hundred years ago, and that was all that mattered to anyone in this town.

God, I can't wait to get out of here.

"Hi!"

He about jumped out of his skin and jerked away from the camera. Emily waved with a huge smile plastered across her face. He just stared, not entirely sure if he was hallucinating. After a beat of silence, her smile wavered. She pulled her lower lip between her teeth, and fuck, the sight of that did something to him.

Talk, you idiot. Talk.

"Um. Hey."

Great. Real smooth.

This wasn't their first conversation, but it might as well have been. The only other time they'd spoken was back during the first week of school. Her mother had driven her over to his house to drop off flowers, and she was just as surprised as him when he opened the door. The new police chief had wanted to send his condolences to the family of his predecessor. If it had been anyone but Emily, Jake would've slammed the door in their face. Instead, he'd gruffly taken the bouquet while she squeaked out an embarrassed *bye*, then fled to the car.

It was the stuff of fairy tales.

Not.

But now she was looking at him with those big doe eyes, and all the ice in him was melting.

Jake shrugged. "What are you, uh, doing here?"

Apparently, that was all the opening she needed because she hopped onto the handrail beside him and started swinging her feet while she spoke. "Well, my sister has decided that the quarterback of the football team, Ian what's-his-name—"

"Ian Winnacker."

"Right, Ian Winnacker is the love of her life. So she dragged me here to watch him play. But then she started talking to the class president, Chris—Chris—"

"Chris Davies."

"Right, Chris Davies. And like five other guys are there hanging on her every word, and I had to get out of there."

"Weren't they hanging on your every word too?"

"Ugh. That made it worse. So I looked around and tried to find someone to talk to who wanted to be here even less than I did. Then I saw you up here, by yourself, scowling into your camera, and I thought—yes! Perfect! Jacob William Henry the Third is my grumpy hero."

It didn't go unnoticed that she remembered his full name. Too bad it was a name he fucking hated.

"Just Jake."

"Okay, *Just Jake*."

She bumped his shoulder with hers. He couldn't fight the grin that passed over his lips, so he ducked his head back behind the camera and pretended to take some casual shots of the crowd for something to do.

"So, you want to be a filmmaker?"

He sent her a teasing glance. "What gave you that idea?"

She grinned and fireworks went off inside his chest. Making her happy was like a drug. He could easily become addicted if he wasn't careful.

And he wasn't.

"What about you?" he asked. "Any big dreams?"

"Oh, I don't know…"

"That's a yes."

She bit her lip again.

Fuck.

He shifted his weight in a lame attempt to hide how much that little maneuver was affecting him. She didn't seem to notice, though, as she tilted her head to the side.

"You promise you won't tell?"

"Who am I going to tell?"

"Nate."

He stopped himself from asking how she knew Nate was his best friend, because he liked that she knew. He liked it more than he should have. "I promise I won't tell anyone, even Nate."

"Okay, then I'll tell you." She leaned so close he could feel the heat of her skin. A bit of her hair fell and tickled his neck. If he'd thought the lip biting was hot, this moment was taking place in a fucking volcano. "I want to move to New York to study fashion and become a jewelry designer."

"Really?"

He turned to look at her. She was so close, his whole world was Emily. There was something cautious in her gaze, something unsure, and he wanted to erase it. She gave a small, almost embarrassed nod. He put his hand on her leg before he even realized what he was doing. She inhaled sharply but didn't move away.

"You're going to do it," he murmured.

She swallowed. "You think so?"

"Yeah. I do."

Trumpets blared as the band started to play the school fight song. He snatched his hand back as if caught. Emily turned toward the field.

"I think they're about to honor your dad."

Jake grunted and returned to the camera, trying to hide the way his jaw clenched. But she noticed. He could feel her gaze on him, could feel her studying him. She didn't ask the questions he knew were swirling in her head, and for the first time, he wondered how much her dad had learned from the other cops or if they were still covering for their old chief, their old quarterback. She had to have asked him about it after dropping off the flowers—something casual like *Hey, Dad, what happened to the old police chief anyway?* And maybe he'd told her about the car crash, and that was it. Or maybe he'd told her everything. And maybe that was why she was there with him, instead of down in the stands with her sister.

And he hated that.

He didn't want her pity.

But he didn't want her to leave either.

"I think Ian just noticed my sister and her gaggle of merry men," Emily said, changing the subject, for which he was truly grateful. She laughed and nudged her chin to where the quarterback stood on the sideline, glaring into the stands.

Jake didn't quite laugh, but he felt lighter, which was something.

Emily must've sensed it, because she kept talking as if to distract Jake from the ceremony taking place at center field.

"I once thought about designing a jewelry line around football," she commented. "There'd be the have-as-many-affairs-as-you-want engagement ring, the caught-in-the-tabloids-please-forgive-me pearls, the keep-'em-quiet diamond studs. Oh, and of course, a gorgeous platinum heart locket for the one woman who actually loves him—his mother."

His lips twitched. "You're terrible."

"I think you like it."

At that, he did smile. Because she was flirting. And now he knew it.

"I do." He turned to look her in the eye. "I really, really do."

Music blares, plucking Jake from his memories and dropping him right back into his own personal hell. Keith Holson comes over the jumbotron, filling SoFi Stadium with his wholesome, fatherly, prime-time voice. Emily emerges from the tunnel in a pleated miniskirt and glorified bra with pom-poms in each hand. The men hoot and holler. Keith cheers. The cameras eat up every second.

Meanwhile Jake is on the sideline, trying not to barf.

He wants to look away, but he can't, and not just for his job. He watches, transfixed, as all twenty remaining men fawn over her. She lets herself be lifted onto one of their shoulders, then carried across the field by another. She applies sunscreen on bare backs, giggles like a lemming, and cheers with each successful pass. When the first touchdown is scored, the suitor runs over and spins her around. She kisses his cheek. With each successful point, the theatrics grow more and more absurd—tossing her over a shoulder, faking a photoshoot, staging a mock proposal—each guy vying for the funniest and most television-worthy celebration while Emily happily goes along for the ride.

It's an out-of-body experience.

The girl he knew is at war with the woman she became, the first too preoccupied with her sketchbook and her dreams to notice all the attention she garnered, and the latter seemingly basking in it.

But this can't be the real her.

He doesn't—he *won't*—believe it.

Which is the only explanation for what happens two hours later, after the blue team wins and all ten of those suitors share a picnic with Emily on the field. Nina gestures toward him. Emily squares her shoulders and closes the distance between them. She needs to select three men for her mini-dates tomorrow—one for breakfast, one for lunch, and one for dinner—but this early in the show the lead only picks one herself and the producer in charge of the suitors picks the other two. Aka, him.

Strangers, Jake reminds himself as she approaches. *Strangers. Strangers.*

"Hey," Emily says, overly cheery. The false tone makes his hackles rise. "Nina sent me—"

"To pick your dates. I know." He crosses his arms and leans his shoulder against the wall, taking her in slowly—the skirt, the top, the spirit ribbons in her hair. A mic pack bulges from her waist, picking up their entire conversation. It's all he can do to keep the sneer from his face. "Anyone you like?"

She grits her teeth, the happy demeanor cracking. "Just tell me your picks."

"I haven't decided yet. I need a little more information."

"Like what?" Her nostrils flare.

He fights a grin. It's always been fun to push her buttons. "Are you a big football fan, then?"

"Sure. Why not?"

"Interesting. What's your favorite team?"

"Georgia."

"Georgia?"

She puts her hands on her hips, not backing down. "That's what I said."

"I didn't know they had a team."

"We do."

"What's the name?"

"The, uh... The..." She scowls. Then her eyes pop wide as a look of triumph fills her entire face. It's adorable and he fucking hates it. "Atlanta!" she exclaims. "The Atlanta Falcons! Ha!"

Touché.

"Did you cheer in high school?" he asks, pushing a little bit further, because his thoughts are still on that night and he can't let go of her yet. "I didn't peg you for the type."

"How is this relevant to my dates tomorrow?"

"Like I said, I want some more information, so I can be sure I'm picking the right guys for you."

"Sure." Her eyebrows rise so high they may detach from her face and start to fly. "I'm sure that's the reason."

"What other reason would I have?"

"Why don't you tell me, *Jackson*?"

"Just Jake."

She snorts and turns her face to the side. But recognition flashes in her honey eyes before she can hide it. As she pulls her lower lip between her teeth, he knows that night is running through her thoughts, the same way it is for him.

Still, she doesn't say what he wants her to.

The reason he was teasing.

The reason he brought them here.

To hear *Okay, Just Jake.*

To hear her admit that she remembers, that maybe somewhere deep inside she also misses the way they used to be, that they were good together once.

Instead, she snaps, "Never mind. Surprise me."

She turns to go.

Jake stands, a rubber band recoiling. He's being an asshole. It's not her fault she's here. It's actually his fault entirely.

"Wait, Em—"

"*Emily.*" She stops and spins on her heels to face him, wrath personified. "My name is Emily. And you know what? You're right. I didn't cheer in high school. I wasn't the type. I couldn't have cared less about football. My first boyfriend was the school loner. He wanted to be a director, a bit like you actually. And you know what he taught me? Even the nerdy boys can break your heart, so you might as well date the ones with muscles and enjoy yourself."

He should admit defeat.

He should apologize.

He should relent.

Instead, he puffs up his chest. "You want meatheads?"

"Bring 'em on."

"Okay. Kevin and Tony are my picks."

"Great."

"Great."

"Good."

"Good."

"Fine."

"Fine."

With a proud lilt of her chin, she stomps away. He tracks her across the field, not looking away, not blinking, until another voice comes through his comm.

"Kevin and Tony?" Nina asks dubiously. "Do you want her to have an awful day?"

Yes.

Jake sighs.

No.

He scrunches his features.

I don't fucking know.

He scowls, and into the mic says, "Just go with it."

CHAPTER NINE

WHEN EMILY WAKES the next day, the sun is shining. Birds are chirping. She does a twirl in her pink flannel pajamas, blissfully happy because she's finally—*finally*—going to have a completely Jake-free day.

Yes!

It's the day of her mini-dates, which means Nina will be coming with her as the lead producer on the dates, and Jake has to stay behind at the mansion to stir up some drama between the guys.

Take that!

There's a knock at the door. "Emily?"

"Come on in, Nina!"

Her producer opens the door and pokes her head through as a slow smile widens her lips. "You look chipper."

"I am. I really am."

"Excited for the dates?"

Not really, but it was as good an excuse as any. "Yup!"

"Great! I can't tell you too much, but hair, makeup, and

wardrobe are coming in now. We're leaving in about an hour for the first date."

"Who's it with?"

"Kevin."

Kevin, Emily thinks. *Kevin. Kevin. My knight in shining not-Jake armor.*

Nothing will burst her bubble today, not even the sight of the precariously empty wardrobe rack filled only with barely there string bikinis. Emily simply picks her favorite one—a high-neck royal-blue two-piece with a slightly sporty edge—and ties a silk scarf around her waist like a sarong before adding a chunky Emily Ann Designs necklace. Nina cuts off the stylist's protest. Displaying her products is in Emily's contract, and the producer is still trying to get on her good side. Besides, the white and cream beads pop perfectly against the swimsuit. For good measure, Emily slips two simple cushion-cut sapphires into her lobes, another Emily Ann original. She managed to get the stones for a steal from an estate sale a few years back—with some polish and a new setting, they were good as new. More importantly, they make her feel good as new, ready for a fresh start, a fresh day, a fresh...everything.

Emily is on a high as she walks across the grass from the guesthouse to the main house. Kevin is waiting for her by the front door, his board shorts low on his tan hips. Who needs a shirt with pecs like that? She tries not to gawk as they settle in the back seat of the limo, pointedly ignoring the cameras aimed at their faces. Kevin finds a bottle of champagne and expertly pops it open. They laugh and sip. Small talk eventually lapses to silence as the ride continues. Still, she's optimistic. It's not until they pull up next to a one-hundred-foot yacht that the problems begin. Not for her, obviously. She grew up on the beach. Her father loves to fish. Boats are in her blood. She's ecstatic. But when she turns to Kevin with an ear-to-ear grin, his face has gone green.

"Are you okay?" she asks politely.

He gulps. "Sure. Yeah, sure."

News flash. He's not okay. Ten seconds into the boat ride, he's already running for the bathroom. Emily chases after him, trying to keep up with the cameraman hot on his tail. There's another behind her, capturing every horrifying moment. The hallway fills with the sound of his retching—the coughing, the gurgling, the wet *splats*. There's no doubt it's a serious projectile situation on the other side of the door. Before long, Emily's feeling queasy too.

I've got to get out of here.

She leaves under the guise of finding him some water and rushes above deck to breathe the fresh air. Then she runs back down with water. Then up again for crackers. Then down. Then up for mints. Then down. Again and again. Until Nina finally stops her.

"He's a lost cause," the producer says and puts her hand across the door Emily was about to duck inside with an armful of fresh towels.

"I feel so bad. The poor guy."

"I do, too." The words are made completely unconvincing by the mirth twinkling in the woman's eyes.

"No, you don't."

"Okay, fine. I don't." Nina shrugs, offering a rueful smile. "This is reality TV gold. But I can assure you, the network won't let us air more than five minutes of this absolute disaster of a date, and we have enough footage for that already. So, you have two options. Continue to run up and down the stairs watching after a guy you've barely spent half an hour with and will probably only spend another half an hour with before you give him the boot, or grab a mimosa, lie in the sun, and bask in an hour of unexpected downtime on us. The PAs can handle him. We paid for a morning on this yacht, and unfortunately for Kevin, the senior crew fully intends to enjoy it. In about fifty-five minutes, we'll be back at the dock. The choice is yours."

Emily hesitates for an admirable half-second before turning longingly toward the bar. A champagne flute already waits on the polished wood, orange juice and champagne bubbling.

"Good choice," Nina whispers.

A stewardess leads her to a lounge chair on the main deck. Emily flops onto the cushion and takes in the sweeping view of the Pacific Ocean. The salty air is familiar. The crashing waves and the wind in her hair remind her of home. But this rich blue color is almost too beautiful to be real. So Emily sips her drink and breathes the scene in.

The next fifty-three minutes are the best fifty-three minutes she's had in a month, and that might be the very reason she's single.

Men are *so* much work.

Take her father, for example, whom she loves dearly and can't help thinking about as the yacht races over the water, stirring up memories of her youth. The man can remember every single detail of an investigation, but ask him where his shoes are? Or his keys? Or his fill-in-the-blank household object? And he'll stare at you blankly before muttering a curse. Gifts have never been his forte. Emily usually steps in for her mother's birthday and their anniversary, plus Christmas and Valentine's Day and Mother's Day. He needs dinner served every night and lunch packed for work—god forbid the chief of police learn how to make a freaking sandwich. And her mother does it happily despite having her own business to run.

Emily can't do that.

She won't.

And the men she meets never seem to get it. They don't understand that starting her own business means late nights working, and a reliance on takeout, and an inability to make *them* the biggest priority in her life. They stare at her blankly when she starts talking about her designs, as if jewelry is a fleeting hobby and not the passion at the core of her personality. They aren't interested in *her*, but in the image of her they made up in their own heads, some ideal she can never quite meet. And that's *before* she goes deeper, before she even thinks of telling them the messy truth.

Only one man ever saw her clearly.

Only one man ever loved her for *her*.

And then he left.

Just like that, Emily's Jake-free day is ruined. His mocking look comes to the forefront of her thoughts, the slow perusal of her cheerleading costume followed by a smarmy raise of his brow, as if he still knew her better than anyone else in the world, as if he still had any right to call her out.

Sure, she felt absurd in pigtails as a grown-ass woman.

Sure, the initial thought of wearing the outfit had her in hives.

Sure, she hated every second of the date and was playing it up for the cameras and for the guys who all gave up so much to be there with her.

But—

Wait a second.

Emily freezes mid-mimosa, a sudden realization striking. She downs the rest of her drink, then stands. The dock is already in view, which means she has less than five minutes before the cameras start rolling again. She finds Nina in two.

"Did you know Kevin gets seasick?"

"I think it's pretty obvious. He's been barfing for like an hour."

"No." Emily shakes her head. "Before, when you were organizing the dates, did you know Kevin gets seasick? Did you know this would happen?"

"Oh..." The producer swallows, winces, offers a weak smile. "I didn't—"

"Did Jake?"

Nina scrunches her brow. "What?"

"Yesterday, when he chose Kevin for me, did he know?"

"Well, that depends."

"On what?"

"On how well he read the files."

Emily sees red.

He knew.

He fucking knew, and he chose Kevin out of spite.

Asshole.

Fury lights up her entire being. It simmers in the

background while she smiles and presents Kevin with a pity puzzle piece as he desperately holds a barf bag to his lips. It sizzles while she's led to the van where wardrobe is waiting. It spits and spews and grows for forty-five minutes before she steps onto the Santa Monica Pier in a pink peplum blouse, ripped jean shorts, white sneakers, sixties-inspired sunglasses, and a chunky turquoise necklace from her own line.

Outside, she's Malibu Barbie. But inside, she's a seething inferno of rage.

She blames the rage for what happens next.

A masculine arm grabs her from behind.

Without thinking, Emily flings her elbow back into his head. The man groans and she twists, on autopilot as she brings her knee to his groin, the lessons drilled into her. He keels over and she pushes on the back of his neck so he flails to the ground. It's only when he rolls onto his back, face pinched in pain, that she realizes he's not Jake.

He's her date.

"Tony!"

Shit!

Emily drops to her knees beside him. Jake was in her head. All that pent-up anger was in her heart. She just reacted.

"I'm so sorry," she gushes.

"Don't be!" Nina calls from the side as a medic rushes in. "That was amazing!"

"Was it?" Tony grumbles as he pushes the medic away and eases to his feet with an aggravated, "I'm fine. I'm fine."

"I'm so sorry, really," Emily repeats, following him up and tentatively putting her hand on his arm. "My father is a police chief, and when my sister and I told him we both wanted to move to New York City after graduation, he made us take self-defense classes with some of the new recruits. I didn't mean— You surprised me! I feel awful."

"Do you?" he snaps, then stops, turning to the side. Emily follows his gaze. The cameras are watching them, red light on and rolling. Suddenly, he laughs, his annoyance vanishing as if it were never there. It's almost frightening how fast his reaction changes. "Don't be sorry! I'm impressed. Let me try this another way."

He stretches out his hand.

Emily shakes it.

And that should reset the date, but it doesn't. Though Tony puts on the charm for the cameras, there's an undercurrent Emily can't help but pick up on. And *god*, she wishes she would stop bringing everything back to Jake, but she can't help it. The last time she played carnival games was with him senior year, and the flashbacks run through her mind like a montage of how it should be.

When she beats Tony at the water gun game and he offers a begrudging congratulations, she closes her eyes and sees Jake. Neon lights reflected in his eyes as he grinned wickedly and leaned in, dragging his nose up the column of her neck as his lips searched for her ear. "That was so fucking sexy."

When Tony bests her at the roll-a-ball derby, he puffs up his chest and chucks his winnings at her like an afterthought. In the back of her mind, she remembers Jake, whooping like an idiot when he finally beat her, then hooking an arm around her neck to pull her close. A laugh was on his lips when he gently teased, "All right, loser. Pick your prize."

When Tony spurts ketchup on her shirt, it's to embarrass her on national television. But back when Jake had nudged her ice cream into her face, it was so he could lean in and lick a wayward drip from her jaw. The resulting shiver that ran down her spine had nothing to do with the cold.

And when they rode the Ferris wheel, Jake didn't cross his arms and turn away the second the cameras shut off. He pulled her onto his lap until she straddled him, then he buried his face in her chest before groaning, "God, I've been waiting to do this all fucking night."

And she deserves that.

She deserves someone whose actions aren't meant to cut her down, the way Tony's have been. She deserves someone who wants to bolster her up, the way Jake once had before the world turned upside down. Emily meant what she said in her speech that first night. She'd rather be alone than settle for someone who makes her feel inadequate. Her own doubts and insecurities do enough of that already. They don't need the help.

Needless to say, Tony doesn't get a puzzle piece at the end of the date. He gets a goodbye handshake, and he's lucky it's not a goodbye kick in the groin.

"Will the viewers think I'm a shrew?" Emily asks Nina as Tony disappears inside his car.

"No."

The earnestness in the response makes Emily turn toward Nina curiously. The producer drops her headphones to her shoulders, disconnecting as much as she can. She's wearing her typical motorcycle boots and a leather jacket despite the heat. The two of them next to each other look as opposite as opposite can be, yet for the first time since coming to California, Emily feels seen, feels understood.

"You're underestimating the viewers," Nina says, stepping closer. "You were a fan before you were the lead. Would you have seen through Tony? The camera picks up more than you know, and I promise you, I don't miss a thing. He was a jerk. You saw it. I saw it. They'll see it too."

"You think so?"

"I do, because you know what makes the love story on our show so satisfying to watch?"

"What?"

"The journey. Every viewer has been in your shoes. Maybe not dating thirty men on live TV, but on a bad date with an asshole who didn't treat them right. Some frogs are just frogs. But you still have to kiss them to find the prince. And when you find your prince, which you will, because there are some great guys here too, you'll give everyone watching hope that they'll find their match too. That's the power of our show. The hope."

Hope, Emily thinks.

Maybe that's what she's been missing. Maybe that's why she can't leave Jake in the past where he belongs, why even on her Jake-free day, his ghost is somehow here, haunting her. She hasn't felt truly hopeful in seven years, and maybe that's what she misses more than anything else—that feeling of running toward something instead of running away.

Hope.

Emily latches on to the word, repeating it like a mantra until it's so big it shoves Kevin and Tony and even Jake away.

She has one date left to salvage the day, and it's time to try something new.

Hope.

When they arrive at the helipad, Ethan is waiting in a black tuxedo, bouncing eagerly on his toes. His green eyes are bright. And as she steps out of her limo, a somewhat immodest amount of leg flashing as the thigh-high slit in her evergreen gown falls open, a boyish grin brings out his dimples.

Henry Cavill and Colin Farrell's love child was right, Emily thinks, Nina's description from the first night coming to mind. *Here goes nothing.*

She waves a bit shyly. He takes her hand and sweeps her into a dramatic spin, the skirt of her dress flaring around her ankles. Somehow she ends up pressed against his chest, two big hands resting on her hips, the weight not unwelcome. He leans down, bringing his lips to her ear.

"You look amazing."

It's exactly the right thing to say and exactly the right way to say it—charming, magnetic, irresistible. His stunt from the first night comes to mind—the spill from the limo and subsequent *Gotcha!* followed by another whispered confession, *And I plan to keep you.*

He's smooth.

Too smooth.

Not-here-for-the-right-reasons smooth.

It's a *Love Match* red flag, she knows. One wrong step and she'll be on a slip-and-slide to heartbreak. Normally she wouldn't dare trust his antics.

But tonight, she wants to hope.

She wants to believe.

So instead of pulling back and refortifying her walls, instead of guarding her heart, Emily lifts onto her toes and presses a soft kiss to his cheek, then whispers, "You don't look so bad yourself."

They load into the helicopter, and she takes one of his hands in both of hers. The door sweeps closed, and they share a grin. She leaves her caution on the launchpad as they soar. The wind and the romance and the magnanimity of the show carry her away. When else will she get a private sunset helicopter ride over Los Angeles? When else will she be serenaded by a string quartet as a handsome man twirls her in circles, the dance floor surrounded by a thousand burning candles? When else will she get a private dinner for two outside the Griffith Observatory, the city skyline twinkling like stars brought down to earth as the moon shines overhead?

Never.

This is the stuff of Hollywood magic, and she's determined to enjoy it, even though the cameras are rolling, the food set before them is cold, and none of it feels quite real. As they settle into their seats, they finally dig into the meat of the date—not the meal, which unlike the wine is there as a prop and not for actual consumption, but the conversation. They move beyond the romantic montage set to music. As a fan, she knows it's time for the *deep reveal*, in which one of them will confess their tragic backstory, leaving the viewers swooning.

As if on script, Ethan leans back to take her in and flirtatiously asks, "How the hell are you single?"

Nina cuts in from the side. "No cursing."

They roll their eyes together, and Ethan asks again. "How in the world are you single?"

It's a testament to the magic of the show that she almost tells him the truth. She's so wrapped up in the evening, so eager to believe in any possible love story, the secret almost rolls off her tongue. But a few hopeful hours aren't enough to undo seven years of hiding. Reality crashes in around her. Jake is there again, the elephant in the room no one else can see. Her throat closes. She remembers the camera, remembers who's watching, remembers why she's been covering up her past.

The spell breaks.

Emily glances away from Ethan's magnetic green eyes.

"I guess for the same reason most people are," she says with a shrug, waiting until her defenses are fortified before looking back at his face. "I dated someone. I loved him. I thought we were the real deal. For life. And then it ended. He left without even saying goodbye. And after that, I was afraid to get hurt again."

It's true, yet not. She *is* afraid to get hurt again, but it's deeper than that. The truth is, after Jake, she doesn't trust anyone will stay. And because of that, she never gives them the chance—to hurt her or to leave her. It's easier to be alone.

"Well, if it makes you feel better..."

Ethan pauses to lean in. He takes Emily's hand and ducks his head, as if saying something in confidence. She knows the move is really to bring them closer together, to set the stage. Because he wants to be the one she can trust? Because he wants to be the hero of her television love story? Because he wants to be the next one to break her? Emily doesn't know. But she does know what's coming next.

"Your ex sounds like an asshole."

Emily laughs on cue, unable to tell what's entirely real anymore. "You're probably right."

"I am. You're a catch, Emily. Everyone can see it. And if you give me a chance, I promise, I won't hurt you like he did. You can trust me."

Can I?

He wets his lips.

He leans in.

Emily glances to the side for a split second, her gaze connecting with Nina's. The producer holds her chin with her fingers, staring at Emily like a specimen to dissect. She knows there's more to the story. She knows Emily is hiding something. She heard the hesitation in her words. Nina said it herself—she misses nothing. And it's not in the woman's nature to let anything go.

Shit, Emily thinks.

Shit. Shit.

Ethan stops an inch before her mouth. He whispers, "Give me a chance, Emily. Ask me to stay."

He probably doesn't even realize how precisely perfect his choice of words is. All she wants is someone who will stay. It means everything.

Ethan might be that man, or he might not be, but right now, it doesn't matter. She's desperate to escape the probing look in Nina's eyes, desperate to keep her secrets safe for one more day, and yes, she's desperate to believe that someone, somewhere, may actually find her worth fighting for.

So she gives in.

To the wine, to the empty stomach, to the romance, no matter how artificial.

Emily answers Ethan with a kiss and loses herself in the feel of his lips.

JEALOUSY BURNS through Jake as Trish pauses the image on the screen—Emily and Ethan locked in a passionate kiss. He can't even pretend it's anything else. Anger. Pain. Bitterness. Desire. They're all there, but the core of this jumbled mess of emotion is good old-fashioned jealousy, something he has absolutely no right to feel.

Trish grins. "We have our first hubby of the season."

"Ethan? Really?" He fights through the knot in his throat, the words coming out far more nonchalant than he feels. Try as he might, he can't pull his eyes away from Emily. No matter where he looks, she's there, in one of the dozen screens littering the video village. Every smile mocks him. Every laugh is at his expense. Filming is supposed to be his happy place, but right now, it's his own personal hell, a prison he can't escape.

"You didn't see the first two dates," Trish comments as she rewinds a few minutes. "They were disasters, which makes Ethan look even more perfect."

"A little *too* perfect, though? He's a typical salesman. We usually weed them out before hometowns."

"Not this season." Trish stops the video. "Here, watch this."

On the big center screen, Emily and Ethan stare at each other through candlelight. Los Angeles twinkles like a starlit sea behind them, the romance palpable.

"He left without saying goodbye," Emily says. Jake knows exactly to whom she's referring. "And after that, I was afraid to get hurt again."

"Your ex sounds like an asshole," Ethan comments.

Emily laughs, deep and true. Once upon a time, the sound was like music in Jake's ear but now it cuts like shattered glass. "You're probably right."

Ethan leans in for a kiss.

Emily looks away. Uncertainty flashes over her features. She has good instincts. She's always seen through bullshit. But then Ethan says four words, four words that make every muscle in her face shift, expression turning from wary to wanting.

"Ask me to stay."

Jake's chest burns as she closes the distance and seals that request with a kiss.

I would have stayed if you asked, he thinks, the past and present mixing so time ceases to exist. *That's why I didn't give you the chance to ask. Because I couldn't stay. I couldn't do that to you.*

The reason he left was so obvious it didn't need to be spelled out, to be spoken. They couldn't be together. They both knew it. She was too good for him. She was going places.

He refused to hold her back. He refused to be like his father. It was better for her if he left. He didn't want to. Lord knows, leaving was the last thing he wanted.

But he almost cost her everything.

All her dreams.

All her hopes.

Her entire future gone in a heartbeat.

Then he got a second chance to do the right thing, and he took it. No turning back. It was the hardest decision he ever made in his life, and if everything hadn't happened the way it had, he might never have had the strength to make it. But he did. And seven years later, he still doesn't know if it was the right choice. At the time, it was the only way he could think of to set her free.

Now, he's the asshole.

The one who broke her.

The one who gets laughed at over wine.

The idiot who let her go.

"You see what I'm seeing?" Trish says, bringing him back to the present as she pauses the image mid-kiss yet again. Another dagger to the gut. "We all know Emily is a bore. She was a bit better in her confessionals today, but she's never going to bring the drama, not the way our show needs. It's up to us. And Ethan? He's perfect. The viewers will see through him long before she does—at least, they will if you do your job right and make sure his real personality comes through in the group scenes. It's been a long time since we've had a villain win the show. I think it's exactly what the season needs."

He hates that he sees her point. If it were anyone except Emily on that screen, he'd be nodding and agreeing without a second thought, and he's not sure he likes what that says about him. When did he stop seeing these people as people but as pawns?

"You think the viewers will want that?" he asks, applying gentle pressure.

"Ethan will be F1," Trish continues, ignoring his pathetic attempt at resistance. "Cooper, the cowboy. Let's get him a mini-date next episode. Make it happen. He's the perfect foil. We get him as F2. Then it's up to Emily to pick good over evil. It's a win-win. If she picks the good guy, people will cheer. If she picks the asshole, then she's the idiot who couldn't see through his buffoonery the way the viewers did, and the cowboy becomes our next lead. Either way, the show comes out on top."

And Emily? he thinks. *What about her?*

Trish couldn't care less.

Jake is dismissed. He drags himself back to his room, then sits in the shadow of his windowsill to look across the lawn at the brightly lit guesthouse. A figure moves behind a gauzy curtain. She's so close, yet so far.

Ask me to stay.

The words flit through his mind, no longer in Ethan's voice, but his own. Jealousy has given way to something far, far worse—longing. It's dangerous to let himself think for even a moment that things could be different. Five more weeks and she'll be gone, probably with a fiancé. And he'll be here, with the same hollow dreams that stopped meaning anything the moment he ducked through her window and drove away.

His phone rings.

Jake turns from the window and looks at the screen lighting up in the dark. *Mom.* She's been calling nonstop. He hasn't picked up because he doesn't know what to say. But now he answers, simply because he wants to hear her voice, to know he's not completely alone.

"Hey, Mom."

She must hear something in the words, because she sighs into the phone. "Oh, Jacob."

Hearing his real name throws him off kilter. Grandpa was William. Dad was Billy. He's Jake. But he'll always be little Jacob to his mother.

The little Jacob she completely screwed over.

Anger surges up his throat, burning with the fury of a rocket entering orbit. It's always been an easier emotion for him to feel, coming too quick, burning too bright. A product of his bloodline. Usually, he tries to fight it.

Not now.

"Don't *oh, Jacob* me, Mom. This is entirely your fault!"

"My fault?"

"Don't play innocent. I know exactly how Mrs. Peters got her intel."

"Oh, that? Well, yes. That was me." She has the decency to sound at least a little repentant. "But I was just spreading a little idle gossip with friends. I had no idea she'd share it with the whole world."

"You didn't?"

"Of course not!"

There's a pause. He's waiting, because he knows his mother and there's no way she's done.

Finally, she mutters, "But I can't exactly say I'm mad about it."

"Mom."

"What? You've been so terrified to see her you haven't come home in seven years. Sue me for hoping the Band-Aid's been ripped off and I might get to spend Christmas in my own house for a change."

"The Band-Aid's been ripped off, all right. I'm helping her find her future husband, for fuck's sake."

"Language."

"Sorry."

"Is that what this is about?"

"What?" he responds gruffly.

"Oh, honey. I'm sorry."

"What?" he snaps. The sympathy in her voice is too much to take.

"You miss her."

Hearing the truth on his mother's lips leaves him sliced open on the operating table, his busted heart visible for the whole world to see. He can't find the words to deny it, not the way he can in his own head. It's easier to lie to himself than to her. It always has been.

"You should tell her," his mother murmurs tentatively, testing the waters.

Jake scoffs.

"I'm serious, honey. She'll never know if you don't tell her. And you'll never know either."

"Never know what?"

"How she'd respond."

Well, if his venture into her room the other night was any

indication, she'd respond by borrowing her father's Glock 22.

"I can't."

"Why not?"

His mom doesn't know all the details. She doesn't know half of them. If she did, she'd be ashamed. So he gives her the one excuse she might understand. "You do remember it's my job to get her engaged in five weeks?"

"Please. These showmances never work out."

"Showmances? Since when do you know the term *showmances*?"

"Stop changing the subject."

"I'm not, Mom. My job is important to me."

"Jacob."

He rolls his eyes at her tone.

"What's really holding you back?"

"Nothing."

Denial permeates the word. She must hear it. A few moments of silence pass. His mother is waiting for an answer he doesn't know how to give.

Finally, she relents.

Or so he thinks as she inhales deeply, the sound of rushing air filling his ear. But when she speaks, it's anything but a surrender.

"You're not your father, Jacob."

She's said this before. She's said it a hundred times. But no matter how many times he hears it, he never quite believes it. He spent one too many nights listening to his father's rants, his mother's cries, the *slap* of a hard palm against a soft cheek, and one too many mornings being told he was the spitting image of his dear old dad. Everyone in town said it. Everyone saw it. Those words carve deep. It's a damage not easily undone. Hell, he moved all the way to Los Angeles and changed his name to Jackson in honor of his maternal grandfather, Jack Moore, and he still can't seem to step out of the man's shadow.

He doesn't fault his mom. He knows the toll abuse can take. He understands the charisma his father held. There was a time Jake saw him as a hero, too. And the bastard was the police chief. Anywhere she went, he would have followed.

Same as Jake had to leave, his mother had to stay.

He gets it.

But he doesn't know how to say any of that without crushing her.

"I've got to go, Mom," he mutters instead, the line thick with tension.

She sighs. "I love you."

"I love you, too."

The silence in his room is suffocating. It rings in his ears, louder and louder, until he finally pulls himself away from the window. The droning doesn't stop. It follows him through the night, into the morning, and all the way to the cocktail party that evening. The room is full of people. Noise bounces off the walls. Still, the buzz grows until he realizes it's not from the quiet. It's from the pressure of everything left unsaid.

Soon, Emily stands at the front of the room. The men are lined up, waiting to be called. Jake stands off to the side behind Fred's camera. The list of suitors fills his clipboard. He mutters the names to the director so he knows where to aim his lens, whose reactions to capture. Down the line they move, until there's only one name left.

"Ja—"

Emily stops, clears her throat. Suddenly, Jake imagines himself somewhere else. In his suit. In the line. Waiting like all the other men. Waiting. Waiting. Then—

Jake.

Her voice fills his head. He walks up, takes the puzzle piece from her hand, and kisses her on the cheek. She's giving him a second chance.

The scene crashes as her real voice fills the room. "James."

Another man moves.

Another man crosses the distance.

Another man pulls her close.

Jake is rooted to the spot. He'll never be her perfect match. Not on TV. Not in real life. Those cards were dealt, and he folded. He'll never be her hero.

But that doesn't mean he has to stay her villain. Maybe a little closure would be better for both of them. An end to the animosity, to the tension, to whatever it is that still simmers between them. Maybe that's the one part of the story he can change, if he tries.

emily

A *TAP, tap, tap* on the window wakes Emily in the morning. The sound is soft but repetitive. After a few minutes, she loses the ability to tune it out.

What the hell is that?

She rolls over in bed and pulls the duvet over her ears to muffle the noise. Her room is still dark, which means it's way too early to be awake. The pecking continues, almost like a beak on glass.

Tap. Tap. Tap.

Did she do something to piss off a bird recently? Because this is a hell of a way to get revenge. Impressive, really, to catch her at her weakest moment.

"Go away," she mumbles into her pillow.

The room quiets.

She sighs in relief. Then—

WHACK!

Emily bolts upright, her head whipping to the window. She almost expects to find a mutilated, feathery carcass stuck to the glass. Instead, there's a yellow Post-it note that reads *Pull me.* She squints, sure she must have read that incorrectly. The sun has barely risen over the horizon. It's hardly light enough to see. She pads across the room for a better look, and finally notices the bit of string taped beneath the note.

Jake.

She has half a mind to crawl back to bed, but her curiosity won't let her. Instead, she reaches beneath the open frame, grabs the line, and reels it in. A small package no bigger than her palm is wrapped in paper and string. She unties it. When a cheap flip phone falls into her lap, she gasps as if she's discovered the Holy Grail. A hasty message is scrawled on the paper. Even if she didn't recognize the handwriting, she'd know who it was from.

I prepaid five hours' worth of calls to NY, and we leave the US in four days for our first stop abroad. It won't work after that, so use it wisely. Consider this a peace offering from a stranger.

PS: Sorry for the early wake-up. I'll have a PA bring you a latte later. Skim milk. One sugar. Two pumps of vanilla. Hopefully your coffee order hasn't changed as much as your sleepwear. I might not recover.

Three seconds pass in stunned silence. A snort escapes as Emily rereads the last few lines one more time, unable to fight her grin. They read almost...flirtatious. Her stomach flutters and she shoves the note under her pillow defiantly. Then she grabs the phone, jumps to her feet, and practically launches herself into the bathroom. The shower seems like overkill, so she stuffs a towel under the door to seal the crack and settles onto the countertop while it rings. The call goes to voicemail three times before Sam finally picks up.

"You're persistent. I'll give you that. And I respect the hustle. But whatever you're selling, I don't want it. Stop calling me."

"Wait, Sam!" Emily grips the phone tighter, wishing she could reach through the receiver and catch her sister before she hangs up. "It's me!"

"...Em?"

"Yes!"

"Em!"

"Sam!"

"How are you calling me? I thought you were on a communication blackout for another five weeks?"

"I am! I mean, I was. But wait, can you talk? I got too excited and totally forgot about the time difference. I can call back later or—"

"Emily Ann Peters, don't you dare hang up that phone."

"Aren't you sleeping?"

Sam chuckles into the phone. "That's cute that you think I sleep. No. I'm obviously at the office. I've been here since five in the morning and there is nothing I want to do more than take a break to talk to my sister before I'm forced to return to this absolutely fascinating and not at all mind-numbing financial model I've been working on for the past week."

"Sounds..."

"Excruciating?"

Sam heaves a big sigh, and Emily smiles as she leans her head back against the wall. "You do remember you chose this profession, right?"

"I chose it for the mountains of cash I'll be making in about ten years when I get promoted to Managing Director and have a team of minions working for me. Until then, it's survival. Actually, speaking of business, don't kill me."

Emily frowns. "What?"

"Just remember, you voluntarily put me in charge of your Etsy shop while you're away."

"Sam—"

"And you love me."

"Sam—"

"And you know I'm brilliant so obviously this is the absolute best decision anyone has ever made while temporarily running a startup jewelry line."

"Spit it out, Sam."

"Even with all the higher stock limits you implemented before going to California, your Etsy store is completely sold out—"

"WHAT?!"

"I know! So I decided to update your website to take direct orders, and I set up preorders for all the pieces I know aren't made from one-of-a-kind stones. Then I blasted it through your social media, which is still absolutely bananas by the way, and voilà, you have two thousand orders on hold."

"Two thousand orders..." Emily trails off into stunned silence. That's more orders than she usually gets in a year, and the season hasn't even started airing yet. They aren't even done filming. Hell, they've barely started! Her throat feels tight, her chest hot. The bathroom is suddenly stifling. "I don't think I can even fill that many orders."

"So hire an assistant."

"It's not that easy," she retorts, her mind already flooding with the what-ifs. What if she can't fill the orders in time?

What if she can't train someone on her techniques? What if this all blows up in her face? What if she becomes a laughingstock? What if she fails? What if she's simply not enough—not smart enough, not savvy enough, not strong enough to pull this off?

"Stop," Sam interrupts.

"Stop what?"

"Stop spiraling. We'll figure this out. I'll help you. Take a moment to breathe, Em. This is your dream, and you're really doing it. Be proud."

"I am."

"Good, because you should be. Now, tell me about the guys. How many have you kissed? How many have you sent home? Did anyone cry? Did anyone beg? God, I wish I was there."

"Yes to the crying. No to the begging."

"And the kissing?"

"I may have made out with a few people."

"You sloot!"

Emily's cheeks flame, but she laughs. "Jealous?"

"Hell to the yes! I would've made out with all of them by now. Tell me everything."

For the next hour, Emily does exactly that. It doesn't matter that her butt starts to go numb from the hard stone counter, or that she starts to shiver from the cool tiles against her back, or that her toes ache from being propped against the towel rack. It feels so good to talk to her sister, to someone she trusts, to someone she knows loves her implicitly, nothing else matters. At least until Sam asks the one question she was *really* hoping she'd be able to avoid.

"How'd you get the phone anyway?"

For a moment, she considers lying. Then that old adage *the cover-up is worse than the crime* filters through her head. If she lies, and Sam sees through it, things will be far, far worse, because it will seem as if she has something to hide.

Which she doesn't.

Jake is...just Jake.

Her ex.

Nothing more, nothing less.

"It was a, um, peace offering. From Jake."

Sam growls under her breath.

"It's not like that." Emily hastens to cut off her twin...then immediately regrets it.

"Not like what?" Sam asks innocently.

Emily rolls her eyes. "Not like whatever it is you're imagining."

"And what do you think I'm imagining?"

"Sam."

"Em."

"He's not trying to win me back."

"Of course not," Sam answers. "He's just seen thirty other men hit on you and make out with you, and he randomly thought, *Huh, now is a really great time to suddenly start being nice to Emily again.*"

"Is that so hard to believe?"

"YES!"

"We have to be around each other for the next five weeks. Is it such a bad thing to be cordial?"

"Cordial is saying hello. Cordial is opening a door. Cordial is respecting your boundaries. Sneaking a contraband phone to the lead of your television show at the risk of being fired because you suddenly realize what a huge mistake you made seven years ago and are scared shitless that the girl you dumped might actually move on with her life is NOT fucking cordial."

"What is it then?"

"Groveling."

Well, that settles that. Emily is *definitely* not telling Sam about how Jake snuck into her bedroom the other night. "I really think you're reading too much into this."

"I really think you're not reading into it enough. Be careful, okay? I don't want you to get hurt again."

"I know, but you've got to trust me."

"I do."

In the following silence, Emily can practically hear her sister's thoughts. *It's him I don't trust.* She sighs. "Love you, sis. I'll call again as soon as I can."

Twenty minutes after they hang up, Nina arrives with hair and makeup. Wardrobe is waiting at the group date location, which, as Emily discovers an hour later when they pull up in the sprinter van, is the famous Paramount Studios. By the time the guys arrive later that morning, she's in a yellow wrap dress with leather booties. A series of thin bangles in silver, gold, and rose gold cover her wrists like cuffs, jingling every time she moves. Some are flat. Some are round. Some are laser cut like latticework, while others are strings of shapes. They're big sellers in her shop because on the inside of each a single word is engraved—*beautiful, strong, graceful, powerful, kind, generous, loved,* and Emily's personal favorite, *enough.* Sometimes, everyone needs a little reminder of their worth.

Today, though, she feels pretty confident as the guys line up before her.

"Welcome to Paramount Studios," she tells them when Nina gives the signal. "It's the only major studio still active in Hollywood, and one of the oldest studios in the world, so I thought it made the perfect stop for our second group date. Today, we're—"

A piercing screech cuts her off.

The men jump.

Emily spins.

A black SUV careens around a corner, then shoots straight for her. There's no time to run. No time to escape. Instead, she puts her hands out in front of her, as if that could possibly do something.

And it does.

The car stops dead, same as they practiced about a hundred times before the guys arrived. The front hood collapses under her palms when she puts a little pressure on the right spots. Then she throws her arms to the side and the car spins wildly across the studio lot. Heat warms her cheeks as the engine explodes, sending a wave of fire into the sky. A wicked grin takes over her face. She feels so badass, it's insane.

The men gape as she dusts off her hands.

"Where was I?" she asks.

Then gunfire *pop pop pop*s. Little dust clouds rise from the pavement, coming closer.

"On second thought, give me a moment."

Emily strips off her wrap dress, revealing the silver-and-gold superhero costume hidden underneath—a leather corset with a miniskirt. Definitely not the most feminist, but Nina assured her she looked ridiculously hot, which come to think of it is also not the most feminist...but whatever. She feels powerful, and that's all that matters.

Three bad guys in ski masks repel down the building at her back. Emily rushes over to meet them. They swap a few coordinated moves, and then the fun stuff begins. She kicks one in the chest and invisible strings launch him into the air, sending him flying. Then she grabs one of their guns and bends it in half before tossing it over to the guy's feet. Another punch sends the second attacker into a brick wall, which crumbles as he falls through it. The third assailant rushes her. Emily still isn't entirely sure how the stuntman pulls it off, even after practicing it so many times, but she sticks her arm out and he cartwheels in the air before landing "unconscious" at her feet.

End scene.

The suitors holler. Emily grins. Even the crew starts clapping, so she gives a little curtsy. When she lifts her head, her gaze goes to Jake before she can stop it. He's there, next to Fred, practically beaming. A tingle warms her chest. They make eye contact and hold it for a second too long. Underneath all the malice, all the anger she can't help but still feel, there's kinship too, a shared history. All those hours Emily spent in front of his camera. All those hours she did homework on his bed while he edited shots at his computer. All those hours they watched movies and dreamed of seeing his name on the big screen. And now they're here, in Paramount Studios, doing the dang thing.

No, she's not an actress.

Yes, this is reality television.

Still, there's shared disbelief.

We actually made it. We're here.

It's their first real moment of connection in seven years and it leaves her stunned. Emily stumbles back a step as her knees go weak. She looks away, turns back to her suitors. Fifteen perfectly eligible and notably handsome men watch her, waiting for their cue. She recovers and returns to script, telling them about the various scenes they'll be filming for the group date. Her voice sounds airy and a bit weak, but hopefully, they'll chalk it up to the moment.

For the rest of the afternoon, she tries her best to focus on the dates.

A half-naked Cooper dressed in nothing but fireman overalls rescues her from a burning building. It's sexy. It's hot. While he carries her in his arms, her rebellious gaze still darts toward Jake behind the camera. The furrow of concentration in his brow reminds her a little of the boy she used to know.

Ethan gets a spy role, and the end of his rescue involves the two of them jumping out of a window onto a massive inflatable cushion. While they're hidden in the voluminous folds, he rolls on top of her and steals a kiss. By the time they pull apart, the camera is about two feet from their faces and the entire crew watches on. They laugh like two kids caught by their parents, but deep down, Emily actually feels a pang of guilt. It's not fair. She's doing nothing wrong. But the sight of Jake's tight lips and clenched jaw twists her insides. He's the only one on set who's looking away.

Ben K. and Michael get superhero scenes similar to hers, but this time, Emily is the damsel in distress. While she waits for her rescue, she watches Jake from the corners of her eyes. He's talking to some of the Paramount employees, hanging on their every word, his focus acute as they point to various places around the set. The yearning on his face makes her wonder what happened to him. He wanted to know why she left New York. Now she wants to know how he came all the way here, made it to Hollywood, but still gave up. Because he did. She sees that now. He settled into this reality TV role and stopped fighting for his dream.

Why?

The air feels different between them as she approaches him at the end of the day, same as she did at the end of the last group date. Instead of being contentious, the mood is almost somber, as if he's also thinking about what was, what is, and how exactly they ended up in this twisted reality where nothing feels quite like it should.

Sam's voice comes back to haunt.

Groveling.

But when Emily stops before Jake and meets his gaze, the emotions circling in his blue eyes are heavy. They weigh him down. It doesn't feel as though he's fighting for her. It feels as though he's letting her go. And she's not sure which option she fears more.

"Here for your dates?" he asks, tone even.

Emily nods.

"You're picking Cooper, I assume?"

She nods again, unable to find her voice.

"Okay. Then I'll add Daniel and Liam. Full disclosure—one of them is actually a nice guy, the other is a dick who ghosted his girlfriend to come on the show. She may or may not be in Los Angeles to confront him. You've been forewarned."

Emily laughs, some of the tension breaking. He smiles at the sound.

"And yes, Nina," he murmurs into his comm. "Before you ask, I got permission from Trish to fill Emily in this time. Don't worry."

He rolls his eyes, then looks down at his clipboard. She knows it's her time to walk away, but she can't make her legs work. Instead, her mouth opens.

"Jake."

At the sound of his name, his smile disappears. The mood turns. Joviality is replaced by seriousness as he lifts his chin and finds Emily's gaze. She doesn't look away.

"Thank you."

The words hold an undercurrent of meaning. She hopes he understands the truth of what she's saying—thank you for the phone, the time with her sister, the peace offering. She's grateful, truly. It's nice to be able to look at him with something more than anger.

He nods subtly, message received, and murmurs a soft, "You're welcome."

Right then, it doesn't feel like groveling or goodbye.

It feels like a truce.

And Emily can live with that.

WHEN THEY RETURN to the mansion late that night, Jake is exhausted. From the physical toll of a day on his feet. From the emotional toll of a day in Emily's presence. From the general heft of spending all day so close to his dream. Paramount Studios doesn't even film that many movies in the Hollywood lot anymore, mostly television shows, but being there, being so close, god it hurt.

One day, he tells himself.

Though he stopped applying for jobs.

Though he stopped studying film.

Though he stopped networking.

Though he settled for this.

Don't get him wrong. *The Love Match* is one of the most popular shows on television. Reality TV is taking over cable. He gets to meet new people. He gets to travel the world. He gets to produce. It's a dream.

It's just not *his* dream.

But it pays the bills. It keeps him busy. It gives him an excuse not to go back to Georgia. And that's been enough.

Until now.

Jake settles in his window seat, same as the night before, wondering when he officially became a stalker. Because that's what he is, sitting there in the dark with his gaze on the small house lit up across the garden and his mind on the girl hiding somewhere inside.

His phone buzzes. Jake looks down, and immediately starts choking as he reads the name across the screen.

Samantha Peters.

Why the hell is she texting him?

He slides open the screen and pulls up the message. A snort barrels up his throat. It's a single GIF of Robert De Niro in a top hat with the words *I'm watching you* flashing across the bottom. He knows the movie immediately—*Meet the Parents*. He knows the message, too.

I'm watching you, Focker.

Only he's pretty sure Sam meant for him to use a different F word. She's a pain in the ass, but damn him if it doesn't make him smile. They were friends, once upon a time, before he broke her sister's heart and she had to deal with the fallout. He knows exactly how to respond.

Jake returns fire with a GIF of Puss in Boots from *Shrek* doing his innocent cat eyes.

His phone buzzes almost immediately. This time he actually laughs out loud when he opens it. It's Chris Tucker from *Rush Hour* in the famous scene where he incorrectly assumes Jackie Chan can't speak English, and screams, *Do you understand the words that are coming out of my mouth?*

Sam's meaning is a little different, but still clear. Jake sends back a GIF of Harrison Ford as Han Solo saying, *Aye, aye, Captain.*

Her next response wipes the grin from his lips.

No GIF.

No teasing.

No camaraderie.

Just five words.

You're going to hurt her.

It's like taking a steak knife right to the heart. His gaze drifts back to the guesthouse, now dark with the late hour. He stands and closes all his curtains. Then he turns his phone off and lies in bed. All night her words churn in his head. All night he tries to craft a response.

I don't want to hurt her.

That was true seven years ago and look what happened.

Nothing's going on.

His heart just combusts every time he sees her.

I've moved on.

Yeah fucking right.

She doesn't want me anyway.

True. But he can't admit it out loud, and especially not to Sam. That would make it real. Instead, he leaves her text unanswered and wishes that will wipe the conversation from his mind, but it doesn't.

Her words follow him all day, while he attempts to play the guys off each other and expose Ethan for the jerk he really is while Emily is off on her dates. They follow him all night, while he hides in the dark using every ounce of self-control he possesses to leave the curtains closed and his eyes on the shadows in his own room. He hears them every time he lays eyes on Emily during the puzzle-piece ceremony—talking to, flirting with, and kissing other men.

You're going to hurt her.

Let her go.

You're going to hurt her.

Let her move on.

You're going to hurt her.

Let her be free.

When he sits on his windowsill late in the evening, his bags packed for the flight to England tomorrow, his hand itching for the seam of the fabric, his mind already picturing the glowing guesthouse on the other side of the curtains, Jake finally hears something else.

The voice still belongs to Sam, but it's from another time, another life, as he's flung back into the past.

"What the FUCK are you doing here?"

Her words were vicious. Her tone was hateful. The venom spewed like lava, pent up for months and finally able to blow. She stood in the front doorway of her parents' home with an oversized sweater hanging from her shoulders, soft flannel pants clinging to her legs, and fuzzy slippers on her feet. He froze where he was—crouched over the front steps, about to put a thick envelope on their doormat. She closed the door behind her and took two steps forward.

"I said, what the fuck are you doing here, Jake?"

He was afraid to look at her because he knew he'd see Emily in her face. She was everywhere in this town—every street, every stop sign, every store holding some memory. He'd been a fool for coming here, for coming home. His mother had begged him. It was Christmas, she'd reasoned. She hadn't wanted to spend the holidays in some cheap hotel in Los Angeles without a single decoration in sight. She'd wanted him home. So he'd come.

Idiot.

He hadn't even lasted twenty-four hours before showing up at Emily's door, his willpower only as strong as the distance between them. When three thousand miles had kept them apart, he could at least pretend he'd moved on. But with nothing more than three blocks standing in his way, he'd had no hope.

I'll leave her a note, he'd reasoned. *I just want to apologize. I just want to explain. She deserves that much from me.*

Of course, in the back of his head, he'd been unable to fight the image of her opening the door and running into his arms—a naive hope. More likely, she would slap him in the face. Still, he would have taken it. He would have taken anything. He'd missed her so goddamn much he couldn't breathe sometimes from the ache. The sight of her would be enough.

Instead, he'd gotten Sam.

Fuck.

He finally looked up. "I'm leaving this for Em. I wasn't going to knock. I'm not trying to stay. It's just a note, to explain, to apologize. I don't even know, but—"

"Take your note," she spat, "and get the fuck off my front porch."

"I'm leaving this for her, Sam. She can decide if she wants to read it or not."

Sam scoffed and yanked the letter from his hand. "You

don't get to make decisions like that anymore, Jake. You don't get to leave her in the dead of night without a word, and then show up four months later trying to get back in her good graces. You don't get to rip her heart to shreds, and then decide one day you'd like to try to put it back together."

"Sam—"

"No." She cut him off and stepped closer. With him on the bottom step and her on the porch, they were at eye level. She jabbed her finger into his chest and stood taller, prouder. He cowered beneath the fury in her eyes. "You have no idea what we've been through these past four months, Jake—what she's been through. You have no fucking idea, because you weren't here. You left. You already made your choice. Emily doesn't want to see you. She doesn't want to hear from you. She sent me out here to get rid of you, so just go. And take your fucking note with you."

She ripped the envelope down the middle and shoved him in the chest. He stumbled back, clutching the fragments of paper as if they were the pieces of his broken heart. Nothing would ever put him back together. But it was what he deserved.

Why had he ever thought he could have a happy ending? After what he'd done?

This was who he was.

Shattered bits. Sharp edges. Poison. Pain.

The memory burns so sharply that Jake's heart aches even now, as he sits on the windowsill in the dark. His hand drops from the curtains. He knows Sam is right. He wishes he could say he never looked back after that idiotic night, but he did. He looked back all the time. That was why he never let less than three thousand miles stand between them again—otherwise the urge to go to her would be too strong, like it is now, with Emily no more than three hundred feet away.

His phone lights up in the dark.

It's an unknown number. The area code matches Los Angeles.

His heart catapults up his throat.

It's too much to dream, too much to hope. He lifts the phone to his ear. "Hello?"

There's a pause, a breath, and then—

"Jake."

At the sound of her voice, his control shatters. He rips the curtains aside. His gaze shoots immediately to the guesthouse. Obviously, she's not in the window. She's on the phone. It's not allowed. Both of them could be in a huge amount of trouble. Still, disappointment floods his system. He wants to see her.

"Jake? Are you there?"

"Yes! Sorry, yes. I'm here. Surprised is all. I, uh, wasn't expecting you to call."

"Yeah, well, I just got off the phone with Sam and we fly to London tomorrow, so I figured I may as well use the last twenty minutes on this bad boy while I still can. Wasn't that what you said? Use it wisely?"

Yes. It was. He just never in a million years thought her interpretation of *wisely* would be to call him. He would have been less surprised to have the floor give out underneath him, which, come to think of it, is exactly how this feels, as if he's tumbling down a black hole with no sense of when he might hit bottom.

Nothing left to lose, he can't help but ask, "Is this wise?"

"No." She laughs softly into the line, and the hairs at the back of his neck rise. "Probably not. But I wanted to say thank you, without the cameras and the microphones and the double meanings. You have no idea how much talking to my sister has meant to me, and it wouldn't have been possible without you."

He's pretty sure he does know how much it means to her, which is exactly why he did it. "No problem."

"Anyway, that's why I was calling. So—"

"Where are you?" he asks, so desperate not to hear goodbye he blurts the first thing that comes to mind.

"Oh, um, in the bathroom. Don't worry, I stuffed a towel under the door. No one can hear me."

"I'm not worried."

"Good."

"I want to be able to picture you while we're talking."

"Oh."

"Are you sitting next to the sink?"

"Yeah."

"Toes on the towel rack?"

"Uh-huh."

"Head back against the tiles?"

"Stop. You're freaking me out. Can you see me?"

"What are you wearing?"

The image of her in his T-shirt and a thong burns the backs of his eyeballs, but her answer is even better. "My pink flannels with the rainbows on them."

He barks out a laugh. "I *knew* you still had those."

"Well, what are you wearing, Mister High-and-Mighty?"

"Boxer briefs."

"Oh..."

She swallows audibly. He grins.

"And a Star Wars T-shirt."

"Ah-ha! Which one?"

"My vintage 1977 logo shirt."

"The one with the rainbow stripes and the jet?"

He can't believe she still remembers. "That's the one."

"Soft."

"It is."

"And where are you sitting?"

"On the window seat in my room."

"Which has a view of..."

"Your room."

She snorts. "I thought you were going to say the ocean or something."

"Not nearly as enticing."

He's riding a thin line. He knows it, but he can't help it. With Emily, he always liked to live a bit dangerously.

To his surprise, Emily doesn't back off. She fights fire with fire. "You have always had a thing for staring at my bedroom window."

"That's because you used to stare back."

Click.

For a second he thinks she hung up, but then he hears the *creak* of a door and he realizes she put the phone down on the counter. A few seconds later, a shadow moves across her curtain. It pulls back, and there she is. It's déjà vu seeing her there in those pink pajamas with her hair hanging loosely around her shoulders and no makeup. She's just Emily, the girl he remembers.

Seven years ago, he would have been on the ground beneath her window. She would have slid it open and giggled under her breath from the nerves while he pulled himself inside. They would have fallen onto the bed in a mess of lips and limbs, knocking a pile of books off her nightstand in their haste before shushing each other to be quiet. It was all laughs and sighs and smiles. He wonders if the bottom button on that shirt is still missing or if she sewed it back on. The plastic was so slippery, and his hands were so shaky, that he finally ripped the stupid thing apart to get to her skin.

Jake flicks on the light in his room.

Emily's searching gaze immediately jumps to the spot.

They stare at each other, no telling for how long. Despite the distance, the tension is thick, at least on his end. Jake's heart pounds. His jaw clenches. His chest feels tight, as if he's running a marathon and can't catch a breath. Does she feel it too? This pressure? This connection?

He'll never know.

Emily turns away from the window and pulls her curtain closed. The light in her room turns off and her outline dissolves into shadows. The phone line goes dead. Fifteen minutes must have passed. His time is up.

Was she on her way back to the bathroom to keep talking, or was she going to hang up on him anyway?

The question haunts him into the night. But Jake does have clarity on one thing.

He let Sam scare him away once before.

He's not going to do it again.

Jake pulls up the conversation with Sam and finally replies. It's what he should have said seven years ago, the first time she spoke in Emily's stead.

It's her decision to make.

Then he blocks Sam's number, turns off his phone, and goes to sleep.

A COLD SHOWER does nothing to dampen the fire under Emily's skin the next morning.

Fucking Jake.

Why did she call him? Why did he answer? Why did he ask her what she was wearing? Why did she walk to the window? And for the love of all things holy, why oh why did the phone have to die?

Frigid water pellets her back, but deep in her core, everything is still molten as the memory draws up. She walked back to the bathroom, fully prepared to continue the stupidly flirty conversation, but when she picked up the phone, her prepaid limit had been reached. With a growl, she wrapped the stupid thing in an old shirt and stuffed it at the base of her suitcase—just in case. Then she went to bed.

At least, that was her intention.

But when she lay down, her fingers found the threads at the bottom of her shirt where the button used to be, and her mind did the rest, drawing up the images of the adorably frustrated knot in his brow as he tried again and again to undo the final button, the wicked gleam in his eye as a new idea struck, the triumphant grin as he ripped and—*pop!*—the shirt finally parted to reveal her bare skin.

Emily had barked out a surprised laugh. Jake's eyes had popped wide in fear. She'd slapped her hands over her mouth in horror as they both froze, waiting, waiting for some sign her mother or father down the hall had heard. They lasted about ten seconds in absolute silence before breaking down into giggles. Jake pulled her into his chest and kissed her. His mouth slipped down her throat and over her collarbone, then followed the path down her stomach.

And *that* was the memory that Emily went to bed with.

A ghost haunting her from the grave.

It's no wonder her dreams went the way they did. Except the dream wasn't a memory. As much as she wishes she could blame past Emily for her wayward imaginings, current Emily was fully at fault. Because the Jake in her dreams didn't sneak into her teenage bedroom. He snuck in here. In boxer briefs and a Star Wars T-shirt. And this time, all the buttons on her shirt popped off as he pulled it apart in his haste to touch her. And the very same shower she's standing in now, trying like hell to cool herself down in, is where his hands dug into her thighs, and her feet hooked around his back, and her spine slammed into the tiles while he caught every last sigh with his lips, keeping them safe and hidden from the world, until—

Shit.

She needs to stop picturing it.

She needs to get out of this shower.

Emily turns the water off, grabs a towel, and stumbles into the bedroom. With a hard yank, she closes the bathroom door firmly behind her, then drops her head back against the wood with a sigh. The cold air draws goose bumps to her skin.

Finally, a little relief.

"Emily?" Nina knocks on the door. "You okay in there?"

"Yeah!" She jerks away from the bathroom as if she's been caught in the act, her heart racing in her chest. "Sorry. I was in the shower. I'm still in a towel, but you can come in if you need to."

Nina pokes her head through the door. "I'm putting an order in for breakfast. I'll leave the menu here. Holler when you know what you want. Oh, and we have the last wardrobe consultation before Europe in about an hour and a half. We're headed to the airport after that, so make sure you're all good to go beforehand. Okay?"

Emily nods, offering a weak smile. "Yup."

Nina's brows twitch. She knows something is off, but she retreats to the hall and pulls the door shut behind her.

Emily throws on her comfiest leggings and an oversized sweatshirt. Then, in case paparazzi happen to be at the airport, she adds one of the embellished headbands she's been working on plus a few bracelets. It never hurts to be prepared.

Breakfast is a massive burrito which is really the exact comfort food she needs right now, even if her stylist is giving her major side-eye while she shoves every morsel into her mouth. *The evening gowns will fit,* she wants to say, *don't worry.* Nina smiles as if amused while she eats her much more

Hollywood-approved egg-white omelet. They're lucky they aren't in Georgia right now or Emily would be housing a plate of biscuits with gravy and a side of cheesy grits.

Mmm, she thinks. *I miss home.*

The drive to the airport feels all sorts of wrong. No phone. No wallet. No ticket. No ID. That's all in Nina's bag. All she's got in her carry-on is a romance novel, a sketchbook, her one-of-a-kind Emily Ann Designs that she would never trust in a checked bag, and some snacks. Not even any good ones. Just some nuts she managed to steal from the mansion and a single dark chocolate bar, which is something, she guesses, but she's a milk chocolate girl. Really, she's a Skittles girl. Or Starburst. Anything sweet and fruity. It's an eleven-hour flight —she needs sugar.

Alas, when they finally get to the airport, Emily feels more like a piece of luggage than a human. Nina and Trish shuttle her through the business-class line, then through security. She sees her ten remaining guys in the normal line with Jake, the assistants, and all the non-senior crew. There's no time to wave. Nina grabs her arm and tugs. On the other side of security, people stare. Some snap photos. It's sort of surreal. But she hardly has time to process it as Trish and Nina urge her along, never stopping, keeping it moving, until the three of them are sitting out of the public eye in the business-class lounge.

And, okay yes, business class is the BOMB, but would one little stop at the newsstand have killed them?

Fred joins them about twenty minutes later with four glasses of free wine.

"To Emily!" he cheers.

She rolls her eyes. "To England!"

"To love," Nina adds with a wink.

Trish grins. "To ratings."

"To taking one for the team."

Emily almost spits out her wine as Jake's voice spills over her shoulder. The sound shoots down her spine and she jolts upright. Wine sloshes over the edge of her glass as she spins. He doesn't seem to notice her overreaction as he casually plops into the open chair next to Fred and takes a long sip, downing half his wine in one gulp.

How is he so unaffected?

How is he so chill?

Emily's heart pounds out of her chest. Her hand shakes as she lifts the glass to her lips and takes a careful sip. Images shuffle through her thoughts—him in the window, him in her bedroom, him in her shower, him in...her.

Nothing happened, she tries to remind herself. *We made eye contact from three hundred feet away. That's it. Everything else was all in my head.*

But was she really the only one?

Did last night mean nothing to him?

Jake puts his glass down and sighs.

"Long morning?" Nina teases gently.

He offers her a glare. "The men are at the gate. The PAs are holding them hostage. The crew has all their equipment. I've done my job."

Nina snorts.

Trish glances at him wryly. "And your reward is free booze and a lay-flat seat for the next eleven hours. No complaining."

"Who said I was complaining?"

"Fred?" Nina asks, as if he's the jury.

The director nods. "Complaining."

"What?"

"Next round's on you."

"It's free."

"My old legs are tired."

Jake rolls his eyes, downs the rest of his drink, and stands. They rattle off orders. Vodka soda. Red wine. Rum and Coke.

"Emily?"

She looks up from her glass.

Jake's gaze is live fire. It physically burns. She swallows as her throat runs dry and all the air in her lungs suctions out. He's not unaffected, she realizes. He's just better at hiding it. With his boss and coworkers so close, he's playing a part. Friendly. Distant. It's why he hasn't looked at her until now. Because he can't without making the room go up in flames.

"Do you want a drink?" he asks, slightly hoarse.

Right. She shakes her head. *Answer him, you dolt.* "No thanks. I'm good."

He turns away before she's even done speaking, cutting the contact. Emily takes out her book. She reads the same sentence ten times in a row until he comes back, so she puts it away and grabs her sketchbook while the four of them talk shop. It's all names she doesn't know, and shorthand she can't decipher. Still, every time he speaks, the sound of his voice makes her jump, the pen cutting across the page. Her sketches are normally flirty and fun, like her jewelry, meant to make the wearer happy, confident, strong. This is something else, all jagged lines and rough edges, lightning made of ink, a reflection of her pulse. Part of her wants to rip it out, crumple it into a ball, and toss it in the trash. The artist in her recognizes something worth keeping. It's new and raw, but there's potential, a kernel of something great if she's brave enough to ever revisit this moment and this feeling and the man sitting across the way.

When their flight is called, she finally looks up.

Jake is staring right at her—not her face, but her hands. She follows his gaze, glancing down, noticing the black smudges now decorating her fingertips.

Before she can stop it, a memory resurfaces.

She had stayed late in the art room after school one day, working on a design, and she completely forgot she was supposed to meet Jake after last period. They'd been on three dates. It was still new, still fragile. The second she realized her mistake, she jolted out of her creative haze and swung toward the door.

He was there, leaning against the frame, a soft smile on his lips, one she guessed he didn't even know was there. A camera hid the rest of his face, but he lowered it the second she spotted him to offer a sheepish grin. Emily didn't mind.

"I'm so sorry," she rushed to say. "I got this new idea for a necklace, and I totally lost track of time. I didn't mean to—"

"Em," he interrupted and stepped forward. "I don't care."

She swallowed and looked up at him through her eyelashes. "Really?"

"As long as you don't care that I was filming you like a creepy stalker."

"I don't care."

"Real answer?" he asked.

She liked the sound of that, the inherent promise to always be truthful with each other. She grinned. "Real answer."

"Good, because all I've been able to think about since watching you eat those strawberries at lunch was making out with you, so…"

He closed in while she laughed and hooked an arm around her waist. Jake lifted her onto the table and stepped between her legs. Making out with a boy in a classroom after hours was *so* not like her, yet with him, it felt like the most natural thing in the world, as if it were exactly what she should be doing, no matter how wrong. The second he put his lips to hers, the rest of the world fell away. Emily kissed him back, running her hands over his cheeks and up into his hair before pulling him closer. When they finally parted, ragged breathing filled the silence. She opened her eyes and a snort immediately barreled through her nose.

"Oh my god, Jake."

Emily folded her lips into her mouth to try to stop from laughing. He watched her, bemused.

"What?"

"I didn't realize…"

She looked down at her hands, and his gaze followed. Charcoal and grease stained her fingertips black—the same fingertips that had just rubbed all over his face. Smudges marred his cheekbones. His hair was wild, slick and sticking out from all sides. He looked as though he'd been mauled by an art student in a classroom after hours—which, obviously, he had.

"You can't leave looking like this."

She tried to pat his hair down and wipe the marks from his skin, but that only made it worse. After a minute, Jake grabbed her hands and flattened her palms to his cheeks before staring at her intently.

"Do you really think I give a shit what anyone else in this damn town thinks about me?"

"But, Jake—"

"You have no idea how sexy you are if you think a little grease is going to stop me."

Then he kissed her again, shutting up her protest. They walked hand in hand out of the school half an hour later to catcalls, the evidence undeniable. That night, he asked her to be his girlfriend. It was...perfect.

Emily closes the sketchbook on her lap. She reaches for the napkin under her drink and tries to wipe both the smudges and the memory from her mind. She can feel Jake's gaze on her face now. He's pleading with her to look up, but she doesn't give him the satisfaction.

It hurts too much.

Because it was so incredibly good before he ruined it.

She needs a break, and thankfully, after a moment, she gets one. Jake slips away to check on the guys while the rest of them pack up and head for the gate. Out of his sight, she can finally breathe, but it doesn't last long. Emily follows Nina, Trish, and Fred onto the plane. The four of them take their seats...and her stomach flips.

Nina and Trish sit in a pod to her left. Fred is in a different pod all the way to her right, next to a stranger. And Emily sits in the middle pod with an open seat to her right—an open seat she desperately prays someone will fill as the rest of the business-class passengers shuffle down the aisle.

No one does.

The line thins, then ends. Flight attendants take drink orders. For a brief, glorious moment, Emily wonders if he's sitting somewhere else.

Then, as if summoned, Jake is suddenly there. Without glancing her way, he drops into the empty seat by her side. As he readjusts, her seat bounces slightly. Every shuffle of clothes and *clink* of metal makes her curious, but she couldn't see him even if she tried. A plastic divider separates the seats. The only thing they share is a drink tray and the air around their legs. Really, it's no big deal that he's there. He could be anyone.

But he's not.

He's Jake.

Every breath. Every sound. Every silent moment is like a reminder.

Jake. Jake. Jake.

When the flight attendant finally puts her wine down on the drink tray, Emily goes for it immediately, not realizing Jake had the same thought. She grabs her glass. He grabs his. The backs of their fingers brush, a match striking flint. The fuse zips up her arm. Fireworks explode inside her chest, stunning her still. A soft gasp escapes her lips.

Does he hear?

Does he know?

Jake doesn't move. Emily doesn't either. Time stretches. No more than an inch of his skin touches hers, but they may as well be naked with the way her body lights up. Every nerve is alert. Her cheeks flush with heat. She can't see him, can't gauge his reaction, but he must feel it. Why else hasn't he pulled away?

Move your hand.

Move your hand.

Move your freaking hand.

She can't. Her arm won't budge. Someone else has possession of her body—the same backstabbing bitch who had control of her dreams the night before.

Jake moves, but not away.

He bends his pointer finger, bringing his knuckle fully against her skin, then lifts it up and drops it down in an unmistakable stroke. Deliberate. Purposeful. Not even close to an accident. Emily feels it everywhere—and she means *everywhere*. She clenches her thighs together as her need skyrockets.

The plane jolts into motion, breaking the spell.

Shit.

What am I doing? What am I doing?

Emily jerks her hand away, bringing her drink with it, and takes a long sip to calm her racing pulse. She glances around to distract herself and meets Nina's gaze. How much did the producer see? Was there even anything to see?

Emily swallows.

Nina's expression is for a moment inscrutable, but it quickly relaxes into an easy smile. She lifts her glass in a silent cheers. Emily does the same, feigning calm. Then she shoves her headphones on and chooses the least romantic movie she can from the list. She has absolutely no idea what it's about, but there's a slimy, putrid alien on the poster and that's enough. She settles into her seat.

At the exact moment she finally feels somewhat back to normal, something sharp scratches her calf.

What the hell?

She jerks her leg to the side and glances out the corner of her eye. Jake is hunched over in his seat. He must've accidentally nudged her with his bag.

Except, ten seconds later it happens again.

She kicks instinctively. He grunts.

This time, instead of the gentle prod, something whacks her leg. There's no mistaking its intentionality. Annoyed, Emily reaches down and grabs the offending item, prepared to start whacking Jake with it, until she sees what it is.

A roll of Starburst.

Something else scrapes her leg with a little jingle.

She knows that sound. Emily reaches down and— *Yes!* It's a king-sized bag of Skittles.

One last item grazes her calf.

Twizzlers.

Her three favorite candies. She shouldn't be surprised— he's taken her to the movies enough times to know what she likes—but she's touched just the same. He didn't have to do this for her. But he did. And it softens her walls that much more.

When Jake puts his drink down on their shared tray, she can't help but notice it's accompanied by a note. Emily reaches for her glass and casually takes the folded bit of paper.

Why are you watching Venom? You hate comic book movies.

She looks at their divider, imagines his smug expression, and sneers.

Butt out, she writes back and drops the note on the tray.

They have the new Julia Roberts movie, he writes.

She doesn't respond.

Another note comes a minute later. *You know you want to.*

She crumples it up.

Come on, he tries one last time. *I'll watch it too. For old time's sake.*

While she reads, she glances over at his screen, which is half-dark from the privacy shield but not so dark she can't see him move through the home screen and pull up the romantic comedy she's been dying to watch for three months.

Fine, she writes, then underlines to get her point across. He might have won the battle, but he didn't win the war.

Or did he?

They press play at the same time. Throughout the movie, notes drift back and forth across their drink tray. Nothing personal. Nothing dramatic. Just little thoughts like *$10 the first kiss happens before we make it twenty minutes into the movie.* Or *JUST ADMIT YOU LOVE EACH OTHER.* Or *Fight! Fight! Fight!* Sometimes she hears him snort through the divider. Sometimes she can't contain her own laugh. It reminds her of being seventeen in the back of his pickup truck, watching movies on his laptop under a blanket with her head against his chest.

It's so wrong, when there are ten men in the back of the plane vying for her heart and an entire crew in seats all around her working to make her dream love story come true.

But it feels right.

It always does with Jake.

When the movie ends, against her better judgment, they pick another. Then another. Somewhere over the Atlantic, the plane goes dark and everyone else falls asleep, but Emily and Jake stay like that, munching on candy, passing notes, and giggling like little kids.

jake

I SHOULDN'T BE HERE.

He's standing in front of Emily's hotel room, knuckles poised to knock.

I really shouldn't be here.

Nina is in the room next door. Trish is in the room next to hers. Fred is across the way. The rest of the hall is filled with crew, and three floors down the guys and the PAs are all tucked away. They're supposed to be sleeping for the next five hours to catch up on rest before the group date this afternoon. Anyone could see him. They could be watching him right now through a peephole and he'd never know.

This isn't worth your job, your future.

Except it is. Because it's Emily.

Jake knocks.

The door swings open.

"Hey—" Emily freezes, visibly recalibrating at the unexpected sight of his face. Jake takes the opportunity to swoop in.

"Get dressed and meet me downstairs in the lobby in five," he whispers.

Her brows knot.

He grabs the knob and pulls the door closed, saying two more words before it shuts. "Trust me."

Then he walks steadily down the hall to the elevator. His heart pounds as he takes it to the ground level. He finds a chair and waits, gaze glued to the metal doors. Time moves like crystallized honey down the side of the bottle, thick and slow. Finally, the doors slide open to reveal Emily in jeans and a fitted navy jacket for the colder London air with one of her colorful floral scarves knotted elegantly around her throat. She scans the lobby as she walks off. He waits until they make eye contact. Then he gets up and strides out the front door, knowing she'll follow. They walk a block like that until he finally slows down to let her catch up.

"What's going on?" she asks. "Nina told me to stay in my room."

"I know."

"And this is very much *not* my room."

"I know."

"So where are you taking me?"

"Technically, I'm not *taking* you anywhere. You came willingly."

She offers a pointed glare. "Where, Jake?"

He glances at her from the corner of his eye, lifting his lip in a half grin. "It's a surprise."

"A surprise," she deadpans. "I hate surprises."

His smile deepens. "I know."

"The last time someone surprised me, it was my mother

on national television telling the whole world about her pathetically single daughter."

"And look how great that turned out."

She rolls her eyes. "The last time *you* surprised me, it was with tickets to an outdoor music festival that ended with the two of us being driven home in separate cop cars."

"One of which was driven by your father."

"Yes…"

"And the other by Big Mike, a man I've known my entire life."

"Your point being?"

"We weren't in any trouble."

She snorts. "You didn't kiss me in public for a month after that night."

"I *said* we weren't in any trouble." He stopped to hail a cab, then met her gaze. "I didn't say I wasn't scared shitless."

She smiles despite herself. There's a war afoot in her eyes, a push and pull he remembers well. It's not the first time he's convinced her to go against her better judgment—and sneaking away with him? It's clearly a bad decision. Still, when a cab finally pulls over, after a moment's hesitation, she follows him inside. He breathes a sigh of relief. Unlike when they were teens, he really wasn't sure what she would do.

"The Tower of London, please," Jake says.

Emily knits her brows, trying to figure out the why, but she's blank.

Good.

He wants to see her face the moment she realizes where he's taking her. It's going to be a feeling money can't buy.

"Have you been here before?" she asks, changing the

subject while she looks out the window and drinks in the sights. "In London, I mean."

"Twice. Both for work."

"It's my first time in Europe," she says softly, like a confession. He wants to take her hand, but he knows that would be too far. She's got no reason to be embarrassed. "Sam comes all the time for work, to meet with clients. She's offered to bring me, but I don't want to be a burden. You know?"

No. He didn't know. She could never be a burden even if she tried.

"We went to Mexico once, just the two of us. And a few places in the Caribbean." She sighs, a sound he can't quite read, neither content nor sad, somewhere in between. "I guess that's one of the reasons I decided to do the show. It's forcing me to finally go to all the amazing places I've never had the courage visit on my own."

Jake raps on the front divider.

"Oi," the cabbie says.

"Can you take the scenic route?" Aka, the more expensive route.

The car immediately switches lanes and they turn down a small side street. Jake points out the window as they pass various landmarks—Buckingham Palace, Westminster Abbey, the Houses of Parliament, Trafalgar Square, St. Paul's Cathedral, and finally, the Tower of London. The conversation is entirely neutral, carefully avoiding the past or anything too deep. Still, the act of being near her and sharing the same air makes it the best twenty minutes he's had in a while. When they step out of the cab, he points out the famous Tower Bridge before they cross over the grass-covered moat, through the entrance gate, and into the walled-off fortress.

"I tried to get a group date set up here when I realized you were going to be the lead," he explains as he guides her through another gate, along perfectly manicured grass, and past the central castle to the far side of the grounds. "But it was too late to get the proper permissions. Hence, my knocking on your door this morning. It's the only open block of time while we're in London, and I knew you'd want to see these while you're here, so…"

He steps to the side, and Emily gasps when she sees the sign. Her eyes go wide. Excitement brightens her entire expression. She bounces on her toes, eager as she clasps her hands in front of her chest. The transformation leaves him weak.

It's worth every risk of being fired to see the joy on her face.

To know he put it there.

"Jake, are we—"

"Come on."

He takes her hand, caution be damned. To his shock, she doesn't slap him away. He knows he's taking advantage of her distracted state of mind, but touching her soft, warm skin feels so good he doesn't care. He leads her down into the vault and hands over the tickets. She practically squeals when they step through the velvet curtain and into another world.

Everything twinkles.

Crowns. Scepters. Mantels. Rings. Swords. Bracelets.

All sparkling in the dark.

Emily drops his hand and darts to the first display. She

drinks in every diamond, every gem, every precious stone—the cuts, the carats, the arrangements, and a million other details he would never pick up on because he doesn't know any better. But she does. This is her passion, her life. She talks in a stream of consciousness as they wander through the displays, her enthusiasm wiping away her walls. When he's walking too fast, she grabs his hand to pull him back. When he goes the wrong way, she tugs on his fingers to bring him closer. Every insignificant touch she makes without thinking leaves him reeling. They're stolen moments he doesn't deserve but greedily takes. Because yes, he wanted to do something nice for her, and yes, he wanted to make amends, and yes, he desperately wanted to see that fervent glow in her eyes one more time, but there's more to it than that. Deep down, he can't deny his selfish desire to be her first experience in London, before the dates begin and the Hollywood magic wipes all memory of him away. Jake basks in her presence, in her undeserved attention, knowing it will end too soon.

And it does.

They take a cab back to the hotel. They delay for ten minutes getting coffees from the shop in the lobby. They run out of excuses and ride the elevator up in silence. Jake walks Emily to her door. She scans her key card. When the light blinks green, she turns the knob and steps inside.

He wants to stop her.

He wants to follow her.

He wants to spin her around, push her against the wall, and do a lot of things he's not allowed to do with her.

He doesn't.

He stands there, rooted to the spot with his heart in his throat.

Until she stops.

She turns.

She looks at him with an invitation in her eyes and pulls her bottom lip between her teeth. Uncertainty flashes alongside her lust.

He steps forward.

Emily doesn't move, not closer to meet him nor to the side to let him in. They stay where they are and stare at each other with mere inches between them, so close he can feel the heat of her body. It brings a static charge to his skin. The air turns electric. Yet the line feels as impassable as ever, fortified by everything left unspoken. They want each other. They've always wanted each other. But will that ever be enough?

A door opens.

Cold air rushes over Jake, shocking him to his senses, and he steps back. It's the move of a guilty man. When he turns to meet Nina's gaze, her narrowed eyes are scrutinizing. He swallows and runs his hand through his hair, unable to stop himself even as he knows it makes him look worse, like someone caught in the act.

But what act?

Nothing happened.

As far as Nina is concerned, he's standing in front of Emily's door, talking to the lead of their show, about their show—so why is she studying him like that?

"Hey, Nina," Emily says, her voice perfectly normal, somehow at ease. "Jake took me to the lobby for some coffee. I hope that's okay? I woke up in desperate need of caffeine and saw him in the hallway, so I pounced. I know you said not to leave my room, but I figured as long as I was with a crew member, it was okay. And it *is* okay, right?"

Nina glances quickly between them, then slowly says, "Of course it's okay. Next time, call my room, though. I could've used a latte." She crosses her arms and leans against the doorframe with a friendly smile on her face. "So what'd you talk about? Catch me up."

"I asked how she feels about the guys," Jake says after swallowing to loosen his throat.

"And...?"

"Well, Ethan and Cooper are her one and two right now."

Nina nods. "Good choices."

"I thought so," Emily chimes in.

"Kevin is at the bottom of the pack. He still hasn't recovered from the barfing fiasco, so we're thinking he should get one of the two one-on-ones this week. Viewers love a redemption story."

"True. I like it."

"The other seven guys are all sort of even."

"So who are we thinking for the second one-on-one?"

Me. Me. Me.

Fire scorches his throat as he physically forces the word back down his throat. It's painful to talk about this, painful to pretend he doesn't care. Worse, it's a pain he brought entirely upon himself.

"Pierre?" Emily suggests.

The sound of another man's name on her lips is like taking a hot poker to the heart.

Nina shakes her head. "No. Save him for France next week. He'll shine on his home turf."

"Frank?" Jake jumps in to stop Emily from giving someone else her favor. Frank's a nice guy—former college swimmer turned marine biologist, good sense of humor, wore a pink flamingo floatie to greet Emily on the first night. Most importantly, he spends six months out of the year in the middle of the ocean studying fish. There's no chance Emily will choose him in the end, but he's good looking and good natured enough to keep viewers entertained. Perfect *The Love Match in Mexico* material.

Nina must have the same thought because she meets Jake's gaze and nods. Mistrust still hides in the corners of her eyes, but they've been convincing enough her suspicions seemed cooled.

For now.

"Good. I'll tell one of the PAs to get the date cards ready. It's almost time to round everyone up, anyway. It's an hour and a half drive to the castle for the group date."

"Castle?" Emily asks.

"You'll see," Nina responds evasively.

"I'm not sure I like the sound of that."

Jake and Nina grin at each other. He slips his producer hat back on, remembering who he is and what he's supposed to be doing there. The group date is a medieval tournament, complete with jousting, sword fights, and good old-fashioned wrestling. Oh, and did he mention costumes? Medieval knights wore tights under their armor, and the women wore corsets plus about five layers of underwear. It's going to be fucking glorious.

"Guys?" Emily glances between them.

Jake offers her a wink, unable to stop himself, then backs slowly away. Nina slinks into her open doorway.

"Guys? Guys!"

"See you in a few hours," he calls before disappearing into his hotel room. As the door closes, he presses his eye to the peephole, needing one more glance. Alone in the hallway, Emily frowns and crosses her arms. Then she rolls her eyes, throws her hands in the air, and vanishes inside her room.

He keeps watching for a few more seconds, imagining her there.

This is the difference. The guys only get the carefully curated Hollywood version of her, but Jake gets the real Emily, frustration and all. It's enough for now, to keep him from losing his mind. But with every day—and every date—that distinction slowly fades. By hometowns, by dream suites, by the final two, it might be gone entirely.

He doesn't know what he'll do then.

But today, he gets to stand on the sideline in his best suit while eight of her suitors get dressed in tights and armor and make complete fools of themselves. Today, he gave Emily an authentic memory to remember. Today, he won.

I'll take it.

emily

CORSETS ARE THE WORSTTTTT.

Emily tugs at the strings crisscrossing her abdomen, hardly able to breathe. She's sitting on an uncomfortable wooden "throne," hair styled in an almost comical number of ringlets, with about ten pounds of skirts holding her in place. The men are lined up below, attempting to ride horses across a medieval arena and knock over a wooden dummy with a lance. It would be pretty funny, if not for one thing. The man in the suit standing directly across from her.

Dammit. Why does he look so good?

Emily can't stop from going back to that moment outside her hotel room. Jake standing before her, his dark hair swooping over his hooded eyes, his jaw set, his body hard. Her hands still tingled from the feel of his skin. Her cheeks still ached from so much smiling. It was so easy to fall back into old habits, so easy to spend a morning by his side. Just thinking about the hungry look in his eyes made her pulse race. He'd been about one second from ripping her clothes off. She'd been about one second from letting him.

What would have happened if Nina hadn't stepped outside?

Nothing, she tries to reassure herself.

Yet in the back of her mind, she can't help but hear Sam's reprimanding voice. *What the HELL happened to revenge?*

What the hell, indeed.

Emily was supposed to make him hurt, to make him pay. Pining over him was *not* part of the deal. Unless, of course, that was Jake's intention all along. Not to make amends. Not to apologize. Not to extend a peace offering from a stranger, as he put it. But to suck her back into his orbit.

Shit.

Jake meets her gaze across the field, as if he can sense his presence in her thoughts. The corner of his lip twitches with a suppressed grin. Suddenly, the morning takes on a new sheen. Sure, he wanted to take her to the crown jewels because he knew she would love it. But he also wanted this moment, right here, with her gaze on him instead of the suitors and her thoughts on their time together instead of on the group date. The trick with the phone had left her thinking of him all night, and now he wanted her thinking of him all day too.

Shit, she thinks again.

A prepaid phone, a few bags of candy, some albeit insanely gorgeous jewels, and she's putty in his hands? *Blech!* She never even put up a fight.

Get your head in the game, Peters.

Emily stands.

Jake frowns and murmurs something into his mic. She's done caring what he thinks. Instead, she turns her attention to the eight ridiculously attractive men who agreed to wear literal tights under suits of armor on national television just for the shot to win her affection. *They* are the ones she should be concerned with. *They* are the ones she should be focused on. *They* haven't broken her heart. *They* don't have ulterior motives.

Okay, well, that last one isn't entirely true. No one goes on reality television without some ulterior motive, but still. Her point stands.

"Good sirs," Emily calls across the field to gain everyone's attention. She puts down the chalkboard, meant to be used to rate the performances from one to ten, and settles her hands on her hips instead. "Seeing as we're not actually in medieval times, who wants to up the ante a little bit?"

Cameras turn. Crew members dart around the sidelines. A buzz fills the air. This is what she's supposed to be doing— making good TV, gaining the audience's favor, building her brand. Not obsessing over Jake.

In his seat by her side, Keith Holson ditches his chalkboard, grabs his mic, and stands up with her. A twinkle lights his eyes. "I think the lady wants to raise the stakes."

"I do," Emily says, leaning into his mic. "I don't want to rate the guys—I mean, noble knights—from one to ten. They're all trying their best, and they're all doing such an amazing job. Some of them have never ridden a horse before. It's not really fair. So I thought the prize should be something a bit more concrete." Nina studies her, unsure. Some of the assistants look at each other. She can read their doubts and sense their excitement fading. *No faith*, she silently chides before meeting Keith's warm, fatherly gaze. "How about a kiss instead?"

The buzz is back.

"A kiss?" Keith repeats, glancing around the field, letting the word linger. He really is a master at manipulating the drama.

"A kiss," Emily says again, trying to copy his style. "To any knight who can unseat his foe."

He turns to the men. "What say you?"

They cheer.

Energy fills the field, from the crew, from the suitors, from her. Emily feels electric. Alive. Jake's watching her, she knows he is, but she doesn't give him the satisfaction of looking back. As the first suitor lines up to take his shot, her heart pounds. This is exactly what she needed. A little excitement. A little fun. A little distraction.

Ben C. gallops down the jousting arena, and—

Misses.

An audible groan comes from the crew, along with some good-natured teasing from the men.

Pierre lines up next, but apparently what they say about the French is true. He's a lover, not a fighter. He hits the dummy with a glancing blow. It barely moves.

Emily sighs.

Maybe this won't be so fun after all.

Ethan's next. He offers her a slow grin, then a wink as he lowers the visor on his helmet. Emily sits forward in her seat. Her pulse elevates. He can barely stay in the saddle. It's clear he's never ridden a horse before by the way he's clutching the pommel for dear life with one hand while hoisting the lance with the other. Yet she knows he'll find a way. It's what he's done from the beginning. Find a way to make a scene, to make a moment, to make his way to her. For camera time? For fame? For romance? She still can't tell, but as his horse picks up speed it hardly matters.

Emily leans forward, gripping the banister with two hands.

Cameras zoom in on her reaction.

She's hooked.

The viewers will be too.

Is that why she's hooked? Is that why she wants this? Everything is so confusing, but right now, every bit of her body wants this kiss from Ethan. Everyone on reality television has ulterior motives—Emily included. She needs Jake to know she's not the doe-eyed seventeen-year-old still in love with him. More importantly, she needs to know it, too.

Ethan closes in on the dummy.

Ten feet.

Five feet.

Two feet.

Right before the lance hits the target, Ethan drops it. The weapon falls to the ground with a *thud*.

Emily gasps.

Her heart sinks.

He doesn't seem bothered. Ethan takes his feet from the stirrups, still focused on the dummy, and throws himself to the side.

He's airborne.

He's a human cannon.

He hits the dummy at full speed. They both fall to the

ground and roll. A second passes. Then two. They're so still it's hard to tell beneath all that armor who's alive and who's made of straw.

"Ethan!" Emily shouts, fear shooting up her throat. She takes off across the field, skirts billowing behind as she lifts them to run.

"A medic!" one of the crew shouts. "Get a medic!"

Emily drops to her knees by his side. The dummy is on top, and she pushes the stupid thing out of the way. Ethan is still. She gently tugs off his helmet.

"Ethan? Ethan!"

His black hair is in disarray. A bead of blood trickles down his forehead. She cups his cheek, relieved to find his skin is still warm.

"Oh my god. Oh my god. Are you okay? Are you hurt? Talk to me, Ethan. Say something!"

His bright green eyes pop open. A dimple digs into his cheek. He says two words. "I won."

Then he reaches up, grabs the back of her head, and pulls her down into a searing kiss. Relief more than anything else makes her laugh against his lips.

"You're an idiot," she whispers.

"You're worth it."

The words make her light up inside. He always manages to say the right thing, the perfect thing. The kiss goes on longer than it should. The cameras suck in every moment.

It's television gold.

And the look in Ethan's eyes as he finally lets her go makes it clear that he knows it—knows his scene will be the one to make the promos, to tug on the heartstrings of millions of women across the country. He got exactly what he wanted.

She did, too.

Across the field, Jake scowls. Storm clouds practically thunder around his head.

I'm not yours, Emily thinks. *Not anymore.*

Two of the next four suitors win kisses. Emily happily grants each one, her ex watching on with an increasingly ominous expression. She can practically hear her sister chanting in the back of her mind.

Revenge.

Revenge.

Cooper is the last to go. He's a cowboy in every sense of the word. At home on his horse. Not bothering to use the reins but guiding the animal with his legs alone. The lance fits naturally in his hand as if it takes no effort to hold. With a click of his tongue and kick of his heels, he takes off at a thunderous gallop down the line. Dust gathers in his wake. He's a renaissance fantasy come to life. Hell, the tights only highlight the bulging muscles in his legs as he rises to a crouch. The tip of the weapon doesn't move. It's steady, unflinching.

Emily's jaw falls open as she watches.

I might be drooling.

Her head drops forward, her eyes glued to him.

Shit. I might actually be drooling. On national TV.

It doesn't even matter. Let the cameras catch her salivating over this god of a man, who cares? Every woman in America will be too—she may as well join them.

He closes in on the target.

Three.

Two.

One.

BAM!

His lance slams into the center of the dummy's chest. Straw explodes. The head flies off. Armor goes sailing in every direction as the thing is completely pulverized.

Cooper doesn't even bother to look back at his handiwork. He knows exactly what he did without having to see it. Instead, he guides his horse around and stops in front of Emily. In slow motion, he takes off his helmet with a self-satisfied grin. Red curls frame his tanned and chiseled face, rugged and boyish and sexy as freaking hell.

"My lady," he says.

Emily can't even breathe as she leans forward. She grips the bannister for dear life as she offers him a kiss. Ever the gentleman, he presses his lips to her cheek. A surprising amount of disappointment floods her chest, until he leans a little closer and whispers, "Want to go somewhere a little more private?"

The mics must pick it up because in her peripheral vision, the crew mobilizes.

They're not fast enough.

Emily nods. Cooper snakes his arm around her waist and yanks her over the railing, corset, skirts, and all, truly like something out of a movie. The second she's settled on his lap, they're off.

"I've never been on a horse before," she screams, burying her face in his chest as she hugs him for dear life.

"I've never kidnapped someone before," he shouts back.

"Good to know we're in this together."

He barks out a laugh and says, "Hold on."

Somehow, they launch into an even faster pace, but she never feels scared, not really. It's a mix of adrenaline, exhilaration, and nerves, but not fear. Caged in by Cooper's arms, she never worries about falling. He's got her. He won't let her get hurt. They've had exactly one solo date in front of cameras and a few group interactions, but she's shocked to realize she trusts him—truly trusts him. Maybe more than Jake. Definitely more than Ethan, or anyone else on this set.

He's good.

He's safe.

Which is why she rips off their mics and throws them to the ground somewhere in the middle of their escape. And why, as the horse slows down, giving her a moment to finally lean back and look up at his handsome face, she says something she never expected to say to any of the men.

"Can I be honest?"

He cocks his head to the side, taking a moment to read her expression. She wishes she knew what it conveyed. "Of course."

"I'm not sure I'm over my ex."

He nods, absorbing that for a moment. Something in his eyes shifts, as if the curtain is pulled aside and the walls are down and finally, without the cameras and the mics and the crew, he can relax. She feels the same. Then he says, "Can I be honest?"

"Of course."

"I didn't pull that stunt because I'm desperate to spend time with you, though I think you're a great girl and I've been having a lot of fun. I just really, really miss being on a horse."

It takes a moment for the words to sink in.

When they do, her reaction is immediate.

Emily laughs hard—harder than she's laughed since waking up to find her mother on *Wake Up, America!* and her world forever changed. It's the kind of laugh that starts in her toes and barrels up her chest until her whole body is quaking. The kind she can't stop once started. And as soon as he hears it, Cooper laughs too. A release. A camaraderie. A confession. Emily drops her head against his chest, and he puts an arm around her waist to keep her from falling as the giggles settle.

"That may have come out wrong," he finally says, his deep voice full of mirth.

"No." Emily pulls back and meets his crystal-clear green eyes with a smile. "It came out exactly right, and I love you for that."

"It's just, I've spent every day of my life on a horse, or near a horse, and when I saw the opening to get a ride in, I—"

"Cooper." Emily covers his lips with her palm, showing he doesn't need to explain. They've spent probably six hours total together, and he's been in love with horses his whole life. She isn't offended in the slightest. "I get it."

He nods, his chin dipping in such a way that for a moment, Emily can't help but envision a cowboy hat on his head, à la Brad Pitt in *Legends of the Fall*.

He really is one attractive man, she thinks, somewhat sadly. Hopefully her next question won't ruin everything.

"Can I ask you one more thing, before the crew tracks us down?"

"Shoot."

"Why did you really come on the show?"

"You want my honest answer?" he asks.

In the back of her mind, she hears Jake's voice. *Real answer?*

It was a game they used to play, to demand the truth from one another. Not the surface-level truth, but the real, deep-down, nitty-gritty, vulnerable truth everyone is afraid to really say. If she asked Jake for a real answer now, about the past, about them, about his feelings, he would give it. She knows that. She still trusts him that much. But unlike when they were seventeen, she's too afraid to ask. She doesn't want to know the truth.

From Jake, at least.

To Cooper, she simply nods.

"I do want to find love," the cowboy says evenly, gauging her reaction. She silently encourages him to continue. "It's not the easiest thing to meet someone when you live on a massive ranch hours away from the rest of the world, but if I'm being honest, was that the main reason I decided to take the casting call? Not exactly."

"What was?"

"The ranch. It's everything to me, to my family, and my father is very resistant to move anything into more modern times. I was hoping that a little publicity, maybe some social media following, some sort of platform would show him that change doesn't always have to be for the worse. I knew the show could give it to me. And I really believe in my heart it's the only way to ensure the business stays alive for my children and their children after that. There's nothing I wouldn't do or try or sacrifice to—"

The sound of an engine cuts him off.

They both turn.

A production van careens around a tree and across the grass, racing toward them. A cameraman hangs out the window, desperate for a shot. Booms poke out like antennae, stretching for audio.

Coopers meets Emily's gaze, waiting for her lead. A question lingers in his eyes. Now that she has the truth, what is she going to do with it?

Jake might be in that van.

He might not.

For once, it doesn't matter. These few moments of honesty meant a lot to her after so many days of constant doubts and double meanings and shrouded intentions. So Emily threads her fingers through Cooper's silky hair and lifts her face. The cowboy closes the distance, understanding his role as he seals their silent pact with a kiss.

It doesn't reach her toes.

It doesn't burn.

It doesn't knock her over the way the briefest glance from Jake seems to do.

But it's a start. To giving someone else a real chance. To moving on. To putting the past in the past and making this opportunity count.

Not for revenge, but for self-preservation.

Seconds later, the van pulls to a stop and the cameramen jump out. With Cooper's help, Emily gives them a show.

jake

"IT WAS FUCKING IRRESPONSIBLE," Jake fumes, his gaze on the computer screen frozen on the shot of Cooper and Emily galloping out of camera range. The sight of it puts him into a rage, puts him back in that moment and those minutes where he had no idea where she was or if she was safe or what the hell was happening to her.

By his side, Nina scoffs.

They're in Trish's hotel room, reviewing the daily footage.

Jake forces his gaze away from Emily's disappearing form and turns to his coworker. "You don't think it was irresponsible? I don't give two shits that the guy grew up on horses. This was a new animal that he had no experience with and a new place that he was unfamiliar with, and he still said fuck it to the waiver he signed. Emily could have been hurt. She could have fallen. She could have broken her fucking neck." He pauses to take a deep breath, aware there's too much emotion in his voice. *Turn it around. Turn it around.* He swallows, regaining his control. "And if the lead gets hurt, the show is over."

Nina arches a brow and pointedly turns her gaze to the second computer screen, currently frozen on the passionate kiss the camera crew interrupted when they finally caught up to the little runaways. "She seemed fine to me."

"That's not the point."

"Then what is?"

"Everything turned out okay, but it might not have. What he did was dangerous—for all of us, but especially for Emily, who we signed a contract to protect."

"News flash, Jake. If that's dangerous, sign about ten million women across America up, because it was also fucking hot. It was everything our show is supposed to be, the sort of scene entire seasons are built around."

"We can't control him anymore. He needs to go."

"He's our F2. He's staying."

"He's a liability."

"He's a leading man."

"He's—"

"Children," Trish interrupts and they fall silent. "You're both right."

Jake's mouth falls open. Nina's does the same. They glance at each other, brows furrowed, as Trish turns to face them.

"What he did was reckless and dangerous, and it could have put the entire network in jeopardy. But it was also the best fucking play I've seen after ten years working on this show. So here's what we're going to do. Cooper stays."

Jake jumps forward. "But—"

Trish holds up her hand. "If we send him home, it would be admitting we lost control of the situation. Rule one of reality television—never cede the storyline. Besides, Nina is right. He's got *leading man* practically written across his forehead. That's our next season, right there. The trick isn't punishing him for pulling a stunt. The trick is bringing him back under our thumb through the guise of a reward."

"Tell him he's F2," Nina says softly, nodding.

"Exactly," Trish confirms. "Jake, you're his handler. Handle him. Tell him he's got next season in the bag. All he has to do is follow the rules. If he listens to us, by this time next year, he'll be the star. No suitor would say no. He'll fall into line."

"Understood." Jake forces the word through gritted teeth.

Trish shuts off the screens.

They're dismissed.

He stomps from the room, prepared to begrudgingly locate Cooper, but when the door closes behind him, Nina stops him with a whisper.

"Jake."

Dark eyes watch him, inscrutable in the dim fluorescent lights. He swallows. "Yeah?"

"Be careful."

Concern, he realizes. That's the emotion in her eyes, edged by something else, judgment or maybe suspicion. He plays dumb. "What do you mean?"

A puff of air slips through her lips as they twitch with a smile. "Jake."

"What?"

She arches her brows as if to say, *You want to play it that way? I can play it that way.* Then she steps closer, getting in his personal space. "I'm only going to remind you of this once, so take it to heart," she murmurs. "The crew is the crew. The cast is the cast. And never the two shall meet. Understand?"

"I know that."

"Do you?"

His heart thuds so loudly he's sure she must hear. "What exactly are you implying, Nina?"

"What exactly are you avoiding, Jake?"

They stare at each other for a prolonged moment, until she shakes her head with a soft laugh. "Oh, Jake, Jake, Jake."

She says his name as if she can read every thought in his head, as if she knows everything. But she couldn't possibly.

She's fishing, he thinks. *She's got to be.*

Well, he's not some puppet to be produced.

"I'm not sure what you think you know, but I'm here to do a job, same as you."

"Then why don't you?" Nina retorts as she pulls open the door to her room. "Go find Cooper. Go secure us a leading man for next season. And leave the worrying about Emily to me. Got it?"

"What do you think I was doing before you stopped me for this little chat?"

"I don't know, Jake," she says, offering him one last opening, one last chance. Then she steps into her room, eying him over her shoulder. "I really don't know."

The door closes.

Jake grits his teeth, glancing once at Emily's closed door

before stomping to the elevator at the end of the hall. The last thing he needs is Nina's suspicion.

What the hell am I doing?

He presses the button for the fifth floor and drops his head back against the wall, then runs his hands over his face and through his hair.

What in the actual hell am I doing?

Giving Em a phone. Passing her notes on the plane. Sneaking her out of the hotel. It's not just playing with fire. It's lighting a stick of dynamite and watching it burn—bound to blow up in his face. And why? For what?

Because it's Emily.

That's exactly why he needs to stop.

God, I'm such a fucking idiot.

It's not about his job. He doesn't give a rat's asshole about the job. Let them fire him for all he cares. He'll find something else. It won't be easy, and he'll have to start over in a lot of ways, but he can do it if he has to. The seven years he put into this career means nothing compared to the seven years of space he put between him and Emily—seven years of space that's rapidly depleting before his very eyes due to his own stupid, selfish behavior.

I'm no good for her.

I almost ruined her life once. I can't do it again.

I destroy everything I touch.

It's the mantra he told himself over and over again in those early days in Los Angeles, when he was hurting and alone and couldn't stop from reaching for the phone, ready to dial the number he would never forget, dying to hear the sound of her breath on the other end of the line.

He would say those words to remember why he left.

He would put down the phone.

He would walk away.

Because they were the truth. He knew it in his soul. She was better off without him. He destroyed the people he loved. He didn't save them. His mother's life ended the day she found out she was pregnant with him. Her love for him kept her trapped in an abusive marriage until the day his father died. Every punch, every kick, every bruise, all because of him. Being a good son had made it worse. Fighting back only made his father hit harder. Even when he tried to fix things, he broke them. It was what he did—what he'd do—if Emily came back into his life.

Just walk away, Jake thinks now as the elevator doors open to the fifth floor. *Let her go. Be a stranger. It's what she asked for. It's what she wants. Just walk the fuck away.*

He steps off the elevator with renewed focus.

For the next three days in London, he concentrates on the job. Emily goes on her solo dates. He hangs back with the men. He watches the footage of her kissing other guys and is absolutely stone faced, pushing his every emotion down so deep it would take an excavator to retrieve them. He keeps his eyes to himself during the puzzle ceremony. Emily doesn't look at him, and he doesn't look at her. He's not her handler. She's not his job.

On the train to Paris, he requests to sit back with the men. During the group date at Giverny, he distracts himself by orchestrating an all-out paint war that probably has Monet rolling over in his grave. Two more solo dates pass while he spends his time ensuring the viewers will understand the true depths of Ethan's assholery. And then it's the next puzzle ceremony, where eight guys will get cut down to six, leaving him that much closer to the end of this fucking nightmare of a season.

A few more hours, and we'll be on our way to Italy.

Just a few more hours.

Jake stands straighter, laser focused on Ethan as the man leans in and whispers something to Frank. Jake lifts his comm to his lips.

"Rajit?" he murmurs, seeing the tall, skinny PA next to Fred by the cameras. "Did the mic pick that up? What did Ethan say?"

"We got it," Rajit says back. "He said, *Nervous, Fish Boy?*"

The two of them had been going at it since Frank got the first one-on-one date back in London. But tonight, it's Ethan, Cooper, and Pierre sitting pretty with the puzzle pieces, while Frank is waiting for the ceremony with the rest. The last thing a smug asshole like Ethan needs is more power going to his head. Kevin is the obvious cut tonight, but another guy will be going home, and in Frank's mind, he's on the chopping block. He's not, of course. If it all goes to plan, Emily is going to send David, the personal trainer from Arizona, packing. But Frank doesn't know that, and neither does Ethan.

"Keep an eye on them," Jake tells Rajit and Fred. "I want a camera crew on the two of them at all times. Something's brewing there. Trish will murder me if we don't get it on film."

"You're right," she interjects. "I will."

Emily walks into the room, her effect immediate. The men fall silent. They sit up straighter. Heads turn. Throats are cleared. Every eye is on her, cast and crew included, as she elegantly crosses the room and asks Ethan for a chat.

Jake doesn't look directly at her.

He can't.

It would be like staring into the sun, painful and blinding with its glory.

So he keeps his focus on Ethan, catching the sly wink he throws in Frank's direction as he escorts Emily from the room. The marine biologist scowls and grabs a drink from the tray.

Bad move, Jake thinks to himself. Alcohol never solves anything. But the producer in him remains silent, aware of the brewing tension in the air. He keeps his professional hat on. He analyzes everything with the detached, clinical gaze of a physician. It's bold of Emily to pull Ethan for the first chat when he already has a puzzle piece. Nina must have suggested it. A producer playing chess while everyone else plays checkers.

The animosity keeps building from there.

When Ethan returns, a smug grin fills his face. He tosses a few more taunts Frank's way, makes fish lips when Emily isn't looking. He thinks he's subtle enough the cameras won't catch it—or he thinks they won't use the footage. Jake told him back in London, right after visiting Cooper's room, that he was on track to become the next male lead. A lie, of course. But ever since, he's been less careful about keeping his true nature off screen, which is, of course, exactly what Jake had been hoping.

Now, Ethan's pushing.

The cameras are rolling.

And his villain edit is falling precisely into place—until the moment Frank snaps.

It happens in a blink.

Jake doesn't even know what finally sets him off, but one minute Ethan is leaning in with a snide comment, and the next Frank's fist is connecting with his face. The pretty boy goes down hard. Emily screams. Cooper jumps in to hold Frank back while Emily falls to her knees at Ethan's side. He's bleeding from the nose, which may be broken. It's the perfect victim scenario. No one will care that Ethan was goading Frank all night. The one who gets violent is the one who goes down. Security is already sneaking in from the side to retrieve Frank from Cooper's hold.

All Jake can think is, *Fuck.*

All his planning, all his narrative building, wasted.

Then Ethan sits up. He touches his fingers to his nose and pulls them away red. Rage flashes in his eyes. He's a man possessed. Emily has her arm around him, trying to help, but he doesn't seem to notice her or seem to care. For the first time since he arrived on set, he finally forgets the cameras are there and the role he's supposed to be playing. The real Ethan comes out and it's not pretty. His sneer wipes all evidence of those charming dimples away.

Ethan shrugs out of Emily's hold, snapping his body away with the sort of force that immediately puts Jake on edge. She shrinks back instinctively. It's a move Jake saw too many times in his childhood—the innate reaction of fear in a woman he cares about, the attempt to look smaller, to hide in her own skin. Jake clenches his fingers into a fist to physically restrain himself as Ethan jumps to his feet.

Cooper senses the impending disaster and tries to stop Ethan. Frank is already being led out by security. The jig is up. Ethan got the better edit. He should let it go. But he won't. He can't. It was too big a blow to his ego. He tries to shirk out of Cooper's hold, but the cowboy's grip is firm. Emily comes up behind both of them. She reaches out her hand. The tips of her fingers graze Ethan's shoulder—Jake is absolutely certain of this. Ethan knows she's right there. He knows she's right behind him.

Still, he drives his elbow into Cooper's gut to force him to let go, and in the process, throws his other elbow high. Emily cries out. Her face whips to the side. She stumbles, holding a hand to her cheek, and drops to the floor.

A second is all it takes.

One second and every wall Jake spent the past seven years building comes crashing down. He doesn't know he's moving. He's not present. He's not aware. One moment he's off to the side of the room with the crew, and the next his fist is connecting with Ethan's face. This time, when Ethan drops, he doesn't get up.

All at once, the trance shatters. Jake stares at his own hand as if it can't possibly belong to him, as if the dull pain in his fingers belongs to someone else. The pounding of his heart gets louder and louder, drumming in his ears, drowning out all other sound, until there's so much pressure in his ears the world becomes silent. He's transfixed by the red speckles across his knuckles.

I hit someone.

The words land like a waterfall on his head, pounding him into the ground with so much force his knees start to give out.

He takes a step to find his balance as his breath comes short. He's only ever hit one other person in his life, and as that man's coffin was being lowered into the ground, Jake made a promise to never touch another person in anger again. After seven years of controlling his emotions, of shunning that side of himself, of fighting his every instinct, he finally lost the battle of wills.

He gave in.

He hit someone.

Suddenly his father is there, watching with that smug expression, staggering and drunk, yet somehow superior. A bead of blood leaks from his swollen lip. When he wipes the spot, his hand comes back crimson and he smiles as if that's exactly what he wanted. Those eerily familiar bright blue eyes freeze Jake to the spot.

I told you, son, he says in a goading tone. *I told you. You're just like me.*

"Jake."

Her tender voice is the only thing that reaches him. It pulls him from the vacuum. Jake looks up, directly into Emily's golden eyes.

"I'm all right," she says, despite the bruise already forming on her cheek. It's the same lie his mother used to tell. "I'm fine."

Jake can't stand to look at her—to know she's seeing him like this. He turns his face to the side as if to hide, and the chaos of the room comes back into full focus. Ethan splayed out on the ground with a medic kneeling over his face. Frank laughing from the side as security forcibly holds him back. Cooper taking Emily by the arm and asking if she's okay. Fred grinning into his camera. Nina gaping at Jake as if he's lost his goddamn mind. The crew all staring at him, watching him, doubting him.

He can't meet their eyes.

He can't catch his breath.

He can't stay here.

So he doesn't. He turns on his heels and walks out of the room without looking back.

emily

THE LOOK in his eyes before he leaves hollows her out. The urge to follow is so strong she actually takes a step before Cooper gently holds her back.

"Don't go."

Emily looks into his caring green eyes and wonders how much he suspects. But there's no judgment in his expression, just worry.

"It'll be worse for him if you leave," Cooper continues softly.

Emily closes her eyes, once again seeing the hurricane brewing in Jake's gaze, the anger and the hatred and the loathing, all directed at the person who least deserves it— himself. Then she nods. Cooper is right. If she chases after him, it'll raise questions. It'll cause more gossip. It'll put a bigger target on his back. As hard as it is, the best thing to do now is lie low.

Cooper lifts his fingers to her cheek, wincing as he gently touches her skin. "You've got a bit of a shiner. Are you okay?"

"I'll be fine." Emily shrugs. The ache in her cheek is dull compared to the throbbing one in her heart. "I was more shocked than anything. It all happened so fast. I'm not even sure how I got hit."

"Ethan." There's a rough edge to the cowboy's voice she's never heard before. "He caught you with his elbow, but he had to know you were right there. He must have sensed you right behind him."

Emily goes still as the scene replays in slow motion. Ethan jumping to his feet to go after Frank. Cooper holding him back. Emily stepping forward to calm him down. She reached out her hand. She touched his shoulder. She made contact. Then a sudden blur. Pain exploding behind her eyes. A cry spilling through her lips. She held a hand to her cheek and stumbled back, her gaze dropping to the floor while the room righted itself. By the time the world came back into focus, Jake was there with his fist raised.

I touched Ethan's shoulder.

I touched him.

He knew.

"You don't think it was an accident?" Emily asks, her voice small.

Cooper's expression turns dark. "It was a risk any good man knows better than to take."

She squeezes his hand. A furrow forms in her brow as her thoughts swirl. Fury and hurt curl in her gut, but mostly what she feels is concern—and not for herself. She'll deal with Ethan later, when he's not moaning on the floor. Because every time she hears him, all she hears is the *crack* of Jake's fist connecting with his face, and all she sees is the horror in

Jake's eyes as he stared disbelieving at his own hand as if it couldn't possibly be connected to his body. He never spoke about his dad with her, but she knew. From her father, from town gossip, from school friends. She knew and maybe it had been a disservice to pretend she didn't.

Maybe it still is.

"Okay, people, listen up." Nina's voice fills the room. "I think we all need a break. Unless anyone objects, we're going to put this puzzle ceremony on hold for a little bit. Guys, Rajit will take you back to your rooms until further notice. Emily, I'm going to have Rita escort you back to yours. Production needs to regroup, and then we'll bring you all back to finish this thing up. Sound good?"

A general consensus emerges. Nina makes eye contact with Emily to confirm her approval. Little does the producer know this is the exact opening she needs. Emily nods, trying her best not to seem too eager as the assigned PA makes her way over. While Rita leads her out, Ethan finally sits up and aggressively demands to talk to Trish. A shiver works its way down Emily's spine at the vitriol in his tone. Clearly, he's not the man she thought he was. But as she leaves the cameras behind, she can't find the energy to care. Every step down the hall leads her closer to the man she actually wants to see.

There's only one problem.

Rita isn't just a guide. She's a babysitter, too.

The second her hotel room door closes, Emily presses her eye to the peephole.

Come on. Come on.

The PA doesn't leave. In fact, Rita leans back against the opposite wall and slides down in a slow-motion collapse against the floor to settle into what appears to be a long-term stakeout.

Shit.

Emily flips around and drops her head against the door.

What am I going to do now?

She reaches her hand to the left and touches the wall. Jake is right next door. He's five feet away. She knows because the walls are paper thin and she's spent the past three nights pretending not to hear him pace across the floor, muttering to himself. But when she presses her ear to the surface now, there's nothing but silence.

You're in there.

I know you're in there.

Emily knocks on the wall.

She's deranged, she knows, officially toeing the line between crazy ex-girlfriend and plain old crazy, but she needs a sign that he's okay. Because yes, he broke her heart when he walked out on her seven years ago. And yes, she's never gotten over it. And yes, she will probably love him for the rest of her life. But—

Wait.

What was the point she was trying to make?

Jake. Jake and his emotionless gaze. Jake punishing himself for crimes that were never his. Despite their history, or maybe because of it, she can't let him drown in those memories, not when the only reason he did what he did was to protect her.

She knocks again.

Still nothing.

"Jake," she forcefully whispers, practically making out with the wall.

Nothing.

"Jake!" she growls.

Nothing.

Her fist meets drywall, and she spins, wildly searching for a chair to break the stupid barrier down. Her gaze snags on the light streaming through the curtains.

The curtains...

Emily runs across the room and throws them apart, revealing the balcony. In a flash, she's outside. Warm sunshine prickles her cheeks. Wind whips her hair. The Eiffel Tower pokes up over the buildings across the street, a view she's spent most of her life dreaming about, but her eyes drop immediately to the man sitting on the balcony to her left. His legs dangle over the edge and his face is firmly pressed against the wrought iron railing. He looks more like he's in jail than in the most romantic city in the world.

"Jake."

This time her voice is soft, almost lost on the breeze. He doesn't even flinch. His usual suit jacket is gone, and the white shirt beneath is rumpled. His hair sticks up in clumps, the oils from his hands leaving it greasy from having run his fingers through it so many times. If she could see his eyes, she knows they'd be bloodshot and dark as the ocean at midnight.

"Jake, look at me."

He doesn't.

He won't.

The only indication he's heard her is the clench of his already tight jaw.

"Jake. Please, look at me."

"No."

His voice hits her like a wrecking ball, taking down every last shred of restraint. It's vacant and cold, no hint of the boy she once knew.

"Talk to me, please."

"Go away, Emily."

Not Em.

Emily.

Just like she wanted, only now at the sound, she wants to reach across the distance between them and absolutely throttle him for using it.

"Jake, if you don't look at me right now, I'll—I'll—"

She cuts off, not even sure how to complete the sentence. As far as threats go, it's pretty much a complete failure. Except that the corner of his mouth twitches just enough that nothing else matters.

"Jake. Jake!"

Before Emily even realizes what she's doing, her foot is on the railing. They're five stories up. The very hard sidewalk very far below them would most certainly kill her if she fell, which really isn't how she always imagined her first trip to Paris. But his balcony is three feet away. Three measly feet! A child could make it. She can practically reach across the distance with her hand.

He must be able to read her mind because the exact moment she lifts herself fully onto the railing, he spins toward her with horror in his eyes.

"Emily, what the hell—"

Too late.

She jumps, possessed by some sort of spider monkey as she sails across the opening to slam fully into his chest. She claws at his shoulders. Her heart pounds as she hooks her ankles behind his back. He catches her with a grunt, and she melts into his chest. For a moment, nothing else matters. It's been seven years since she's let him get this close. His breath tickles her neck. His warmth sinks into her skin. His scent wraps around her, a fresh ocean breeze blowing through the trees, wild and untamable. Suddenly she's back in high school with her heart in her throat, except this isn't a boy. He's a man, muscular and hard in all the right places. Fire zips down her spine at the way his large fingers dig into her thighs. Now, she's back in her dream, back in the shower, back with his skin on her skin and a moan on her lips. She's one breath from shifting her face, bringing their lips closer, until...he goes and ruins it.

"What the fuck, Em!"

Jake sets her down firmly and holds her at arm's length. He grips her shoulders with a reprimanding look in his eyes.

"What the fuck was that? Are you kidding me? You could have died! You could have—"

"But I didn't. And now, you're looking at me."

She grins. He glowers.

"You shouldn't be here."

"Oh?" she asks innocently and reaches for the railing. "Should I go back the way I came?"

"Stop."

He takes her by the hand. An electric shock zips up her arm, as if she's touching live wires instead of skin. When he tugs gently, she turns back to him, looking first at their joined hands then up to his face. He feels it too. There's no denying the want in his eyes, not with her. She's seen this passionate glance too many times before. His blue eyes turn to molten sapphire, burning their way through her. Jake strokes the inside of her palm. His calloused thumb gently scratches her skin in a touch she can feel all the way to her core. Then he blinks and forces his gaze away.

"Come on."

He guides her inside his room. They march toward the door. She's so caught up in the feel of him, it takes her a second to realize what he's doing.

"Wait!"

"You need to leave."

"Rita is sitting in the hallway."

"What?" He freezes.

"Rita? The PA?"

"Yes, I know who she is. Why is she—"

"I think she's guarding my door. Or maybe yours."

"Fuck," he mutters and drops her hand to run his fingers through his hair. His muscles pull against his white button-down, revealing rippled contours, toned biceps, and a broad chest. She averts her eyes, but those backstabbing jerks jump to the exact wrong place—the sliver of hard, tan skin visible above his belt. A smattering of dark hair follows a defined curve, guiding her directly to his zipper. Her throat runs dry.

Stupid untucked shirt.

"I'll go out and send her away. Give me a minute."

He's almost out of reach before Emily's trance breaks and his words reach her brain. "Jake, stop. I came here to talk to you."

She grabs for him. He shakes her off, but stops walking. It's something, at least.

"I don't want to talk."

"Since when has that ever stopped me?"

"This is different."

He speaks to the wall, refusing to look at her. Or maybe he simply can't. Emily walks into the path of his gaze and forces his hand. "Why?"

He turns away with his jaw clenched. "Because you don't understand."

"I understand more than you know."

"I can't talk about this."

"Why, Jake?"

"Because I can't!" he shouts. The words emerge from somewhere deep inside his chest, raw and aching.

Emily reaches out to comfort him, but he flinches back. He still won't meet her eyes. Maybe she's overstepping. Maybe she should respect his boundaries. Or maybe she needs to show him that she's not afraid of the darkness that's always been inside of him. She'll admit that at seventeen, she found it intriguing, mysterious, even brooding. Now her more mature heart aches for everything he's had to endure. She can't walk away. Even if she should, she just...can't.

"I know about your father, Jake."

He sucks in a sharp breath.

She barrels on. "And you're right. Even though I know what a monster he was, I don't understand everything you and your mom went through. I can't. I never will. But I know you, maybe better than anyone else in the world. I know you,

Jake. And you're not him. I don't need all the details to know that."

"Em…"

His voice cracks and he stumbles. The backs of his knees hit the side of the bed and he drops down onto the mattress. She steps between his legs and cradles his face with her palms. His lashes are wet with unshed tears. She arches his face until he looks at her—really looks at her.

"You hit someone, and it's obviously ripping you to shreds inside. That alone tells me you're nothing like your dad. You didn't act out of some urge for violence. You did it to protect me, Jake. Please, stop punishing yourself on my account. It was a mistake, nothing more, and it's not who you are. You're a good person, Jake. You are."

He reaches up to hold her hands against his cheeks and takes a shuddering breath. A battle rages in his eyes. He wants to believe her—he wants it so badly—but she can see he doesn't. The shadows in his gaze are too deep for her words to penetrate.

She keeps trying.

She has to.

"You set up a monthly movie night at the nursing home for your grandfather, and then kept it going three years after he passed. You went to every school spirit event even though they made you die a little inside each time just because you wanted everyone else to have those memories for the video yearbook. You did more chores than any seventeen-year-old I've ever known—mowing the lawn, taking out the trash, clearing the leaves, doing the dishes—all so your mom's life could be a little bit easier. And you believed in me, Jake.

Always. Even when I didn't believe in myself. You were ready to drop everything for me. I know you were. I know you would have, if things had gone differently."

He threads his fingers through hers, tightening them around her palms as their gazes lock. It's the closest they've come to talking about the past, about what really happened between them. A lump forms in the back of her throat. It's full of the what-ifs—questions she's never been able to get rid of, even after seven years of wondering, because deep down she wants the other life, the one she thought they were going to have until it all fell apart.

Does he feel the same?

Once upon a time, she would have said yes. But now, after the way he left, she's not so sure. The movie of what might have been plays in his eyes. To her, it's a happy film, his favorite kind. She could stand there and watch it all day. But Jake closes his eyes as if unable to bear the sight of it. His brows pinch with pain. It makes her chest ache in an all-too-familiar way. *She* would have been happy in that other life, but not him, and that's the crux of their problem.

Seven years and nothing's changed.

Emily drops her hands from his face, but she doesn't leave. She's always had a weakness for antiques—maybe that's why she's never been able to walk away. But he isn't a diamond that needs a new setting. He's not so easily fixed.

Still, she dips her head back into his line of sight.

He refuses to meet her gaze.

"If you don't believe me, maybe you'll believe someone else," Emily says, distancing the conversation from them and their past back into safer ground. "My dad is a police chief, remember? He knows how to read people, and he knew all about your father. But he never once told me to watch out for you. He never once said you were bad news. He never once asked me not to go out with you. He knew you weren't your father, Jake. He trusted you, and that's not something he does lightly."

"I know."

It's the first he's spoken in minutes, and if anything, he sounds worse. More broken. More bruised. As if the ghost of his father were there in the room throwing punches.

"He did trust me," Jake says, finally meeting her eyes. "And look what I did, Em. Look what I did with his trust."

She's not entirely sure which grievance he's referring to, but it doesn't matter. For the first time since waking up alone in her bed that fateful morning, her anger simply melts away. It's been a constant in her life for seven years, always churning, like a pit of lava that appeared crusted over and sealed, yet bubbled under the surface. And now it's gone. Because the look on his face is so shattered she can't be mad anymore. He hates himself enough for both of them.

"Jake."

She puts her hand on his leg to comfort him. The muscles beneath her palm tense and flex. Then he sighs, giving in as his whole body relaxes into her touch. Before she knows what's happening, his cheek presses against her stomach. His arms wrap around her waist. He holds on to her for dear life, as if she's the only thing keeping him alive, keeping him going. Emily hugs him to her chest, bending at the waist to wrap him closer. She doesn't care if it's a good idea or a bad one, she's just aware that he needs her right now. He's battling more demons than she ever realized existed.

She's never seen Jake cry.

But even though he doesn't make a sound, she knows he's sobbing. His entire body trembles in her arms.

The moment is splintered by a knock at the door.

He flinches back with a sharp inhale and rubs at his eyes, visibly rebuilding his walls.

The knock sounds again, this time accompanied by a voice. "Jackson."

It's Trish.

"Fuck," he mutters before launching to his feet and pulling her with him. "Coming!"

His hold is firm but never painful, gentle even if coercing. It's clear he's innately aware of what lines can and can't be crossed. How did she never notice how carefully he always handled her? It's so obvious now that he's restraining himself, that he could so easily overpower her but never would. Emily goes along with his obvious plan and huddles in the closet, hiding between a few of his suit jackets. The smell of him overwhelms her, comforting as an old blanket. Jake meets her eyes once before sliding the door closed.

"Don't say anything."

Then she's in the dark, barely able to see him through a sliver in the sliding door. He steps out of sight for a moment. The hinges creak as the door swings open. He's back in view by the time it clicks closed.

"Give me an explanation right now or you're fired," Trish says, her tone ominous. Emily can't see her, but she can imagine the hard lines along her porcelain face. The executive producer is fearsome to behold even under the most mundane circumstances.

Jake shifts his weight, obviously uncomfortable, then straightens his shoulders when his decision is made.

"My father was abusive," he says, tone firm but detached in a way maybe no one but Emily would ever notice. His fingers curl into a fist by his side, clenching once before flexing. It's the only indication that this topic is so very difficult for him to discuss that the mere mention is cutting him up inside. Does Trish notice? Does she care? "When I saw Ethan's elbow connect with Emily's face, I just reacted," he continues. "I honestly don't even remember getting from point A to point B. One second I was with the crew, and the next he was on the ground. I'm not proud of what happened. I'm actually horrified by it. So you can trust me when I say, please fire me if you feel like that's what you need to do. I understand. My behavior was indefensible."

He stops talking and waits.

The silence stretches from one second into two.

Emily tries to hold perfectly still in her hiding spot, but her every breath sounds like roaring thunder in the quiet. Her heart pounds. Her palms start to sweat. There was a reason Jake was always the one sneaking into her house in the middle of the night. She wasn't made for this. Already, her muscles are beginning to cramp as adrenaline floods her system.

Finally, Trish sighs.

"Thank you for your honesty." It's the warmest Emily has ever heard the executive producer sound, which is to say, a few degrees above freezing. But still. "Don't beat yourself up. I've seen worse punches, and you got lucky this time. We convinced Ethan to sign an NDA as well as an agreement not to sue so long as we delete the footage of everything that happened after Frank's punch. He thinks he'll come out the victor to the viewers, which is exactly what we want him to think anyway. Nina didn't have time to get a read on Emily before Rita escorted her out, but my gut feeling is that if he apologizes profusely enough, she'll keep him."

Jake's face turns dark. "You want him to stay?"

"Want him to stay?" Trish scoffs.

Emily leans a little closer, fully absorbed in the conversation. It's the first time she's heard the producers speak as if she's not there, because, well, as far as Trish knows, she's not. It's a tantalizing peek behind the curtain.

"He's our season," Trish continues. "You know that. We haven't had a villain win in years. The viewers will eat it up."

Villain? Emily thinks. All the hours she's spent chatting with Nina run through her mind. Never once has her handler had a bad thing to say about Ethan. She's always been encouraging, talking about how attractive he is, how romantic their dates are. On some level, Emily knew it was bullshit, but to hear it out loud is something else. All the man's red flags flash before her eyes like a billboard in Times Square, suddenly so obvious she can't believe she didn't notice them until tonight. He's self-involved. He's not there for the right reasons. He wants to be famous. He doesn't care one iota about her. He's using her to climb the Hollywood ladder. He's manipulative and deceitful and a con.

He's the villain.

Of course he's the freaking villain—and she was playing right into their hands!

Dammit!

"What if Emily doesn't forgive him?" Jake finally asks. He knows she's right there listening, and he's trying to give her an out. "What if she sends him home?"

"Then it's your ass on the line, Jake, for messing up my storyline."

He juts his chin forward, about to speak, but she cuts in.

"My room. Five minutes. Nina and Fred are already on their way there, setting up a video conference with Nick and network execs. It's ultimately not my call if you get to keep your job, so I'd come prepared with answers for the hell Legal is about to put you through. You can tell them what you told me or not. That's up to you. But you'll need to tell them something. And I'll do what I can to help you."

"Thanks, Trish."

"Don't thank me yet."

A *whoosh* followed by a solid *thud* indicates the door has opened and closed. Not a moment later, the closet slides open.

Before Jake has time to say anything, Emily emerges from his suit jackets and stands before him. She stares into his unreadable eyes. This is the moment she's been waiting for since finding him standing outside her window in a suit and headset like some nightmare made to haunt her. This is her revenge. All she has to do is rightfully send Ethan home, and Jake will lose his job. She can make him pay the ultimate price for leaving her seven years ago, for choosing this life over the one they could have had, for throwing everything away. In the back of her mind, Sam chants.

Do it. Do it. Do it.

And yet, when she opens her mouth, something else tumbles out instead. "I'll keep him."

"What?"

"Ethan," she explains, her mind clear for the first time in weeks—heck, years. She doesn't want to hurt Jake. She never did. "I'll pretend to forgive him. I'll let him paint the whole thing as an accident. I'll keep him until the end like Trish wants."

"Em." He steps forward and she holds up her hand to stop him.

"I didn't say he'd win, I just said I'd keep him until the end, and then I'll send him home on my terms. Trish will get her show, I promise. You don't have to worry."

"Fuck it, Em. I don't care about the show."

Jake steps closer, until the hand Emily raised to stop him is pressed firmly to his chest. His heart thuds against her palm, the pace increasing the longer they touch. He reaches up to gently cup her cheek, his thumb scraping over the same line of skin Cooper touched back in the puzzle ceremony room. Her bruise. She shivers, not from pain, but from how deeply the tenderness in Jake's caress penetrates. He misreads her and drops his hand away immediately.

"Don't keep him for me."

"Maybe I'm keeping him for me."

Jake arches a brow. Emily arches right back.

Voices filter in from the hallway, reminding them both of the timeline Trish gave. Emily melts back into the closet, out of sight.

"Go, Jake. And send Rita away if you can. I'll walk out the door as soon as the coast is clear."

"The door. You promise?"

There's a slight twinkle in his eyes that makes her heart sing. She shoves him playfully on the shoulder.

"Just go."

He chuckles softly. The deep, throaty sound stays with her long after he leaves. It makes home in the spot where her anger once lived like a new sprout after a forest fire, the first sign of life in a once-barren place.

CHAPTER EIGHTEEN

JAKE EMERGES from the van completely confused. He sweeps his gaze along the steep cliffs fanning the road, then down to the deep ravine echoing with the splash of rushing water, then back to the arch bridge stretched before him. One lane is closed to traffic, filled instead by his crew. Emily and Ethan have the first solo date in Italy, and they're going bungee jumping. The location isn't what's confusing him—he was briefed this morning. The question running through his mind is, *Why the hell am I here?*

Nina handles the solo dates.

Jake stays back at the house to handle the men.

That's how it is. That's how it's always been as long as he's been working for the show—the suitor handler stays with the suitors. The fact that he's here means Nina is up to something, and it can't be good.

"Jake!"

Speak of the devil.

Nina signals him over to the production tent near the foot

of the bridge. It's currently filled with four different displays all showing various camera angles of the site. Fred and Trish are deep in discussion, pointing at something on the screens. A pit forms in Jake's stomach.

"Jake, how tall would you say Ethan is?" Nina asks when he steps beneath the awning.

He furrows his brows. "I don't know. Six-two?"

"And how tall would you say you are?"

He narrows his eyes at her.

She grins. "How tall?"

"Six-two," he mutters.

"And would you say the two of you have similar builds?"

"I guess."

He shifts his weight, glancing to where Trish and Fred are still whispering quietly, pointing at various parts of the ravine. The camera angles, he can't help but notice, are all zoomed out, distance shots. Nothing close up.

"But he has black hair," Jake says, all too aware where this is leading.

Nina slaps him on the back. "And we have makeup artists."

"You want me to jump?" he finally blurts, cutting to the chase. "What happened? Did he chicken out? Why not use it? I've never known you to shy away from a good story."

"It is a good story," Trish intercedes, "but it's not the story we need."

"What—"

Nina cuts him off. "Ethan won't jump because of his nose. You're the one who broke his nose. So, you're jumping. This way he can save face with the viewers, and we can hold up our end of the so-called bargain helping him get to the finals."

"And Emily?" Jake asks, fighting for one last chance.

"Mad at us for even bringing Ethan on this date. She said we were being irresponsible and reckless. She's in deep, I guess. Which is good for us, but bad for you, because she already agreed to the swap."

His thoughts jump back to his hotel room the day before, to Emily's promise. *I'll keep him.*

He sneers.

She's doing this for him, not for Ethan, as if his job is some wonderful thing worth saving and not the epitome of manipulative Hollywood bullshit. He almost wishes he did get fired to save them both the trouble, but when Nick heard about his antics he laughed and actually offered a pay raise. The network execs shot that down pretty quickly, giving Jake a stern warning. All in all, the meeting in Trish's room lasted no more than half an hour. Then they returned to set to finish filming the puzzle ceremony. Off camera, Ethan fawned over Emily and she forgave him. On camera, she gave a speech denouncing Frank's actions and explaining that violence was never, ever the answer. No one else went home. Then television glamor took over as champagne magically appeared and they toasted to the new adventures waiting in Italy. It was all smiles and laughter and cheer. The fight was forgotten—for everyone except Jake.

It took everything he had to make it through the night.

Then he retreated to his room. But instead of a reprieve, Emily was right there with him. The muffled thump of her footsteps filtered through the thin wall, as did the musical sound of her laughter. Her words from earlier replayed torturously in his mind.

I know you, Jake. And you're not him.

You're a good person.

You were ready to drop everything for me.

He was. God, she didn't even know how ready. Seven years later, he still had the file on his computer, titled *Emily*. It was full of all the movie clips he made that year. Shots of her. Shots of them. Mock interviews. Goofing around. The happiest ten months of his life were documented as if in mockery of what his world then became. And then there was the short film he still couldn't bring himself to open after all these years. He'd finished it that night before crawling into Emily's room. He was going to play it for her before getting down on one knee, with a Ring Pop in his pocket and a thousand promises in his heart.

She had no idea how ready he was to drop everything for her, how much he wanted to, how lucky he felt that her world was falling apart so he could selfishly keep her.

Then she told him the news.

And everything changed.

Jake wanted to believe what Emily said yesterday in his room. He wanted to believe it with everything in him. But he couldn't. And then she put the final nail in the coffin.

He knew you weren't your father, Jake. He trusted you.

And look what I did, Jake thinks again, his answer still the same as it was twenty-four hours before. *Look what I did with that trust.*

Almost the exact thing his father had, as if he were the man reincarnated.

"You afraid of heights, Jake?" Nina asks, bringing him back to the production tent, and the bridge, and the unavoidable present.

"No."

"Good. Oh, and one more thing." Nina points to where one of the wardrobe consultants is standing with what can only be described as a flesh-tone banana-hammock dangling from her finger. "Did I mention it's a nude bungee jump?"

"You've got to be fucking kidding me," Jake grumbles under his breath as Nina shoves him toward the bridge, her laughter echoing in his wake.

The wardrobe consultant smiles weakly as he approaches, the apology ripe on her face. He practically bares his teeth as he pinches the offending fabric between his pointer finger and thumb, holding it as far away from himself as possible—as if *that* would do anything.

"No one wore this, right?" he asks.

"No," she answers quickly. "No, no. Here's a robe, too."

She shoves it into his chest. With a growl, Jake stalks over to the changing tent. Curse words pour from his lips as he strips off his suit. They only get louder as he pulls the thong up his legs, barely able to get situated in the minuscule strip of fabric. How do women wear these things? Why? It's as if he has floss between his butt cheeks, or a permanent wedgie.

I can't believe this, he thinks as he shrugs on the robe, which doesn't even reach his knees. *I can't fucking believe this.*

He exits the changing tent to an immediate roar of applause. Everyone in the crew is standing there, forming a makeshift aisle to the bungee-jumping platform. Emily waits at the other end in a fluffy white robe. It's some sort of twisted nightmare reality of his wildest dreams. Suddenly, the truth smacks him in the face. He forgot in all of his annoyance that she would be there too. Nude. Pressed up against him. Soft and warm in all the right places.

Fucking hell.

"I hate all of you," he announces as he stomps forward.

Emily covers her mouth with her hand to stifle a laugh. He glares at her. A deep chuckle draws his attention over her shoulder to where Ethan watches, a smug expression on his face—well, as smug as an expression can be when a thick bandage stretches from cheek to cheek, not quite able to cover the bruised skin underneath.

Jake almost—*almost*—smiles.

With a different childhood, maybe he would have.

Instead, the instinct fades as soon as it comes. Breaking another man's nose is nothing to be proud of, nothing to gloat about. And with that sour reprimand in the back of his mind, he finally notices what Ethan is wearing. A plush white floor-length robe to match Emily's. Warm. Comfortable. Not flashing an indecent amount of leg to the general public.

Asshole, he thinks, before the truth strikes like lightning down his spine, a burning flash of jealousy. *They already shot the lead-up.*

That's why Ethan looks smug. Because he already stood in this spot with Emily, bodies pressed tight, skin against skin, talking for the cameras, bonding over the fake nerves, maybe even sharing a kiss. He saw her every curve. He probably felt half of them, the pervert. At the end of the day, he gets the glory and the girl, while Jake gets humiliated in front of his entire crew.

Great. Just great.

"Take it off, Jake," Nina calls suggestively from his left.

"This is sexual harassment," he shouts back.

"Report me to HR."

She steps in front of him with two makeup artists and a bungee instructor, blocking his view of Emily. A Cheshire cat smile paints her lips as she crosses her arms, scrunching the sleeves of her leather jacket, and notches her chin in his direction.

"I wasn't being an asshole," she comments, then amends, "I wasn't *just* being an asshole. We have to get your makeup done and harness on. So, take it off."

Someone whistles behind him.

Soft snickering follows.

Nina lifts her fingers to her mouth in a half-hearted attempt to stifle her grin, and one thing becomes glaringly clear to Jake. Seventy-five percent of his coworkers *are* about to see him in a thong. It *will* be embarrassing. But if he owns it, there's a slight chance it won't haunt him for the rest of his life. With that in mind, Jake turns to his audience.

"You want a show?" he says, throwing his arms to the side.

A round of catcalls ensues. Someone starts a slow clap—he thinks it's that traitor Greg, who is still bitter about being passed over on Jake's promotion—and soon the entire crew joins in, giving him a beat. Jake whips one edge of his robe to the side to flash some leg. Then he grabs the extra bit of belt and swings it around suggestively while he waggles his eyebrows. Hoots and hollers ring out as he loosens the tie. He shrugs one shoulder free, revealing some tan, toned skin with a laugh. He's not ashamed of his body. It's come a long way since high school, thanks in no small part to his discovery of the meditative powers of surfing when he moved to LA. Five mornings a week on the water does a lot for the soul, but it does even more for the body. He's got muscles. He's fit. And he's suddenly very aware of Emily behind him as the top of the robe falls, completely baring his upper body to the crowd.

Jake may or may not flex.

Sue me.

The clapping reaches an almost ridiculous roar as he holds the final bit of knot. He's a producer at heart and can't help but draw the moment out in a deliberate pause.

"Take it off," someone shouts. It sounds suspiciously like Trish, but the voice is drowned out as more people yell, the words turning into a chant. "Take it off. Take it off."

The network execs would have a stroke if they were here. But they're not. All Jake can do is own it.

He yanks the robe completely off and tosses it directly at Nina, who laughs and smoothly sidesteps the projectile. Then she cups her fingers around her mouth and yells. "That's the whitest ass cheek I've ever seen!"

Humiliation complete.

"Laugh all you want." Jake shrugs. "But someone here is going to spend hours up close and personal with this white ass cheek to make sure not a single speck of it winds up on cable TV."

"Not me," Nina says cheerfully, then signals the makeup team to step forward as the crowd starts to disperse.

He turns toward them and catches sight of Emily. It's as if the rest of the world disappears. Everything goes quiet.

Everyone fades except for her, and those honey eyes currently devouring every inch of his exposed skin. Goose bumps rise along his flesh, as if her gaze were a physical thing. He can *feel* it as she traces the ridges of his abdomen. His muscles flex and stretch in response, as if it were her fingers and not her eyes blazing a path across his chest. An adorable blush fills her cheeks when her gaze dips for a prolonged moment. Hunger flashes as she pulls her lower lip between her teeth. His stomach clenches at the sight, his body reacting before he can stop it. Because it's impossible to watch her watch him like that and not be visibly turned on.

No. No.

Fuck.

No.

She snaps her gaze up, making him question exactly how obvious his impending hard-on is becoming. The eye contact lasts for an excruciatingly drawn-out two-point-five seconds before a makeup artist steps between them.

Thank god.

Everything is so much easier when he doesn't have to look at her. He can breathe. He can think. He can review in painful detail all the reasons why they can't be together. A bandage gets taped across his nose. Some sort of oil is rubbed in his hair. He doesn't want to know what all the brushes gently patting his bare skin are even doing. A few minutes later, his transformation into a sniveling asshole is complete. The bungee instructor comes over with a harness and tightens all the straps. Then...his brief reprieve ends.

Jake is wholly unprepared for the sight that greets him when he finally turns back toward the platform.

Emily.

Naked.

In the blinding sunlight.

A cough barrels up his chest and he doubles over, flashing what he's sure must be a rather unattractive view of his ass crack to everyone standing behind him, but he can't help it. The air is quite literally sucked from his lungs. He heaves, trying to catch his breath.

It's nothing I haven't seen, he tries to reason.

Which is true.

But he hasn't seen it outside of his dreams in seven years and apparently that makes all the difference. Because…fuck, she looks good. More than good. Like a goddess. An apparition. A—

"You okay?" Nina slaps him on the back, hard. "Come on. We're losing daylight, and we shot Ethan's scene half an hour ago. I don't want the light to change too much between takes."

She shoves him and he stumbles forward. His every muscle locks up as he approaches Emily. She has her arms crossed to cover her chest, but it does little to stop his imagination from filling in the view. A nude thong stretches across her hips beneath the harness. Uncertainty lights her eyes.

The instructor guides him closer, too close, nothing but two inches of suddenly hot air between their bodies as more straps are tied and carabiners secured. Nina provides instruction from the side, one eye on a screen and one eye on them to make sure the poses match.

"Jake, get closer."

He does, sucking in a breath as their thighs graze. Emily gasps softly.

"Emily, drop your arms and put them around him like you were doing with Ethan."

Emily swallows, not looking at him as she unfolds her arms and seals the distance between them, hugging him fully against her. Her breasts press flush to his chest. Logically, he knows there's a set of pasties between them, but logic doesn't mean a hell of a lot at the moment. Blood rushes like a forest fire through his veins.

"Jake, put your left arm around her."

He tries to keep some semblance of distance between them and hugs her by the shoulders, but Nina quickly calls him out.

"Not like that, you idiot. Have you never held a woman before? Around her hips."

He grits his teeth, fighting the way his body responds as his arms slide around the small of her back. Involuntarily, he digs his fingers into her skin, itching to lay claim.

Perfect.

That's how this feels.

Fucking perfect.

Jake rests his chin on her head, relishing the moment, and without prompting, Emily nuzzles into his chest. Her hair falls like silk across his skin. Her cheek is hot where it touches his pec. She sighs, softening just enough to make him wonder if the same thoughts are running through her head.

He doesn't ever want to move, to leave. It's everything he's been missing.

And for the next thirty seconds, it's his.

The instructor steps back. The cameras zoom in. A countdown begins, matching the thud of his heart. He's never wanted time to stop so badly in his life—not because he's scared of the drop, but because he knows once it's over, he'll never be here with her again.

"Ten," the crew shouts. "Nine."

He tightens his hold, squeezing her to him as if to never let go.

"Six. Five."

"I'm sorry about this," he whispers into her hair in one last desperate attempt to fool himself into believing the lines between them still exist.

"Don't be," she whispers back, burying her face deeper into his chest. Her heart pounds so hard he can feel it against his skin. *Thud. Thud. Thud.* She digs her fingers into his back and shifts ever so slightly. Her lips brush hotly over his flesh as she confesses, "It was my idea."

"One!"

The world tilts on its axis and they fall.

emily

THEY WERE ONLY TOUCHING for five minutes, but three days later Emily still can't scrub the feel of Jake from her skin. She's trying. Oh, she's trying. With a loofah. With other men's kisses. With a very sassy internal dialogue. Nothing's working. Every time she closes her eyes, he's there, with his chest hard against her breasts, his hands firm around her waist, his breath hot on her neck, and his heart loud in her ear. They'd been in that position a hundred times before—hell, in more intimate positions—and yet, it had felt different after so many years apart. More significant. More tense. More deliciously sensual. Something about the crowd around them, the secret history between them, the cool air on their skin, and the rising heat within all merged to create a new experience, one that was dangerously exciting.

Then they fell.

All the lines between them disappeared in an instant. Emily screamed into his chest. He hollered into her hair. Their arms tightened. Their legs squeezed. Every ounce of space between them disappeared as they clung to each other for dear life, the trust between them as strong as it had been all those years before.

As suddenly as it came, it was over.

The adrenaline faded.

The walls resurrected.

He barely looked at her as the boat retrieved them. He didn't say a word—maybe because they were mic'd, but Emily suspected that was an excuse. He wanted to keep her at arm's length.

Why?

Seven years ago, she thought she understood. He wanted to go to LA. He had dreams, a future to seize. He didn't want to be stuck in their small town, clinging to the past with his high school girlfriend. When the opening came, he ran. It hurt like hell, but she understood. She had New York. She had dreams, too. They'd known from the start they were on diverging paths. Maybe they could have made it work if he had wanted to, but he didn't, and that was okay. Sort of. Maybe. Not really, but she got it.

Now, Emily is just confused.

He wants her, physically if not emotionally. That much is obvious. So why is he still determined to push her away? They're older. They're more established. No one will have to give up their dreams. Her job is flexible. She can move to LA. Heck, she'll be a pseudo-celebrity in a matter of months. Maybe she *should* be in LA. Maybe it'll be better for her business. Or maybe—

Stop, she silently commands. *Just stop.*

Emily falls back against the bed and throws her arms

over her face in surrender. *Move to Los Angeles? What the hell am I thinking? This is insane. I'm insane. HE DOESN'T WANT ME.*

But on some level, he does.

And that's what makes it so damn frustrating.

"Emily!" Nina calls as she knocks on the door. "You ready?"

"Almost!" Emily squeaks back as she rolls half-naked from the mattress. It's their last night in Rome before they leave tomorrow to start filming the hometown dates. Most of the supporting staff will return to LA, not needed for the remainder of the season, so it's tradition to have a big send-off celebration. The suitors have to stay locked up in their towers, but apparently, the lead is always invited to join.

After her terrible solo date with David where she sent him home before even making it to dinner—a real shame, because the vineyard was gorgeous and Emily could have enjoyed about ten more glasses of wine if not for his incessant attempts to grope her—and a long, albeit entertaining, group date watching the guys pretend to be gladiators in the *actual* Coliseum—she's still pinching herself about that one—both leading to the excruciating puzzle ceremony that concluded about an hour earlier, Emily isn't really in the mood to go out. All she wants to do is curl up in her robe, order about six helpings of tiramisu off the room service menu, and pass the F out.

Instead...

"Emily," Nina sing-songs.

"Two minutes! I promise!"

Her makeup from filming is still intact. The elaborate

updo her stylist insisted on won't come out without the help of a chainsaw. All she needs is an outfit.

Easy.

Simple.

Except when she slides open the closet door, nothing works. Her shirts are too colorful. Her dresses are too patterned. Everything is bright. Everything is cheerful. Everything is so *Emily Ann Peters* when all she wants to do is crawl out of her skin and be someone else for one night. Not Jake's ex. Not the lead of the show. Not the bubbly, sweet girl too afraid to push buttons. Someone no one knows. Someone unpredictable. Someone new.

She pulls open the door.

Nina gives her once over. "You're in a bra."

"I am."

"I'm not sure that's going to work for dinner when the Pope lives like five blocks away."

Emily rolls her eyes. "Can I borrow something?"

"What?"

"I don't know. A skirt? A dress? Anything."

Nina eyes her again, brow furrowed, then shrugs. "Give me one sec."

True to her words, she returns no more than a minute later and shoves a black bundle into Emily's arms.

"Try this."

Emily throws on the skintight black racerback tank, then slides the ruched leather miniskirt up her legs. She's taller than Nina, so it's a bit shorter on her, but when she looks in the mirror a grin widens her lips. Her legs look long as hell, especially with the added inches from her leather booties. More importantly, she feels sexy as hell. Edgier. Different. But not too different, especially after slipping on a crystal-covered gold headband from her line and her electric-blue motorcycle jacket. Emily adds on a pair of studs and slides a few of her affirmation bangles over her wrist like a soldier preparing for battle—*beautiful, strong, confident, enough.* Then she heads for the door.

"You look like moto-Barbie," Nina says, then grins. "I like it. Let's go."

Everyone is waiting in the lobby. Jake does a double take as she steps off the elevator. His gaze drops to her legs and stays there, as if mesmerized by every inch of her exposed skin. A flush warms her cheeks. When he finally meets her eyes, the message in his is clear.

You're not playing fair.

He's got a weakness for her legs—always has, always will. It's why she wore so many miniskirts in high school.

Emily smiles back. *Nope.*

He turns away with a scowl and follows the group out the door, careful to keep his distance. They sit at opposite ends of the table at the restaurant—Emily with Nina and Trish, Jake all the way at the other end with the assistants. She sneaks peeks while they eat, noticing for the first time how slowly he sips his wine while the people around him guzzle. At the end of the meal, he declines the limoncello. Everyone else sports the bright eyes of a healthy buzz—heck, Emily herself is feeling nice and tipsy—but not Jake.

It brings her back to high school. How many times did he volunteer to be designated driver? Had she ever seen him well and truly drunk? A beer or two maybe, but never more than that, while some of their classmates were passed out on the front lawn. Back then, she never noticed how strange that was, too consumed by her own fun to take note.

Now she wonders.

Now she questions.

Without her anger to blind her, Emily can't help but think back to the look in his eyes after he ran from the puzzle ceremony and the hollow sound of his voice as he later confessed, *Look what I did with that trust.* Is that what's holding him back? What's always held him back?

Is he afraid of himself?

Afraid what he'll do if he lets go?

She hates that for him.

A fire stokes to life deep in her gut, made of desperation and determination. It's a need she can't fight, this desire to burn his fear away. As their boisterous group wanders down the cobbled streets of Rome, her focus stays on Jake. He's the only one not shouting loudly, the only one not smiling, still at heart the boy who preferred to stand at the top of the bleachers filming everyone else's fun rather than partake in the fun himself.

When they come upon the Trevi Fountain, he hangs back while the assistants all rush to find a place next to the water. Against the dark night sky, the marble gleams. Beneath the towering columns of a palazzo facade, Neptune stands like a giant on his chariot, being pulled out to sea. The water glows an unnatural blue, casting everyone's faces in a cerulean haze.

All her life, Emily dreamed of standing here. Yet instead of clamoring for a spot, she takes the opening and walks over to Jake while the rest of the crew is distracted.

"Are you okay?"

"Huh?" He turns to her, blinking, as if returning from another world. "Yeah, I'm fine."

"You seem quiet."

He grins, a charming grin to be sure, but shadows hang in the corners of his eyes. "I'm always quiet."

"You weren't quiet yesterday."

"Yeah, well..." He shrugs. "I guess the nude thong brought something out in me. Consider me back in boxer briefs and returned to normal."

"Jake."

"Aren't you going to throw a coin in?" He changes the subject and returns his gaze to the fountain as he shoves his hands into his pockets. "According to legend, the first coin ensures a return trip to Rome."

"And the second, a love affair," Emily says, studying the slight clench in his jaw. "And the third, a marriage. I read that in the guidebook, too."

"Well, you're set to be engaged in about three weeks. I'd say your odds are pretty good."

There's an edge to his words. Bitterness? Anger? Whatever the reason, it's clear he doesn't want her to go through with it. It's also clear he's too stubborn to admit why.

Tell me, Jake.

Let me in.

He doesn't. He won't.

Emily fumbles with her purse, trying to cover the shaking of her hands, and pulls out two coins. "What do you say?"

He stares at her open palm for a moment, then looks back to the group without meeting her eyes. "Go on without me."

The others are starting to walk back. It's not the time to confront him, so she closes her fist around the coins and gives him the space he wants. "Fine. I will."

The second she turns around, she can feel his eyes on her back, like two laser beams pointed straight at her heart, burning their way beneath her skin. No uninterested man would watch her the way he does. His gaze is tangible. The whole walk to the water, he tracks her. She tries to ignore it, to play his game, and asks one of the assistants to take a photo of her as she throws her coin into the fountain. The second coin sits in her palm like a weight, meant for Jake.

One for a return trip.

Two for a love affair.

As if pulled by a magnet, Emily looks to him. This time, he doesn't look away. They're fifty feet apart but he might as well be right next to her with the way her heart leaps out of her chest. He's waiting to see what she'll do.

Emily throws the second coin over her shoulder.

The heat in his eyes flares.

Give in, she wants to shout. *Just give in.*

He turns his back instead.

Maybe I'm wrong, Emily thinks as they continue on their way to the club where Trish rented a private room. *Maybe he's not afraid of himself. Maybe he just doesn't want me, at least not enough. Maybe this is exactly the same as it was seven years ago, and once again he's putting his job first.*

She needs to know.

She can't wait another seven years for the answers to her

questions. She won't spend another seven years wondering. She needs to know once and for all if Jake is willing to risk everything for her. And if he's not, then she needs to say goodbye.

Which is why, when Nina walks over with a shot of tequila, Emily downs it without thinking. And why she does another with Fred, then another with Rita. The more in control Jake is—standing in the corner of the room with his arms crossed, brooding silently, looking far more attractive than he has any right to look—the more out of control Emily becomes. A dance battle with an assistant. A dare to slap Trish on the ass. A round of drinks that somehow ends with her and Nina back-to-back, grinding with each other on top of the bar.

"I had no idea you were this fun!" the producer shouts.

"Me neither!"

Another shot finds her hand and she knocks it back. As the song ends, one of the very handsome Italian bartenders offers to help her down. He reaches up and slides his hands suggestively over her exposed thighs on the way to finding her waist. She giggles as if it's the funniest thing in the world. Then suddenly, a large, familiar hand finds hers and yanks. Emily falls backward with a yelp, sure she's about to eat it on the dance floor. Instead, two solid arms catch her and hold her securely against a warm chest.

"You need some air," Jake growls as he stalks across the room.

Emily grins triumphantly into the nook of his neck. It took longer than she thought it would, but deep down, she knew if she went far enough, he would swoop in to protect her, the way he always did before.

You do still care, she silently goads as they burst through the door and into the crisp evening air. *Ha!*

He puts her down the second they're alone, then steps back to keep a solid three feet between them. Goose bumps rise along her exposed arms and legs, her jacket discarded somewhere inside and the weather cooler now than when they arrived. But inside, she's all fire.

"What the hell was that, Jake?"

"Me, stopping you from getting groped."

"Maybe I wanted to get groped."

"By the lecherous bartender staring up your skirt for the past ten minutes?"

"So you *were* watching."

His nostrils flare. "Em."

"What, Jake? What? I'm all ears."

He clenches his jaw and turns his face to the side.

"Cat got your tongue?" she presses. "Nothing to say now that you brought me outside, alone, where no one else is around to hear?"

He looks back at her sharply.

"Tell me," she demands.

He swallows, his brows drawing together.

"Just tell me," she says, her tone softening as she reaches out to close the space between them. Liquid courage thrums through her veins. She presses her palm flat against his abs and he draws in a quick breath, as if in pain. Yet the look in his eyes is all pleasure. Emily steps closer and runs her hand slowly up his chest, not breaking eye contact as her fingers slide into his hair. He's rigid and stiff, as tense as a rubber band at the brink of snapping. One push and she'll shove him over the edge. One push and maybe he'll finally let go.

Emily leans up to press her body flush to his, emboldened by the shadows wrapped around them and the silence of the street. And yes, okay, by the copious amounts of alcohol in her blood.

"Or better yet," she whispers, her lips on his ear. "Show me."

Jake shudders as if in surrender and pushes her back until she hits the wall. Her shoulders scrape against the rough stone of the building's facade while his hands come to either side of her face. She's caged between his arms. He doesn't touch her except to bring their foreheads together, and they breathe across the silence.

In.

Out.

In.

Out.

Emily waits, too afraid to move, to speak, sure that anything she does will only scare him, a turtle retreating back into its shell.

After the longest minute of her life, he lowers his right arm. At first, she thinks he's turning away and disappointment floods through her. It's replaced almost immediately by a sudden rush of nerves as his fingers gently graze the inside of her wrist. Her heart pounds in her chest but she remains stock still as he slowly trails his touch up her arm. The path scorches as if drawn by dynamite as he moves past her elbow, across her shoulder, over her collarbone, up the column of her throat, until finally, his thumb comes to rest on the center of her lower lip. He tugs it ever so slightly into a pout.

"Em," he murmurs. The sound makes her shiver.

He's still fighting it, still resisting.

Until suddenly he's not.

Jake grabs the back of her neck and closes the distance between them. He devours her, his mouth hungry and urgent as he lays claim to her lips, wiping all thought of any other man away. She grips the front of his shirt and pulls him closer, then tilts her head to deepen the kiss. Seven years of pent-up sexual tension explodes in an instant. His touch is fire. It sets her aflame as he drags his lips across her jaw and down her throat, to the spot near the base of her neck he clearly remembers. Her head falls back against the stone with a sigh. He slides his hand down her side and brushes the edge of her breast on the way to her hip, making her burn deep in her core. She needs something to do, something to hold, so she threads her fingers into his hair and drags her nails along his scalp until he groans. But she doesn't have time to appreciate the deep rumble in his chest before his lips are back on hers, searing all conscious thought away. There's only him and his mouth and his hands. Time fades as she loses herself in the moment, uncaring of the risks, of the consequences, of all the ways he once broke her.

But Jake remembers.

He retreats, panting. "We can't do this."

"We already are," she says and pulls him back, because when they're kissing, nothing else matters.

"You're drunk," he says against her lips.

"Only a little."

"I made a promise."

"Who cares?"

"Me," he says and rips himself back. The sudden rush of cool air is like a slap to the face. "I care, Em. I made a promise—"

"Seven years ago," she retorts, unable to believe he's falling back on this as an excuse. "When I was seventeen, sober, and a virgin. And you damn well know I'm none of those things now."

"That doesn't change what I said to you that night. I meant it then, and I mean it now. I never want to be someone you regret in the morning."

"Too late, Jake," she seethes as she pushes past him. "You already are."

He hooks her around the waist, not letting her go so easily. "What does that mean?"

"What do you think?"

"Are you seriously mad at me for not taking advantage of you?"

"Yes!" But because that comes out wrong, she then mutters, "No." But that's not right either, so she releases a frustrated growl and jabs a finger in the center of his chest. "I'm mad at you for taking advantage of me all the times I didn't want you to, but not the one time I did."

"You're talking in riddles."

"You're being purposefully obtuse."

He gapes at her.

"Sneaking into my bedroom," Emily snaps. "Giving me the cell phone. Passing me notes on the plane. Luring me out of the hotel to take me to the crown jewels, my practical mothership. Come on. You knew exactly what you were doing. Don't feign innocence now."

He looks down, the guilt written across his face.

"So yeah," she continues, driving the point home, "I'm pissed. Pissed that you tried so hard to rope me back in, just to what? Turn your back and leave? Well, news flash. I saw that movie already. I didn't need a sequel."

"I wasn't—" he sputters. "I didn't—"

"Real answer, Jake."

He freezes.

"Real answer," she demands again, invoking something sacred between them. Up until now she's been too afraid for the truth, but she needs it. Like her lungs need air, she needs it in order to breathe. Right now, she's choking on the questions, drowning in them.

"Don't do this, Em," he begs.

"What do you want, Jake?" she presses, refusing to give him the out. All she needs to hear is a single word, three letters, and nothing else will matter.

You.

I want you.

She wills the words into existence, but she can't be the only one. He has to say them. He has to mean them.

Jake stares at her, his jaw set in a stubborn line, and she knows, even before he does, what his answer will be.

"If you leave, I won't be here waiting like I was before. It's over. For real. I mean it, Jake. I can't do this anymore."

He stands tall.

He steps back.

All the emotion in his gaze vanishes, as if sucked through a vacuum back behind his impenetrable wall, leaving her empty.

"Don't walk away," she whispers, hating how she pleads. "Not again."

"I have to."

CHAPTER TWENTY

TEARING himself away from her warm embrace was the hardest thing Jake's ever done, and now here he is doing it again. Each step is more painful than the last, but he forces himself down the block, around the corner, and out of her life for good.

Fucking idiot.

Why did he do this to her? To them? He should have listened when she asked to be strangers. He should have kept his distance. He should have stayed the fuck away.

But he didn't.

Because at heart, he'll always be Jacob William Henry III. A screwup. A life destroyer. The spitting image of his old man. And Emily deserves so much more than that, so much more than him. She deserves someone like Cooper, rugged American hero, nice, safe. Someone good, something Jake will never be. Each excruciating step he takes away from her is a step she can take closer to the better option.

By the time he returns to his hotel room, he's numb. The

moment he turned his back on her, his heart fell out of his chest and shattered into a million tiny pieces. It's now scattered across the streets of Rome. He feels nothing as he stares at the shadows on his ceiling. Nothing as the hours pass. Nothing as the sun peeks through the curtains, signaling a new day.

He goes through the motions at the airport. Emily won't look at him. But he looks at her, taking in her bloodshot eyes, her puffy cheeks, and her shaky voice. *Way too much alcohol,* she tells the others, but he knows the truth. It's him. What he did. What he always does. A visual manifestation of the pain he's caused her, and will continue to cause her, if he doesn't back the fuck up and leave her alone.

So he does.

For the next week, during the hometown dates, he lets Nina take the lead. He films B-roll. He interviews the families. He interviews the guys. He keeps out of Emily's way, not saying a word to her over the course of the eight-day schedule. Four different men in four different cities give impassioned speeches about wanting to propose to the woman he loves, the woman he will always love, the woman he will spend his entire life dreaming of marrying—and he feels nothing. He's dead inside. Robotic. A visitor in his own body.

They fly to South Africa.

Ethan gets the first solo date—a hike up Table Mountain with a sweeping view of Cape Town, followed by a wine tour and an overnight stay in the dream suite, which for this date is a private cabin for two nestled within the grapevines.

Gorgeous.

Romantic.

Emily turns it down. And even then, Jake feels nothing. Not delight. Not relief. He's completely detached as she slips the invitation back in the envelope and explains she doesn't think it's right to share a night together when there are still two other men vying for her heart.

Trish releases a sound of disgust, muttering about ratings.

He can't even muster a nod of agreement.

They fly to their next destination, Victoria Falls, where Pierre gets his chance at the dream suite. The two of them literally spend an hour making out in the Devil's Pool at the edge of the falls with a rainbow reflecting in the mists at their back. It's the sort of scenery that's a producer's dream. But Emily returns to the thousand-dollar-a-night suite at the River Lodge all on her own, using the same excuse as before.

It wouldn't be right.

They fly to the Okavango Delta in Botswana for their final international stop before the men are cut down to two—a romantic safari. Jake spends four hours in an open-top jeep coming face-to-face with lions, zebras, giraffes, antelope, and even a leopard.

He hardly bats an eye.

Dinner that night is a romantic candlelit platform for two at the edge of the game lodge. The lowering sun paints the sky an almost unbelievable tapestry of deep reds, purples, and yellows. Elephants roam in the background. Warthogs gather near the edge of the deck. In the distance, a lion roars. Emily and Cooper sit with wine while the meal is served. From his spot beside Fred, Jake watches the picture-perfect night unfold from behind the lens. A beautiful woman. A dream man. Smiles. Laughter. Romance. It's everything *The Love Match* is supposed to be, and everything he wants for her. The envelope to the dream suite rests against a vase, a gentle reminder throughout the evening that this doesn't have to be the end. Emily waits as long as possible until Nina finally prompts her from the side to keep things moving. They are, after all, on a schedule, and the camp employees can only guard for lions for so long—something Jake honestly never thought he would say.

Emily grabs the envelope, holding it tightly between her fingers as she looks up at Cooper. "I think you know what this is."

The cowboy offers a relaxed smile. "I have an idea."

"Before I open it, I need to tell you something. Something I've been putting off saying. Something I honestly haven't spoken about with anyone in seven years."

For the first time in days, the hollow void in Jake's chest pings with life.

Seven years?

He steps away from the camera, so he can look at her without a lens between them. If Emily sees him behind Cooper's shoulder, she gives no indication. She just wrings the envelope between her fingers, the image of nerves. Around him, the crew shifts their feet. A subtle buzz fills the air at the shift in her demeanor. With Ethan and Pierre, she cut right to the chase, telling them no. This is different. This is a storyline. This is the saving grace of what's usually the most-watched episode of the season but has so far been a dud.

To Jake, it's an Achilles' heel.

Because he knows where this is going before she even opens her mouth. When she finally does speak, it only confirms his suspicions.

"I told you about my ex, remember?" Emily says, her voice soft, but in the perfect silence it carries all the weight of a scream.

Cooper nods, a draw to his brows.

Fred leans over and mutters to Jake. "When did she mention the ex?"

Jake mutely shakes his head as his throat runs dry. A knot forms in the pit of his stomach, growing larger and larger as his nerves swarm. For days, he's felt nothing. But now the dam breaks. Suddenly, he feels everything at once. Fear. Hurt. Longing. Desperation. Pain. Most of all, apprehension. Because he knows what story she's about to tell. He already lived it. And he's spent seven years trying his best not to go back.

"We met when I was seventeen," Emily continues. "It was our senior year of high school. We started dating in October. By Thanksgiving, we were inseparable. By Christmas, we were in love."

A million memories flash before Jake's eyes. Emily beside him on the bleachers. Emily running down the hallway and into his arms. Emily catching snowflakes on her tongue. Emily laughing with his mother over mashed potatoes. Emily looking into his eyes, silently promising him forever.

"He got accepted to a school in California. I was headed to the Fashion Institute in New York. We spent the entire spring planning a long-distance relationship, then the entire summer pretending fall would never come. It felt…" She pauses to take a breath and looks up at the star-studded sky before releasing a sigh. "It felt destined, the way I suppose all first loves feel. Like fate brought us together. Like nothing would ever tear us apart. Like it was us against the world. Like we were simply meant to be. And I really thought we were, until I realized one night that I was two weeks late for my period."

A hushed silence falls over the crew. Trish is undoubtedly grinning. Nina's eyes are probably glowing. It's everything they've been waiting for—something newsworthy. Something unexpected. Drama worth building an entire season around.

If the lead were anyone else, Jake would be right there with them. Instead, he was back in his childhood bedroom with his head on the pillow, absently scrolling through his phone, unaware that in two seconds he was going to get a call that would change his entire life.

He'd just turned the light off when it rang.

The screen lit up with her name.

He smiled, the way he always did at the thought of her, and rolled onto his side before answering, prepared to settle in for her call.

Except... "Jake!"

Her voice was panicked, too sharp, almost a shriek. He sat up immediately. "Em?"

"Oh my god, Jake. You have to come here. Now. Please. I'm freaking out. I'm— We're— This can't be happening. Oh my god. Oh my god. Oh my—"

"Em," he said sternly, his heart ready to leap out of his chest. "What's going on? Take a breath. Tell me."

"I can't do this over the phone. You have to come here. I'm in my room. Please. I need you."

"I'm on my way."

He hung up the phone, practically jumped out of his window, and stuffed his shoes on as he stumbled across the lawn to his truck. He trembled as he drove. His entire body buzzed.

What did I do?

What did I do?

He parked in his usual spot two houses down and sprinted to her window. It was already open, so he pulled himself inside, falling to the floor with a *thud* in his haste. He expected a joke at his expense, but the room was deathly silent. Emily hadn't even turned when he came in. She sat cross-legged on her bed, staring at something on the mattress. As he walked closer, his heart sank to his feet. Two white test strips sat in a line atop her vibrant floral bedspread. He didn't have to look any closer to know what they said. She told him anyway.

"They're both positive."

Her voice was a hushed whisper, scratchy from tears. He said nothing as he sat next to her and gathered her in his arms. She collapsed against his chest, the sobs pulled from somewhere deep inside now that he was there.

"What are we going to do?" she kept saying, again and again and again.

He kissed her forehead and smoothed over her hair as he held her close, as if the tighter he held her the more he could prove he never wanted to let go. "We'll figure it out, Em. I promise, we'll figure it out."

He stayed in her room all night. Eventually she fell asleep, but he didn't. A flood of mixed emotions kept him awake until dawn, the most prominent thought leaving him guilt-ridden with joy while wearing a T-shirt still wet from her tears.

We don't have to say goodbye now.

We can be together forever.

Back in the present, Emily drops the bomb Jake knows is coming. "I was pregnant."

She swallows, her gaze still locked on Cooper's, and it's wrong. It's all so wrong. Jake should be the one holding her hand. He should be the one staring into her eyes. They should be alone somewhere, revisiting this together, not at opposite ends of a crowded platform, filming a show for ten million other people to see.

"I'll admit, I absolutely freaked out at first." She laughs, but the sound is empty. "Some people might not understand my choice when the dreams I'd been working so hard for were on the verge of coming true—New York and FIT and my future. Some people might have chosen differently, which is their right and I wouldn't fault them for it. But the second I saw the positive tests, I knew I'd keep the baby. How could I not when it was me and him and this terrifying yet somehow beautiful life we'd made? And my ex was so good at calming me down. He told me we'd be in it together, that he'd be there every step of the way. For that first week, we didn't tell anyone. It was summer, so every minute we weren't working, we spent together planning the future. I was going to postpone school for a year. He was going to transfer somewhere local. We were going to do it, become a family, raise a baby, even though we were only kids ourselves. Then finally I couldn't keep it from my sister any longer. Twin telepathy and all that. She knew something was up, and when she cornered me in the bathroom, I spilled my guts. The first thing she made me do was schedule an appointment with my gynecologist. I don't know why the thought never crossed my mind. It was so obvious when she said it. My ex drove me to the office the next day. My doctor took a blood sample to confirm the pregnancy. She said the results would be back in twenty-four hours, then we'd go from there. That was that, and I left. I didn't think anything of it until I got the call the next day."

Something within Jake snaps. His shoulders hunch. His spine bends. The weight of the world suddenly becomes too much, and he staggers back until he finds a post to lean on.

This is the moment that broke him.

Not the call to tell him she was pregnant, but the one to tell them she wasn't.

They were together when her doctor called. He was leaning against her headboard, supposedly reading up on the Savannah College of Art and Design where he was going to try to arrange a transfer, but actually fiddling one last time with the secret movie project he'd spent the past week working on for her. His fingers shook. His heart thrummed. Emily was oblivious. She sat at her desk and tinkered with some of the jewelry her grandmother had left her. Country music played softly in the background. They were both so focused they weren't really talking, just enjoying each other's presence. In the quiet, the vibration of her phone sounded almost impossibly loud. Still, he didn't even look over when she answered.

"Hi, Dr. Copeland. Yes, this is Emily. You have the results

back? Yes, I— What?"

She inhaled sharply. Her hand covered her mouth to stifle a gasp.

Jake jerked his head up.

Tears were already forming in her eyes. Before he could reach her, they started falling down her cheeks. The lines glistened in the light of her room.

"Uh-huh. Okay. Yeah. Uh-huh. Tomorrow. Thank you, Dr. Copeland."

She hung up and swiveled in her chair.

His heart was in his throat as he knelt before her, waiting. He kept his hands on her thighs to comfort her. It took everything within him not to fall apart, to be strong for her, because he knew by the look on her face, the news was bad. A second passed in silence. It might as well have been an hour. It was the sort of quiet that defied time, sucking in everything around it, until nothing existed outside the void. Finally, when he couldn't take it any longer, just when he was about to ask, Emily spoke.

"I'm not pregnant."

He flinched. "What?"

"The tests I took were false positives. I'm not pregnant."

"How?"

"I'm going back to her office for some follow-up testing tomorrow. I could have a hormone imbalance. But she said the blood test is accurate. I'm not pregnant."

"So there's no baby?" he asked dumbly, but he couldn't help it. His brain was slow. His lips felt fat. They'd spent the past week building a life together that to him seemed utterly perfect, and now, before his very eyes, it was crumbling.

"No," she whispered, then collapsed into his arms.

He couldn't say how long he held her, only that at one point she leaned back, looked him in the eye, and murmured, "I guess, this is a good thing, right? I don't know why I'm crying. It's—"

She broke off, her voice catching on the words. He gripped the back of her neck and pulled her close again, because he understood. God, she had no idea how well he understood. It was a loss. Even if the baby had never existed, in their minds it had, and now that dream was gone. The plans about getting an apartment together. Gone. The plans about staying in Georgia together. Gone. Talking about names, getting ahead of themselves and looking up baby clothes, picturing a family. Gone. Gone. Gone.

Eventually, they ended up on her bed. Emily curled into his side and buried her face against his chest. He ran his fingers through her hair, trying to soothe her even as his own soul felt ripped apart.

"Will you stay tonight? Will you just stay and hold me?" she asked, her voice on the verge of sleep. "I don't want to be alone."

"I'm here, Em," he told her and she relaxed fully against him. He kissed her forehead. "I'm here and I won't let go."

It was the last thing he said to her before she showed up unexpectedly in his life seven years later. Words she needed to hear. Words he wanted more than anything to believe. Words he knew were a lie even as they left his lips.

"The doctor said I wasn't pregnant, that I never had been," Emily tells Cooper now. Her voice is oddly detached while Jake feels swept away in an onslaught of feeling. The emotions he stifled for the past seven years surge over him at once, leaving him adrift. "They were false positives. And you would think an eighteen-year-old getting that news would be thrilled, but I wasn't. I was...destroyed. That might sound silly, to be wrecked by something that never existed in the first place, but—"

Her voice finally catches.

Cooper swoops in and takes both of her hands in his, ever the gentleman. "It doesn't."

"I loved my ex with everything I had, so I guess, the thought of losing him to long distance scared me more than the thought of having a family together, no matter how premature. After spending the week dreaming up this new life together, I felt like someone had swept the rug out from underneath me, like I was falling, and he was the only one who'd be able to catch me. But he didn't. He left instead. When I woke up the next morning, he was gone. And I never heard from him again."

A look of pure disgust twists Cooper's face.

Bile rises in Jake's throat.

"God, what a fucking asshole," Nina leans over and whispers. Jake has no idea when she came to stand right next to him, but he can't deny the truth in her words.

He is a fucking asshole.

He always has been.

And that's why he left. Because that phone call—that *fucking* phone call—was reality slapping him in the face. He didn't deserve a girl like her. He would never deserve the life they'd been dreaming of, all white picket fences and matching Christmas pajamas. While Emily sobbed in his arms, Jake thought about his parents, about the phone call his mother received at eighteen, about the life she was roped into against her will, about the man she had never been able to escape. But Emily could escape. Emily could get out of this town, and away from his family curse. She could achieve her dreams. She could be so much more. All he needed to do was get out of her way.

It was the second chance his mom never had.

He wouldn't take it from Emily.

So he held her the whole night, not sleeping a wink. His arms cramped from how tightly he wrapped himself around her. And then, when the sun slipped over the horizon, he snuck out the window. He got into his truck. And he drove until there was no more land to drive on.

"I would never—" Cooper rushes to say, but Emily stops him with a smile.

"I know. I'm not telling you this because I think you would ever do that. I'm telling you this because I wanted to explain why I've been holding back, why I haven't been ready. For a long time, I was so angry, but I'm not anymore. I'm not... anything. I'm ready to put the past in the past, to say goodbye and move on with my life."

Emily looks over Cooper's shoulder and finds Jake's eyes immediately, as if she was aware of his presence the entire time. It suddenly becomes clear none of this speech was for the cowboy, or the show. It was for him.

It was goodbye.

Jake holds her gaze.

A wrecking ball obliterates his heart, but he doesn't move. He just stares back, silently saying goodbye, because this is what he wants. For her to move on. For her to be with someone better, even if it breaks him into a thousand irreparable pieces.

She returns her focus to Cooper.

Jake clenches his jaw to fight the knot rising in his throat and the words threatening to spill out. He won't ruin this for her. He won't.

"Back to the envelope," Emily says with a forced laugh. Some of the tension in the air eases. "I want to give this to you, Cooper. I want to take the next step with you. I want to see where the night brings us, but only if you can make me a promise. You have to promise me that I'm enough for you. Because I know what it's like to be found wanting, to wake up alone because the other person needed more. My ex was prepared to stay with me if I was pregnant, but the second he found out I wasn't, he left. Because I wasn't enough for him on my own. He didn't want me just for me. And I can't go through that again."

Wait, what?

Jake straightens. He looks around, wondering if he's in a dream. Did everyone else hear what she said or did he imagine it?

That's not—

You can't honestly believe—

Cooper takes the envelope. He says something, but Jake can't hear what it is. His ears are plugged. Sounds warp and morph as if he's a hundred feet underwater, wading through the muck.

Not enough?

He thought it was obvious why he left. That it was about

him. About who he was. About his past. About his shortcomings. Never about her.

She's perfect.

She's beautiful.

She's— She's—

A guilt unlike any he's ever known rushes through him. It's unimaginable that she could think for a second, let alone for seven years, that his leaving had anything to do with her and not everything to do with him.

He has to tell her.

He has to explain.

Jake jumps forward just as Fred yells, "Cut!"

The entire crew moves into action. Suddenly the platform swarms with people. He loses sight of Emily in the crowd. He runs forward, shoving a PA out of the way.

But he's too late.

One of the camp guards throws an arm around his waist to hold him back. They're only supposed to cross over the boardwalk in small groups. The guidelines are strict to ensure everyone's safety. In the dark, there's danger of lions or leopards hunting prey—humans potentially being that prey.

Ten feet ahead, Nina, a cameraman, and a sound guy follow Cooper and Emily to the dream suite at the far end of the camp. One guide leads them and one follows at their back. Jake can do nothing as he watches them walk away.

Twenty feet.

Thirty feet.

Forty feet.

Gone.

COOPER'S strong hand grips her hip as he rolls her over in the bed. His broad chest weighs her down as their bodies mold together. She tangles her fingers in his hair and drops her head back while he trails kisses down the side of her neck.

It would all be incredibly romantic if not for two things.

One, as ridiculously hot as he is, she doesn't feel that way about him at all. And two, there's a camera about five feet from her face, sort of killing whatever mood might have existed in the first place.

As Cooper works his way down her throat to her collarbone, Emily finally can't help it anymore and looks directly in the bulbous black lens, the way she's been told many, many times she's not supposed to do.

"Are we done yet? I thought the whole point of a dream suite was to be *alone*." Her tone drops suggestively at the end of that sentence and Nina smirks.

"Yeah, we've got enough I think," she says and taps Phil,

the cameraman, on the shoulder. Finally, the little red dot on the side blinks off.

They're free.

Cooper immediately rolls off of her, offering an apologetic grin as she straightens her shirt and sits up. But the show isn't quite over yet. Emily takes his hand and kisses the top side of his palm, then gives Nina a pointed glare over his fingers.

"We're going. We're going," the producer says and ushers her crew from the room. Before she leaves, though, she turns around in the doorway. "Wake-up is at 7 a.m. sharp tomorrow. We're coming in without knocking, so whatever state you're in is the state America will see you in. Then we'll split you up. Emily, you'll have about two hours with hair, makeup, and wardrobe before the final puzzle ceremony, which will be quick. No private conversations unless you really need to. Then as soon as we're done filming, we're headed to the airstrip and our final destination of the season. Got it?"

"Got it."

Nina lingers for another moment. Emily throws a pillow at her head. The producer ducks with a laugh and closes the door behind her. Then finally, *finally*, they're gloriously, blissfully alone. Emily turns to Cooper and lowers her voice to the barest whisper.

"Do you trust me?"

He knots his brows. "Yes."

"Then go with it."

Emily waits thirty seconds, the time she imagines it takes Phil to get his camera back on and pointed at the front door. She's seen enough seasons of *The Love Match* to know that just because the crew left the room doesn't mean they've stopped filming. And she intends to give them a show.

"Oh, Cooper!" she suddenly exclaims in a passionate voice.

He quickly covers his mouth to stifle a laugh. She grabs him by the arm and pulls him to his feet. They stumble into the wall close to the door with an audible *thud*.

"Cooper!"

He smirks, then with a low growl that actually does give her stomach a little flurry, he says, "Emily. My god, Emily."

"Cooper."

She knocks a book off a countertop, trying not to laugh as it smacks the floor. Getting into it now, Cooper grabs her around the waist. He hoists her into the air and carries her across the room, which brings them directly in front of the not-so-opaque curtains. If she were a betting woman, she would guess Phil is knee deep in African grasses right now, less concerned with a lion attack than with the verbal lashing Trish would give him if he missed this shot.

"Cooper!"

"Emily!"

He pushes her back against the curtain, their bodies no doubt silhouetted by the soft lamplight. Emily throws her hands above her head and passionately grabs a fistful of fabric. Suddenly, something snaps. They both tumble to the floor in a fit of giggles, half the curtain dropping behind them. It must look absurd from the other side of the glass. She throws in an overly loud gasp of pleasure before Cooper helps her to her feet.

Emily quickly turns off all the lights but one, a small

lantern by the bed bright enough to still see Cooper's face. They quiet down while they wait for Nina and company to get bored. He stands watch by the door, peeking through the spyhole. After about five minutes, footsteps *thud* softly down the raised walkway outside the door.

"They're gone," he says, turning back to her. "Now, want to tell me what that was all about?"

"In a minute." Emily jumps to her feet. "First, we have to finish setting the scene."

She tosses one set of the silk pajamas to him and takes the other. They turn back-to-back and quickly change. Then Emily grabs their clothes. She hangs her bra over the lamp and his boxers off the bedpost. Their shirts and pants get discarded in a trail leading from the front door of the suite. She empties a nearby countertop and gently places the books along the ground in what she hopes looks like the arc of a passionate table clear. He scatters the pillows about the floor, but something is still missing.

"Rip this," Emily says, passing him her shirt.

Cooper obliges and buttons pop off, flying everywhere. The sight draws her back to Jake, to her pink pajamas, her missing button, and her dream. Emily grabs a pillow and tears it down the center in a momentary fit of rage. Feathers explode in every direction. Cooper blows one from his lip and stares at her with a brow raised.

"I'll pay for damages," she mutters with a wince.

"Don't you think this might be excessive?" he asks, eying the destruction while Emily tosses the feathers about the room. "This will be broadcast to about ten million people, remember? I don't care for me. Hell, this will probably work in my favor. But you're a woman, and as unfair as it might be in this day and age, you'll be judged harshly—"

"I don't care," she interrupts and takes his hand before leading him to the bed. Emily sits cross-legged on the cushy mattress. Cooper joins her, leaning against the headboard with his long legs stretched before him and his red curls unruly. His lips are a bit swollen from their on-camera makeout session and they're framed by a jaw that can only be described as chiseled. He truly is a handsome, handsome man. Life would be so much easier if she would just lean over, kiss him, and make this a true crime scene.

But she doesn't.

Stupid, stupid girl that she is, her heart belongs to someone else. Tonight was the first step in goodbye, but it will take some time before she's in any place to open herself up to someone new, which is why she's made a decision.

"I'm not picking anyone at the end of the show."

"What?" His jaw drops.

"Tomorrow at the puzzle ceremony, I'm sending Pierre home. You and Ethan will be the final two, and I'm going to turn down both of your proposals. Ethan is a jerk and he has it coming, but you've been so sweet, Cooper. So wonderful to me. So much fun to be around. And—"

"Such a great friend?" he concludes.

"Yes," she says softly, not sure how he'll react. "The only person I've been able to call a friend through this whole process. And okay, we're friends who have on occasion made out and gone on extremely romantic dates together, but—"

"Friends, nonetheless." He smiles ruefully. "I know, Emily. I may be a cowboy, but I'm smart enough to know when a woman is kissing me because she wants to, and when she's kissing me just for show."

"I'm sorry."

"Don't be." He shrugs. "Everyone is using everyone on this set, and I don't mean that in a bad way. I told you the real reason I'm here. And maybe there was a chance for us in the beginning, but honestly, I feel the same way now. We're friends...who occasionally make out and go on romantic dates in front of ten million people."

She snorts.

He chuckles.

There's a moment of comfortable, companionable silence before he finally gestures around the room. "So why all this if you're not planning to pick me?"

"Because I want America to pick you. I want the producers to make you the next lead, not Ethan. I want to help you, and your family, and your ranch, because you might not get it, but you've been a huge help to me. Being able to talk to you, being able to finally share my story publicly after keeping it in for so long, to have you not only listen but understand—it's meant more than you'll ever know. And all this," she says, waving her hand toward the chaos, "will ensure you win. You were the perfect gentleman all season, but the good guy doesn't always get the girl. You needed some edge. *This* is your edge."

"I might never hear the end of it back home." He shakes his head with a lopsided grin, and she rolls her eyes.

"You'll survive. Besides," she adds, "I'm the one who will spend the rest of her life known to America as the idiot who turned you down."

"And what are you going to say?"

"The truth." She shrugs and looks down to pick at an imaginary loose nail. "That I'm in no place to be in a relationship right now. That I need to focus on myself. That I'm a little bit broken, and I need time to heal before I can be the sort of partner I want to be for someone else."

"Hey." He reaches over and squeezes her fingers. "Your ex was the idiot."

"Can I admit to something embarrassing?"

"More embarrassing than ten million people thinking we spent a sordid night tearing this place apart? Shoot."

"I think I did this a little bit for him, too."

"To make him jealous?"

"No," she says quickly. "No, I wouldn't use you like that. More to say goodbye."

Emily pauses. Her thoughts drift back to the dinner and the momentary blip of eye contact she allowed herself to share with Jake. He was stoic and unmoving, with his jaw set, his arms crossed, and his expression hard. But she could tell, underneath it all, that he was breaking, same as she. The only difference was she wasn't afraid to admit it.

"Because he left the way he did, I never got to share my piece," she continues softly. "I never got closure. I never got to tell him how it made me feel, how damaged he left me. So I told you, and the world, and maybe the message will get to him somehow. I don't know what he thinks, and frankly, I no longer care. I needed to do that for me, so I can finally leave the past in the past. He's not going to fight for me, and I need to stop hoping he will."

Cooper thinks for a moment, studying her kindly. "You know what you said about not being enough?"

She nods, unable to speak from the sudden, sharp pain in her chest.

"I don't think that's why he left."

"You don't—"

"I know." Cooper holds up both his hands in surrender. "I know. I don't know him. I don't know the situation. But I know you, Emily. You're a sweetheart, and fun, and exciting, and damn near perfect even if you didn't fall madly in love with me. I can't imagine anyone thinking you aren't enough for them. I broke a girl's heart once—I mean, really broke. She thought I was proposing, and instead of giving her a ring I told her goodbye. But it had nothing to do with her. It rarely does. It was me, all me. My insecurities. My doubts. My issues. You say I'm a gentleman, but that's not who they see me as back home. I'm a screwup, a playboy. And I tried to use this girl to prove to my father I'd mended my ways, but my mom saw through the act. When she got sick, she made me promise I wouldn't drag this girl down the aisle to prove a point. She wanted me to find love, real love. So I ended it, breaking her heart and proving to my father I was exactly who he thought I was. My ex got engaged a year later, and now she has two kids. Because she was an angel, and I was the devil who messed everything up. You're the angel, Emily. Trust me on that."

She doesn't even realize she's crying until Cooper reaches up to gently wipe away her tears. It just makes more fall, and more, the floodgates unleashed. He gathers her in his arms, holding her close the way Sam would have if she were there, the way a friend would.

She's crying for Jake, but she's crying for herself, too, for all the things she's too afraid to say. Though she doesn't want to admit it, Jake isn't the only one running. He walked away from her, twice now, but Emily never chased after. There's so much Cooper doesn't know. So much she hid from the cameras. So much she's kept inside for the past seven years. No one outside of her family knows the truth, and she's still too scared to be honest.

About what happened in New York.

About why she left school.

Why she never picked up the phone to call Jake.

Why she watched him walk down the streets of Rome, too terrified to follow.

Emily is a coward, same as he is. And she'll keep running, and running, and running, until someone finally comes along who is strong enough to catch her.

jake

"WHAT THE FUCK..."

The words are out of his mouth before he can stop them as the door to the dream suite swings open. Books lie scattered across the floor. Clothes are tossed about the room. A black lace bra he really doesn't want to be staring at hangs from a lamp, so obviously, he can't stop staring at it. And are those feathers? FEATHERS?!

"What the *fuck*, indeed," Nina muses by his side. Then she whispers to Phil, "Are you getting this?"

The cameraman grins. "Yup."

"Did an animal get in here?" Jake growls and kicks at a pile of feathers.

"A sex animal." Nina laughs, then points to a pair of boxers dangling off a chair. "Get that. And that." She nods toward a pillow that's been ripped in half. Her eyes widen at a pile of buttons on the floor. "Ooh, and that."

"I'm getting it," Phil mutters.

Nina, not realizing Jake has moved far past producer mode

and into an actual panic attack, nudges him with her shoulder. "I had no idea the cowboy had it in him. Trish is going to love this. The only thing better than an all-American boy is an all-American boy who can fuck like America's dirty little secret."

"Jesus," Jake snaps.

He did *not* need that mental picture. In fact, he's been spending the past five minutes doing everything in his power to fight that mental picture. But now that it's there, he can't unsee it. Emily and Cooper on that cleared-off table. Emily and Cooper up against those messed-up curtains. Emily and Cooper doing god knows what with that torn pillow. Emily and Cooper naked in bed.

Except that one isn't just in his head.

It's real.

Right in front of him.

Burning his eyes.

Cooper sleeps bare chested, and Emily is curled into his side. Her hair is strewn across his pecs. Her face is buried against his skin. Her arm stretches across his abs as if hugging him closer. She looks happy, peaceful.

It makes Jake want to die. And he really thinks he might. The pressure in his chest builds and builds the longer he stares, but he can't look away. His gaze is glued to her elegant hand, framed by a defined six-pack. His lungs swell, bigger and bigger. His head pounds. Any moment, he might explode, a real-life case of spontaneous combustion—the result of having his every bad decision shoved directly in his face.

"Rise and shine, lovebirds," Nina finally croons once Phil is done capturing the scene.

Cooper's eyes open immediately. The asshole is obviously a morning person. But it does give Jake some satisfaction when Emily simply groans and pulls the covers up over her head. That satisfaction disappears the moment Cooper offers a slow, smug smile and pulls her an inch closer.

This is what you wanted, Jake tries to remind himself. *This is what you asked for.*

But it's not. It's really not. He wanted them to ride off into the sunset, out of sight and out of mind, like the ending of a classic western. He did NOT want to have their all-night sex fest shoved into his face first thing in the fucking morning.

Message received loud and clear.

She's moved on.

The truth couldn't be more obvious if it hit him in the face with a ten-inch cast-iron frying pan. In fact, it feels like it has.

"Time to wake up," Nina says again, clearly enjoying herself.

A muffled sound erupts from the lump of down comforter. It sounds like, "Go away."

"I told you seven, and it's seven."

"You're evil."

"I'm prompt. And on a schedule, so get up. Are you decent? We need to film a quick goodbye, then get the place packed up."

Neither Cooper nor Emily responds, clearly still in the throes of postcoital bliss. Nina, being Nina, gives them ten seconds and then rips the covers off.

Thank FUCK they're wearing clothes.

Jake might pass out from the relief.

It's not much, a pair of silk pajama pants for Cooper and a

matching tank-and-shorts set for Emily, but it's clothes. If he'd been greeted by their bare asses, he really might have died from the shock.

Emily glares at Nina, sticks her tongue out at the camera, and barely offers Jake a passing glance before she rolls from the bed and wraps herself in a plush robe. Cooper remains shirtless. The guy is carved from fucking marble, so Jake doesn't blame him, but it doesn't keep his blood from boiling as Phil records their chaste kiss goodbye at the door.

All Jake wants to do is take Emily by the arm, lead her away, and confess everything that's been bubbling in the back of his throat since the moment he heard the words *I wasn't enough for him*. He's so racked with guilt he barely slept. His hands have been fidgety all morning. He's jumpy. He's on edge. She's gone seven years thinking the absolute worst thing he can imagine, and he doesn't want to wait another second longer to tell her the truth.

But when? How?

Nina shoves him and Cooper toward the door, and Jake goes on autopilot. He takes Cooper to his room, then checks on Ethan and Pierre. He finds Fred, then Trish, desperate to distract himself when all he wants to do is bust into Emily's room and force Nina to give them a minute alone. All throughout the puzzle ceremony, he searches for some opportunity to get close to her, but there isn't one. They're separated for the private propeller flights to Maun. Jake goes with the guys and Nina flies with Emily. Then they're quickly ushered through the small, chaotic airport and onto their flight to Johannesburg. Because of a delay, they need to run to catch their next flight to Dubai. By the time they get there, bleary eyed and exhausted, it's one more flight to the Maldives and a boat ride to their resort. He can't find a single moment to catch Emily alone. Nina accompanies her to the bathroom, to the lounge, to the newsstand. They travel in separate vehicles and boats. Jake is constantly shoved in with Ethan and Cooper, the two people he least wants to see in the world—one because he's an asshole, and the other because he's Mr. Perfect, which is honestly a hundred times worse.

By the time Jake checks the men in, Emily and Nina are nowhere in sight. As the lead, Emily gets to stay in a private two-bedroom bungalow over the water where they'll be filming with her family when they arrive in the morning. Nina, Trish, Fred, and Emily's camera crew are in the four-bedroom water bungalow next door, while he, Ethan, Cooper, and their camera crew are in a private bungalow way back in the jungle, with the barest glimpse of water visible through the trees. As soon as he puts the guys in their rooms, he follows the path to the beach and plops into the sand to stare across the ocean at the bungalows glowing beneath the stars. Emily's is the second to last. He can tell by the crew parked on the walkway outside her front door, and by the sight of Nina on her phone in the neighboring villa. Emily's curtains are drawn but her light is on, providing tantalizing hints of movement in the room beyond.

She's so close he can taste her.

Yet so fucking far away.

Jake knows the drill. A camera will be set on her front door all night in case anyone gets any ideas—it wouldn't be the first time one of the finalists snuck into the lead's bedroom. She'll be under constant supervision until the proposals, which means he may never get to tell her what he's had no idea she's been waiting seven years to hear.

She's enough.

She's more than enough.

She's too much—too perfect, too good, too beautiful, too talented, too kind, too everything when compared to the likes of him.

Jake's so wrapped up in his thoughts, he jumps when his phone rings. The word *Mom* flashes across the screen as if in accusation. His first instinct is to ignore the call. He's been carefully avoiding her for more than a month—what's one more day? But then he remembers by sunrise, Emily's family will be here. She told ten million people what he did. There's no way she won't tell her parents the truth before it airs, and if he knows Emily, she'll do it tomorrow. In less than twenty-four hours, her parents will know everything, and they'll take it home with them.

His mother deserves to know the truth about her son from his own lips.

So he answers.

"Oh, Jacob, you picked up." Her warm voice comes over the line, full of delighted surprise. That feeling will soon change. "Jacob?"

He tries to respond, but his throat is full of cotton balls, clogged and dry. His tongue sticks to the roof of his mouth, unable to form sound.

How can he tell her?

What can he say?

He's her prince, her only child, her son. She's never seen

the truth of him, but now she will. Now she'll see what everyone else does. He's the spitting image of his dad.

It will ruin her.

It will ruin them.

"Jacob, are you there?"

"I got Emily pregnant."

The confession comes out soft but clear. His voice is raw, his tone hollow. The sound is pulled from somewhere deep, forced up a scratchy throat and thrown into the world like a hammer into glass, shattering everything in its wake. Four little words, then brutal silence.

"That was quick," his mother finally says. "When we spoke a few weeks ago, it didn't sound like you were ready to tell her how you feel. What happened? What changed?"

She doesn't get it.

She doesn't understand.

"Not now," Jake says, tripping over the words while his lips stick to his teeth. He swallows the glue in his mouth and forces himself to continue. "Seven years ago. You always wondered why I left in the middle of the night. You thought it was because we broke up, but that's not why. I got Emily pregnant. Or I thought I did. We were going to move in together. We were going to be a family. I was about to propose. Then she got a call from her doctor. They were false positives. There was no baby. So I left." He finishes softly, hardly even a whisper. "I just left in the middle of the night without ever telling her why."

His mother doesn't respond. She just breathes on the other side of the line. And because he can't stand the quiet, the judgment of everything left unsaid, he keeps going.

"That's not even the worst part, Mom. She thinks I left because of her. Because I didn't want her if there was no baby. Because she wasn't enough for me on her own. How can she think that? How can she have spent seven years thinking that when she was my whole life? I would have gone anywhere with her. I would have done anything for her. And I did. I didn't leave for me. I left for her. How can she not see that? It's so obvious. It's so—"

"Jacob."

He was lost in his own thoughts, in his memories. He forgot his mother was on the line, but he remembers now as her demanding tone cuts through his rambling. He's never heard her so firm. She was always the gentle touch after his father's hard hand, not the one delivering the blow.

"What do you mean, you left for her?"

He swallows thickly. "You know what I mean."

"I don't."

"You do, Mom," he murmurs, digging his free hand into the sand and crushing the grains between his fingers. "You don't have to pretend for me anymore."

"I'm not pretending anything. Tell me what you mean, Jacob. Now."

"I left so she could be free of me," he whispers. "I wreck people, Mom. It's what I do. It's who I am. I wrecked you, and—"

"No."

"Yes," he urged. "Don't tell me you wouldn't go back if you could. If you got the same chance Emily did when you were eighteen. Don't tell me, deep down, you don't wish that Dad had walked away, that you both could have walked away."

"I don't, Jacob."

"You must."

"I don't," she repeats, the sound echoing in his skull. It's the first time he's ever heard her raise her voice. "I don't, and I know that, Jacob, because I had that chance and I chose you. You're the best thing that ever happened to me. I knew I wanted you the moment I found out about you. It wasn't the fifties, my god. I had options. I chose you, and for better or worse, I chose your father. I knew the man he was, and I loved him in spite of it. That was my mistake, not yours. Never yours. I've told you this a thousand times before, but I'll say it again in case this one time maybe it gets through. You're not him."

That's his cue to hang up, to run away, to end the conversation before it has a chance to end him. But he doesn't. For the first time in his life, he grips the phone tighter and asks his mom the one question he's always been too scared to face.

"How, Mom? How do you know that?"

"Because, my darling boy, whenever I was scared, or lonely, or hurt, you were the person I ran to. You were my angel, my protector. Nothing bad could ever touch me when I was with you. And maybe that wasn't fair of me to put that pressure on you when you were a child, but I did, and that's my burden to bear. I should have made it clear, Jacob. I'll make it clear now. I was seventeen the first time your father hit me. It wasn't something you caused, something you could change. It was who he was. And the second you were big enough to challenge him, you did. Because that's who you are. You don't wreck people, honey. You save them. You saved me."

"I destroyed Emily."

"You made a mistake."

"I walked out on her when she needed me most, Mom. I abandoned her. And worse, I spent seven years praising my own righteousness in doing it."

He doesn't realize he's crying until the salt reaches his lips. They're tears he has no right to shed, hurt he has no right to feel.

"Did you apologize?"

"Where would I even start?"

"With *I'm sorry*."

"It won't be enough, Mom."

"How will you know if you never try?"

He doesn't have an answer.

"*I'm* sorry, Jacob," his mother continues, in the gentle, lulling voice he knows so well. "I'm sorry I never protected you, not just from your father's fists, but from his ugliness as well. I should have done more. I could have done more. But I didn't. And I'll never forgive myself for that. From now on, I promise, I'll do everything in my power to make sure you understand how wonderful you are. I don't want you to spend your life the way I've spent mine, running and hiding, thinking I deserved every hit I got dealt. I want more than that for you. Don't let the fear of turning into your father keep you from living. Please, Jacob, go to her. Talk to her. Face her. Be the man I know you to be. Be brave. Be braver than me."

"What if I can't be?"

"Then I guess what you said is true." She sighs, a sad, loving sound. "If you're not willing to fight for her, you don't deserve her anyway. Good night, darling. Good luck."

The phone clicks.

He stares at the dark screen.

In the quiet, a flashback plays like a movie across his thoughts. Him and Emily alone on the streets of Rome. His lips on her throat. Her voice in his ear.

Tell me.

Just tell me.

Real answer, Jake.

Real answer.

What do you want?

Don't walk away.

He didn't see it then, but he sees it now, in her pleas, in his mother's parting words. Emily isn't asking for him to be something he's not. She isn't asking for him to be better, or different, or even good. All she wants, all she's ever wanted since the moment he left, is to be chosen. In her mind, he picked Los Angeles over her. Then he picked this show over her. She thinks she isn't as important as his career, when the truth is, he doesn't give a fuck about anything but her. He never has.

And the only thing left to do is to prove it.

To choose her.

To put her first, above his ego and his fear.

To confront the worst mistake he's ever made and face the very real possibility of her rejection, because nothing is more important to him than making sure Emily doesn't spend another second of her life thinking she's anything less than perfect.

Jake looks up.

He's no longer alone on the beach. A shadowy figure

stands in the shallows a few feet away, the same one that's been haunting him his whole life. As a child, he cowered. As a teen, he raged. But when he stares at the ghost of his father now, he feels nothing. The man is dead. He's gone. And it's time for Jake to leave him where he belongs—in the past.

Seven years ago, he walked away from the love of his life. It was torturous, the hardest thing he'd ever done.

This is easy.

Jake is calm as he stands and shrugs out of his suit jacket. His pulse is even as he kicks off his shoes and digs his toes into the sand. When he walks through the phantom, it dissipates on impact, no power but the power he'd given it. Then he's in the water. The surf is tranquil, almost glassy. His arms slice through liquid obsidian. Jake loses himself in the stroke, his body burning in a familiar way after so many mornings spent surfing off the California coast. The glow of her villa guides him forward. Nothing else matters. Not the creatures lurking beneath the surface. Not the cameras looming above. Not the emotional cargo left behind. There's nothing but him, and this swim, and the place to which he's finally, after seven years, returning.

Home.

Because that's what she is. That's what she'll always be.

His home.

CHAPTER TWENTY-THREE

emily

IT STARTS as a tickle at the back of her neck, this sense she's not alone. Emily turns to the door, waiting for Nina to burst through, or Trish, or Fred, or any number of crew. She's restless. On edge. She's spent the past hour pacing across the living room of her suite, staring down at the glass floor while fish dart beneath her feet. Yes, actual fish. From the ocean. Because this is the most amazing hotel room she's ever seen—it has a freaking water slide!—in the most beautiful place she's ever been—a literal paradise!—and yet, a storm cloud hovers overhead. Tomorrow her family comes. And while she itches to wrap Sam in the biggest bear hug and finally fill her in on the past few weeks, the rest is terrifying. Her parents don't know the truth. They never have. They thought the bloodwork request from her gynecologist came after a routine checkup, not a pregnancy scare. They thought the breakup with Jake had been like that of any other teen romance. And while everything that came after made her experience with Jake feel almost trivial in hindsight, she's scared shitless to tell them she spent the majority of her senior year in high school sneaking her boyfriend into her room while they were sleeping.

She can almost hear her mother now. *Emily Ann Peters, I am incredibly disappointed in your behavior. What were you thinking?*

The same thing every teenager with raging hormones, a serious boyfriend, and a single-story home was probably thinking, but still.

And okay, she's now an adult in her twenties, living in her own apartment, running her own business, and faking a passionate love affair on national TV. They can't ground her, or take away her cell phone, or revoke her driving privileges anymore. But that word, *disappointed*, rings in her head like a gong, shattering rational thought.

Emily glances at the clock.

Ten more hours and they'll be here. She should sleep. Or at least rest. Or maybe throw open the door and figure out why her skin is crawling with the unmistakable sensation of being watched. Except...the tingle isn't coming from the direction of the front door.

Huh?

She follows the feeling.

Her head turns toward the back porch as if pulled by a string. Shadows dance on the other side of the curtains. She turns off her light, sinking her room into darkness. The silhouette of a man outlined by moonlight plays over the fabric. Her heart pinches with anticipation. She knows immediately who the phantom presence belongs to, but when she throws open the curtains to confront Jake, the sight of him takes her breath away.

Rivulets of water stream from his dark hair. Glistening droplets cascade down hooded brows, over defined cheekbones, and along a razor-sharp jaw to drip from his chin. His eyes are closed, giving her gaze the freedom to roam unwatched. The fabric of his white button-down clings to him like a second skin. Hard ridges line his abdomen. Muscles cord up his arms. A smattering of dark hair covers his chiseled chest. It's everything she saw at the bungee jump, yet somehow more now that they're alone in the moonlight. The sheer expanse of him overwhelms. The Jake she knew was always tall, if a little gangly, but in the seven years they've been apart, he's grown into his frame. He's filled it out in all the best ways.

She can almost see herself holding on to his broad shoulders for dear life, can almost feel her nails digging into his skin. Her fingers stretch forward of their own accord, itching to touch, but instead they hit glass. The soft *tap* of her nails is just enough to draw his attention. Jake's deep blue eyes spring open and sharpen on her immediately.

Electricity crackles between them.

It always has.

It always will.

But she's done playing games.

Emily regains control of her wayward hand and opens the sliding door. A rush of cool night air brings a shiver to her skin.

"What are—"

She begins to tell him off, but he silences her with two rushed words. "You're enough."

His voice is so overcome with emotion it emerges as a rough growl, and that deep rumble touches Emily in a place that's been dead for seven years.

She freezes.

"Em, how could you even— How could you think—"

He breaks off and steps closer before bracing his hands against the doorframe, as if physically holding himself back from her. Hard muscles flex along his arms. Suddenly, she's surrounded by him, his heat, his breath, his essence. The salty scent in the air takes her back in time, to another life. Jake leans closer, capturing her gaze with his so she can't look away. The deep hue of his eyes matches the midnight sky overhead, but where one is blanketed in sparkling stars, the other is dark and stormy, a tumultuous sea ready to pull her under.

He takes a deep breath.

She holds hers.

"You were everything, Em," Jake whispers. The soft confession hits her with the force of a tsunami. She can't move, can't run. She's caught in the wave with no control over her senses. The rest of the world is swept away until nothing exists outside of this moment with him. "I didn't leave because you weren't enough for me, and I can't stand that you've spent seven years thinking I did. I left because you were too much. Too driven. Too talented. Too amazing to be stuck in some little podunk town with the likes of me. There was nothing I wanted more—and I mean, absolutely nothing—than to put a ring on your finger, and call you mine, and start a family with you, no matter how young we were. I wanted it all. I was so selfish. I wanted every little piece you could give me. And then we got that call, and it was like reality took a sledgehammer to my dreams. I knew I had to leave. Can't you see why I had to leave?"

His voice cracks. His gaze turns pleading. He leans even closer, his body vibrating with the exertion of holding himself back.

Emily remains paralyzed, caught between her desire to run into his arms and her equally strong desire to run away—from him, from the truth she's still not sure she's ready to tell, from these beautiful words she's been waiting seven years to hear.

Are they enough?

After everything that's happened, can anything possibly be enough?

"You were the sun, Em," Jake continues. "You made everything you touched brighter, better, more alive. And I was the dark cloud keeping you from shining. You almost lost everything because of me, and I promised myself I would never let that happen again. So I left. And I realize now, I should have stayed. I should have explained. I should have been clear. But I wasn't strong enough then—hell, I'm barely strong enough now—to look you in the eyes before I walked away. I knew if I didn't leave then, before the sun had time to rise, before you had time to wake up, I never would. And then you'd never be free of me. I couldn't let that happen. I couldn't put myself first. I couldn't—"

He breaks off and looks away. The veins in his neck bulge.

His jaw clenches. He turns out to sea, gaze glassy and distant, as he softly completes his sentence.

"I couldn't be like him."

The ache in the words finally breaks her stupor. She steps closer, unable to stop herself from brushing the backs of her fingers over the tense muscles in his cheek. They soften immediately, responding to her touch.

"Jake."

He turns back to her, looking more like a lost little boy than ever, and she understands. Without needing to hear it, she understands on a level she never did before. Still, he swallows his hesitation and forces back the dark shadows in his eyes.

"My mom was eighteen when she got pregnant with me," he murmurs. She wants to tell him to stop, that he doesn't need to explain, but she can tell from his expression he does. Not for her, but for him. "She knew my dad for her whole life. They were neighbors. She was shy and reserved. He was the center of attention. She loved him long before he even knew she existed, and when they got together their junior year, he could tell instantly the type of hold he already had on her. He got high off stringing her along, off seeing how far he could push things, how far she'd let him go. My mother never told him no. He was the love of her life, but to him, she was little more than a game. Until he got injured. He was drunk driving. It was completely his fault that he shattered his throwing arm. But he blamed the world. And when he found out my mother got into college, he blamed her, too. I'm not even sure my mom knows the truth, but he told me once in a drunken rage that I was no mistake. He meant for me to happen. He tried for weeks to make me happen, cajoling her to be reckless, taking off his condoms, doing whatever it took. Because he couldn't bear the thought of my pathetic mother daring to leave him behind. And I know—I *know*—our relationship was different. That *we* were different. But when you got that call, all I could think was I had to do the one thing my father never could. I had to prove I wasn't like him. I had to walk away, so you could go to New York and follow your dreams and be whoever you were meant to be without my baggage holding you back."

At the mention of New York, she goes rigid.

Jake doesn't seem to notice. He drops his hand from the frame and cups her face, running his thumb tenderly across her cheek. Then he slides his fingers through her hair to grip the back of her neck and angles her head up so she can't look away.

"I wanted the world for you, Em," he says, his blue eyes drinking her in as if memorizing every detail of her face. The goodbye in his expression makes her heart thunder in protest. "I still do. And I don't think I'll ever forgive myself for not being the man who can give it to you."

You were, she thinks. *You are.*

But he's already dropping his arm from the door, already stepping back toward the water, already turning away while she stands there mutely, the words caught in her throat. Because she doesn't know how to begin to tell him about the mess he left behind, about the things he missed, about the secrets she's been keeping all this time.

A wood board creaks beneath his weight.

Emily snaps into action.

"Jake, stop."

He turns back and stares at her over his shoulder. The hope in his eyes is so overpowering it washes everything else away. Emily forgets her doubts, her fears. The confession tumbles back down her throat, swallowed by a sudden rush of desire. Her mind is blank and her heart is full as she slowly reaches out and laces her fingers through his.

"You're all wet," she says lamely. "You must be cold."

The heat in his gaze is enough to set the world ablaze, but he doesn't argue as she tugs him toward the door. They don't break eye contact as she leads him inside. They don't speak either, as if under a spell, enchanted by the moon and the stars and this little slice of time that seems to exist outside of the world. Emily steps back and back and back, deeper into the shadows. The silvery glow seeping through the windows is the only source of light as she leads Jake across the open living room and through her bedroom door. She doesn't stop until her calves hit the mattress, and even then, she only lets go in order to reach for the top button of his shirt.

It brings back a memory.

She smiles.

But unlike when they were seventeen, hurried and fumbling, Emily takes her time working her way down the center of his chest. The pads of her fingers brush hot skin as she goes. She relishes in each stolen touch. The whole time Jake watches her as if worried he might be in a dream, afraid to speak and wake himself up. As the last button slips loose, Emily meets his awed gaze. She runs her palms slowly up his abs and over his pecs, feasting on the sound of his sharp inhale. Her hands work their way across his shoulders and down the hard muscles of his arms until his shirt hits the floor with a wet *slap*. Emily reaches for his belt and Jake audibly swallows. Metal clinks softly as she undoes the buckle, then the button. In the silence, the hum of his zipper thunders. Jake's stomach tenses in delicious anticipation, and Emily can't help but run her fingers over the trail of dark hair disappearing into his boxers. She traces the elastic edge, but instead of dipping inside to feel the source of that bulge, she pushes his wet pants down his legs, bending until they hit the floor. He kicks them off the rest of the way as she rises, the air smoldering between them.

Then she stops.

"Jake," Emily says, but the words catch in her throat. She tries to swallow the knot away but it won't budge. There's so much to tell him, so much to say, yet she can't. She's stuck on the precipice of before and after, not quite brave enough to meet him on the other side of her fear.

Jake chose her.

He's here.

He stopped running.

After seven years, she's still not sure she can do the same.

He watches her with a question in his gaze as the silence stretches. Emily wets her lips, then holds the bottom one between her teeth while she wavers, unsure what to say. The motion draws his attention to her mouth. He's hardly moved since they entered her room, but he does now, as if on instinct, unable to stop himself from gliding his thumb across her skin and gently tugging her lip free. Caught up in the sudden rush of heat stirred by his touch, Emily plants a soft kiss on the pad of his thumb. It's not enough to satisfy the tight clench of her desire. So she draws his finger fully into her mouth and tastes him with her tongue before sucking gently on the tip.

Jake's eyes go black with need.

Tomorrow, she decides. Tomorrow, she'll tell him everything.

Tonight is magic, and she refuses to ruin it.

"Real answer," Emily quietly demands as she takes his hand in both of hers and clutches his large fingers as though they're a lifeline.

Jake doesn't have to ask. He knows exactly what she means.

"I love you," he says, tone tender but firm, leaving no room for doubt. "I always have. I always will. And if you give me another chance, I promise I will never leave you again. You're everything, Em. Every. Fucking. Thing. I mean it."

"Then touch me, Jake."

She lowers his hand to her breast and holds it there as her heart races. His eyes roll into the back of his head before he closes them with a groan, overwhelmed with pleasure.

She wants to meet him there.

She needs to meet him there.

"Touch me until I believe you."

As if he's waited seven years for the invitation, he slides his hands down to her ass before she even has time to breathe and lifts her against him. The proof of his desire is rock hard against her stomach, undeniable. He grips the backs of her thighs and wraps her legs around him. She crosses her ankles behind his back to squeeze him to her core. A growl pulls free of his lips as he buries his head in her neck.

"I missed you, Em," he whispers against her throat before

pressing his lips to that spot below her ear he must remember drives her wild. Her body clenches instinctively. With a soft laugh, he nips at her skin. "I missed you so goddamn much."

But he doesn't rush.

The Jake of seven years ago would have tumbled into the pillows, ripping at her clothes, desperate to be inside her. This Jake takes his time, savoring every moment, every touch. He cradles her back as he slowly leans forward, perfectly in control as he lays her down on the bed. His lips work their way from her mouth to her throat to her collarbone. His hands dip lower, brushing her breasts, caressing her stomach, gripping her hips. His fingers find the hem of her silk top and sink underneath, hot against her bare skin. Emily gasps, on fire. Jake grins against her neck and continues his slow perusal, feeling every inch of her with such purpose, such care, his every stroke silently insisting she's someone to be cherished, someone to be worshipped. Emily twists her fingers in his hair, growing more inflamed and more impatient with each passing second. He ignores the silent plea and slips her shirt over her head. His focus shifts to her chest, sucking and licking until the meaning of her tight grip changes entirely.

When she doesn't think she can stand it anymore, he kisses a trail down the center of her stomach, pausing to dip his tongue in her navel as he curls his fingers beneath the hem of her silk shorts. He edges lower and lower, but never quite low enough before he slinks off the bed. He meets her eyes as he slowly strips her naked.

Jake stops to breathe in the sight of her, his gaze hungry as it roves over every bared inch lying before him. Emily doesn't move. She can't. It's nothing he hasn't seen, and yet, this moment feels a thousand times more charged.

"You're perfect," he whispers, suddenly hoarse. "So fucking perfect."

She's not.

If it weren't so dark in here, he'd see the three small scars across her abdomen. They're smooth after so many years of healing, but still visible, still there, a reminder every time she looks in the mirror that she might never be enough for anybody, not even herself.

As if sensing she's in her own head, he grabs her by the ankles and yanks. Emily yelps as she slides down the bed, the sudden movement jarring after so much unrushed attention. Her head falls back against the mattress as she laughs.

"That's a new move," she teases. "Something you learned in LA?"

"I just came up with it." Jake grins as he moves his palms slowly over her calves and up her thighs, spreading them. The mirth dies on her lips, replaced with breathless anticipation. "I did learn other things, though."

He kneels on the floor and places her legs over his shoulders, then dips his head so all she can see is a mess of brown hair. The first lick elicits a sharp inhale. The second leaves her gasping. A few more and Emily is lost in him, no longer in this room or on this earth, let alone inside her own head. She twists the sheets in her fists, biting her lip to keep from breaking as he takes her higher and higher. The stars drop from the sky, sparkling across the ceiling as her back arches in a burst of pure pleasure. His name spills from her lips in a piercing cry.

"Jake!"

It only urges him on. His grip on her hips tightens. His mouth turns ravaging. Emily strains beneath him, overwhelmed.

"Jake. Jake. My god, Jake!"

With her body still trembling, he settles his weight over her and whispers, "That's my favorite fucking sound in the world, Em."

And then he proves it, by making her say it again, and again, and again.

CHAPTER TWENTY-FOUR

THE SUN IS STARTING to rise when Jake stirs. The sky is painted in pastel shades. Palm trees sway in dark silhouettes. Light sparkles along the calm ocean surface. It's probably the most beautiful place he's ever seen, yet it doesn't hold a candle to the sight that waits as he looks down at the woman nestled against his chest. Her auburn hair is as jumbled as a bird's nest and her swollen lips are parted in peaceful sleep. A bit of drool leaks from one edge.

Emily.

His Emily.

It's the first time he's ever been able to sit and spend the dawn basking in her presence, not worried about slipping out the window without her parents seeing or getting home before his mother wakes up. Sure, in typical *them* fashion, he did sneak into her bedroom and technically he isn't supposed to be here, but it doesn't matter the way it used to when they were teenagers. This time, he relishes getting caught. He welcomes it. He's ready for the two of them to finally step into the light.

Which is why he eventually eases out of her embrace. Emily offers a sleepy protest, but he tucks the blanket back around her and presses a soft kiss to her brow, lulling her back to sleep. She's not a morning person. She needs her eight hours. Besides, this is his task and his alone.

It's time to quit the show.

For her, yes. But also for him.

Working in reality television has been another punishment he thought he deserved. But he doesn't. He gets it now. The sins of the father don't have to be the sins of the son. He's a different man. A better man. And he deserves to chase his dreams just as much as Emily.

Ever since he was five years old, he's wanted to direct movies.

And he's finally, *finally*, unafraid to do it.

Working for *The Love Match* has been a great stepping stone in the industry, but he's too comfortable here. He needs the drive, the literal hunger, the desperation that will force him to take every interview and every chance without accepting *no* for an answer.

So he's done.

It's time to find Trish—alone.

Emily might kill him for leaving again or she might be relieved to find him gone in the bright light of day. The fact that he's not sure tells him everything he needs to know. She never said *I love you*. She never said *I forgive you*. She said *Touch me until I believe you*. And he did. Lord knows he did everything he could, but this is still her choice to make, and there's only one way to ensure all her options remain available. He has to confess. He has to take the fall for everything that happened last night. He has to let her finish the season without the pressure of his presence, so she can choose Cooper if she wants, or she can choose to be alone, or she can choose him, the same way he's chosen her.

Of course, he's not the same complete idiot he was seven years ago.

This time, he leaves a note.

Dear Em,

Last night meant more to me than you'll ever know. I love you. And in finally finding the courage to say that out loud after seven years of silence, I found the courage to admit other things as well. I want more than this illicit romance for us.

So, I've left to find Trish.

I'm quitting the show. For you, and for me. I'm going to tell her the truth about us. I'm going to take all the blame. I don't want my actions to hurt your business or your brand, and it's in their best interest to let you finish the season without the scandal this would cause for the network. I'll probably have to sign an NDA and then security will probably escort me off the property. You won't see me again until you get back home.

But Em, I'll be waiting.

I'm not running. I'm not leaving.

Even if you choose Cooper (which trust me, I get), I'll be waiting for you for as long as it takes for you to come find me.

I love you.

Real answer.

Yours forever, Jake

With one last look, he settles the letter on her bedside table. Then he leaves her bedroom and walks quietly to the front door. Phil nearly falls off the dock when Jake emerges from the suite. Luckily, his camera is safely on the planks by his toes or it might be ten feet under right about now.

"Where did— How did—"

"Do you have a key to Trish's bungalow?" Jake asks, ignoring the sputtered confusion. "I need to talk to her."

"I do. But—"

"Great."

Jake marches to the villa next door and waits for Phil to catch up.

"Were you in there all night?" the cameraman mutters as he fumbles for the key.

Jake ignores him, utterly focused on the task ahead.

Phil probably takes his silence for confirmation, which honestly, it is.

"How'd you get past me?" he asks, as he slides the fob before the scanner. The door clicks, and he grabs Jake's arm. "I gotta know. Nina's going to kill me for the missing footage."

"I swam," Jake tells him as he reaches for the door.

"Dammit." Phil's mouth drops open. His gaze darts to the distant shore on the other side of the lagoon. "You really swam?"

"I really swam."

Then Jake is inside.

"Trish?" he calls.

"In here."

She doesn't sound surprised. If anything, she sounds as though she's been expecting him. That suspicion is confirmed when he walks around the corner into the shared living room to find Trish, Nina, and Fred all waiting on the couches, the mood somber. A computer sits open on the coffee table. Nick and a network exec stare at him from across the globe.

"You already know," Jake says into the silence.

No one bothers to respond.

"How?"

"Please," Nina scoffs, her annoyance ripe. "Give us some credit. We read people for a living. And you're not that stealthy, *Jacob*. We've known about your past with Emily since before we left LA. All I had to do was get ahold of her old yearbook and talk to some of her high school friends to verify it."

"But you never said—"

"We hoped it would never come to this," Trish intercedes.

"Yeah," Nina adds. "We *hoped* you'd be able to keep it in your pants for six weeks."

Trish cuts her a sharp look, and the producer drops back into the cushions with a frown. "You're our colleague, Jake.

Some would even call you a friend. We gave you ample opportunity to be honest with us, and when it became clear that wouldn't happen, we decided to wait and give you the benefit of the doubt that your relationship with Miss Peters would remain professional. Obviously, if the information the resort security provided us with is accurate, that's no longer the case. Did you spend the night in her room?"

"Yes."

"Was your purpose for being there professional?"

"Definitely not."

"Then you've left us no choice. You're fired."

"You don't have to fire me—"

"Yes, jackass," Nick adds from the computer. "We do."

"That's not what I mean." Jake shakes his head. "I quit."

Nina scoffs and rolls her eyes. Fred grins. Trish pinches her brow with a sigh. From the coffee table, the network exec chimes in.

"Can you repeat that for me on the record?"

Jake walks to the computer and loudly states into the microphone. "I quit."

"Don't be hasty," Trish comments.

Jake turns to her. "I'm not. Trust me, I'm not. I've never been more sure about anything in my entire life. You and Nick gave me my first job in Hollywood. I've been working here ever since. I owe my entire career to both of you, and to this show. I don't want to leave on a sour note. I don't want to burn any bridges on my way out. I just want to go. You don't need to pay me any severance. I'll sign anything you want. I won't put up a fight. All I ask is that you don't punish Emily for any of this. Please. I'm the one who made a mess of our relationship seven years ago, and it's entirely my fault I didn't realize my mistakes until now. The exposure of this show will be huge for her brand. I don't want to taint that. She'll finish the season. You'll get your ending. No one outside the people in this room ever needs to know what happened."

"And when the tabloids snap a photo of the two of you hot and heavy in a week?" Nick asks, cynical as ever. In this one instance, Jake doesn't blame him.

"They won't."

Nick rolls his eyes with a scoff.

"Come on," Jake pushes. "You guys have all spent the past five weeks studying Emily's every move, lamenting behind her back about how boring and well behaved she is. You know her. You know that she's a good person. You all hate her a little bit for that, and admire her a little bit too. She's nothing like us. We're assholes." He grins, and from the couch, Nina grins too. "All of us. Assholes. But she's not. So if I was asking you to trust me, then sure, I could see why you never would. But I'm asking you to trust her. I'm not even sure she'll pick me. But if she does, I think we all know she'll do it the right way."

"So that's it?" Nick asks. "That's your plan? To walk out of here with nothing and pray she comes to find you?"

Jake shrugs. "Pretty much."

"Jesus Christ."

"It's sweet," Fred comments supportively.

"It's asinine," Nina says.

"It's none of our business," Trish cuts in. "What is our business is the paperwork. If this is really what you want, then sign here."

Jake does.

"And here."

He does.

"And here."

He does.

Trish shuffles the papers together and nods. "Security is waiting outside to escort you to your room and then off the premises. We've booked you a seat on the next flight out. I'll send a PA to collect your computer once you're back in LA."

"That's it?"

"That's it."

He turns to leave.

"Oh, and Jake?"

He meets Trish's eyes over his shoulder, unable to quite read her expression. "Yeah?"

"If you need a reference, don't call me for six months. I'm not saying anything until I see how this plays out on national TV."

He laughs softly. "Will do."

Then he walks to the front hall. Simple. Easy. Far easier than he ever imagined. Almost *too* easy. An eerie tingle drips down the back of his neck as he reaches for the door and swings it open. A sixth sense tells him to pause. He waits a moment and angles his neck back toward the shared living room, listening intently. One second passes. Then two. Right when he's about to shrug it off and leave, Nick's voice finally breaks the silence.

"Now that that's over, can we get back to the task at hand? The sister is late. Her plane won't land for another two hours.

How in the hell are we going to make this call to the doctor's office happen without her?"

Jake's heart leaps into his throat.

He shuts the door and marches back inside.

"Call? What call?"

"Fuck," Nick mutters.

Nina winces.

Trish offers him a hard stare. "You wanted out. You're out, Jake."

"What doctor's office?" he demands. "What call?"

"We didn't include you in this for a reason, Jake," Nina says and stands before walking over to grab his forearm. "You can't handle it. So turn around, let security escort you to the airport, and go home."

"Nina." He fights free of her hold. "What call?"

She clenches her jaw stubbornly. The show comes first.

"Fred," he implores, turning to the one crew member he always thought put the people over the production. "What doctor's office? What call? Please, if something's going on you need to tell me. I have to know."

The older man scrunches his face, as if fighting the instinct to relent, and remains silent. They all do.

"Please."

Jake looks at each of them, these people he's spent the past four years of his life with, living and breathing this show. And it hits him all at once. They're not his friends. They never were. Despite all the time they've spent together scheming other people in and out of love, they don't know him. He doesn't know them. And nothing is more important to any of them than the almighty ratings.

"Please," he desperately repeats. "She's the love of my life."

Nina sighs, the first crack he's ever seen in her demeanor. Trish shoots her a warning look, but she ignores it to glance at him. The barest hint of remorse softens her gaze. "We don't know, okay? Even if we wanted to tell you, we couldn't, which is why we're waiting on the sister. Health records are sealed. You know that, Jake. We have no idea what the call is about or who the doctor is. We're working on a hunch here."

"What hunch?"

She crosses her arms and turns her face to the side. That little peace offering is all he's going to get, but it's not nearly enough. With a sneer, Jake scans the couches and the tables for any clue, any sign as to where they think the storyline is going. But there's nothing. All he knows is this—they were planning to use Sam to ambush Emily with some call from a doctor's office, but now they can't because her plane is two hours late.

Her plane, he thinks. *Landing at the airport.*

At the airport...

The airport.

"Fuck it," Jake mutters and turns his back on the past four years of his life. The second he opens the door, two security guards take him by the arms and usher him down the boardwalk. He's half tempted to make a mad dash for Emily's door, but he knows it would only end badly, and he can't afford to waste any time.

Every second is precious.

It'll take him fifteen minutes to pack his stuff. The boat ride to the main island is about an hour and a half, and then it's a short walk to the airport. If he gets through security quickly, he'll have about five minutes to intercept Sam as she's getting off the plane. Convincing her to talk to him will, of course, be another matter entirely, but it's his only shot.

He can't miss.

He won't.

CHAPTER TWENTY-FIVE

EMILY WAKES up sore in all the right places, wishing there were some way to give the sport of surfing and the state of California the huge *thank you* they're due. Because, well, shit. Jake learned a lot in their seven years apart, and she fully intends to take advantage of his new prowess—making up for lost time and all that jazz.

Except...she can't.

When she rolls over, the bed is empty. Emily sits up and hugs the sheet to her chest, suddenly cold as she stares at the vacant room. Outside, the sun sparkles off the water beneath a cloudless sky. A literal paradise beckons. Inside, a nightmare looms.

She's alone.

Again.

The déjà vu washes over her like a sudden-onset flu. She feels hot and feverish, then inexplicably frigid. A chill sends goose bumps down her arms, leaving them trembling. Nausea pulls at her gut. Vomit threatens at the back of her throat.

Emily vaults off the bed and surges toward the bathroom, sure she's about to be sick. It's not until she's kneeling with her head in the toilet that rational thought takes over.

He probably didn't want to get caught.

He's probably back in his room, pretending nothing happened.

She'll see him in an hour.

Emily sits back on her heels and wipes her mouth. The words *He's not gone* play like a mantra in the back of her thoughts. Because he isn't. He can't be. After everything he said to her last night, after everything that happened, he wouldn't just leave again without an explanation, without a reason.

He's here. Somewhere.

He has to be.

The *click* of a door reverberates loudly in the silence of her room. Emily launches to her feet, flushes the toilet, and springs from the bathroom.

"Ja—"

The words catch in her throat when she's greeted by the sight of Nina standing next to her nightstand, staring at her bed with a scowl as if she knows what transpired there last night. The producer jolts and clutches her clipboard as Emily skids into the room.

"Rough night?" She arches her brow.

Emily swallows. "You could say that."

"Have no fear, makeup is on the way."

Emily lets out a pathetically squeaky laugh as the smile on her face wobbles with unshed tears. Nina steps closer with a frown and puts her hand on Emily's shoulder.

"Hey, are you okay?"

"Me? Sure. Yeah, sure."

Nina snorts. "That was convincing."

"You haven't, um—" Emily stops herself, aware how crazy the question will sound first thing in the morning with her hair looking the way it does and her mouth obviously swollen. She's being ridiculous. Jake snuck out to go back to his room. He clearly doesn't want anyone to find out what happened. Anything she says to Nina will be suspicious. Still...

"Haven't what?" Nina presses, her eyes blank.

The question spills out in a rush. "You haven't seen Jake, have you?"

"Jake?"

"Yeah."

"Why?"

"I, um..." Emily glances about the room and draws in a deep breath. She looks back to Nina, sure the producer must see her heart pounding against her thin camisole. "I had a question I wanted to ask him about the guys. It's no big deal, I was just wondering if maybe you'd seen him. Or could, I don't know, send him over here...maybe?"

"He was a no-show for our meeting with Trish this morning," Nina comments with a shrug.

Emily's heart literally stops beating. Pain flares across her chest from the lack of oxygen as her body shuts down. A single word spills airily from her lips. "What?"

"I wouldn't sweat it," the producer hurries to say. "He probably overslept or something. I only meant I haven't seen him. But I'll send him over if I do."

A knock interrupts.

"That's makeup!"

Nina runs to the door. Emily is glued to the spot.

He probably overslept.

Except he didn't. Emily knows he didn't. If he overslept, she would have woken up still wrapped in his arms, warm and cozy and blissfully happy. Instead, her breath comes in short spurts as a panic attack begins to wreak havoc on her system. If he'd left to keep what happened between them a secret, he would have been at that meeting. Nothing would have stopped him from being at that meeting.

But he wasn't.

You're everything, Em. The deep rasp of his voice fills the back of her mind, even now sending a shiver down her spine. *Every. Fucking. Thing. I mean it.*

He said that less than eight hours ago.

How can he be gone?

He isn't.

He can't be.

Emily holds on to that flimsy thought as she's guided to a chair. The makeup artist works brushes and sponges across her skin, but she hardly feels them. As if caught in Medusa's trap, her insides slowly turn to stone, growing harder, colder, number with each passing moment.

"We should review the schedule," Nina says from over her shoulder, unaware that Emily is slowly shutting down. "Your sister's flight got delayed. It's not landing for another hour and a half, then it'll take her another two hours to get her bags and get here on the boat, plus another forty-five minutes for hair and makeup. Long story short, we're filming Cooper's scene without her. Your parents will be here in about half an hour—they're getting their makeup done now—so we'll film the reunion and give you guys a little time to catch up before Cooper arrives. Then he'll come here, chat with your folks, ask for your dad's permission to propose, yada yada. Before you know it, the two of you will be off on your final date night of the season. Sound good?"

Emily doesn't react.

Nina finds her gaze in the mirror. "I said, sound good?"

"Sure."

A look of concern passes briefly over Nina's face. She opens her mouth as if to say something, then closes it. After a final prolonged glance, she turns and walks away. Emily hears her mumbling something into her comms as she disappears around the corner, but she doesn't have the energy to ask what it is.

Instead, she sits there and spirals.

When Emily's parents arrive, her father immediately senses something is wrong. It's hard to get anything past the chief of police. But with the cameras in their faces, he's uncertain. He waits for her move. Emily hugs them fiercely and feigns ignorance, putting on a fake smile. The sound of her voice is comically high pitched as she does her best to cover the knot sitting at the back of her throat. She must be a terrible actress because after only two minutes, her mother's expression also shifts to one of concern.

"Honey?" she murmurs.

Emily swallows and fights down the sobs threatening to spill over. She opens her mouth to respond, but her lips tremble. Nothing emerges. She pushes for any sound, any reaction. An almost maniacal laugh bursts out, so far beyond the edge of reason she may as well be drowning in the deep end of the crazy pool. Nina offers a probing glance while Phil peeks over the rim of his camera with a question in his gaze.

Alarms flash in her mother's eyes. She immediately reaches across the distance to curl her warm fingers around Emily's ice-cold ones. "Honey, what's wrong?"

Emily doesn't trust herself to speak. She just shakes her head. Phil's camera hums quietly as he zooms the lens in. Her mother must hear it, because she glances nervously to the side. But as history proves, the attention of millions isn't enough to sway Tina Peters when it comes to her daughter's well-being. She shoos her husband away and scoots over on the couch to peer closely at Emily's face, trying to discern the reason for her turmoil.

It's too much.

All Emily wants to do is fall into her mother's familiar embrace and let it all out, but she can't. Not with the cameras rolling. And even without them, her mother wouldn't understand.

"I—" She cuts off. "I—"

"Sweetheart, whatever it is, you can tell me," her mother murmurs, love woven through the words. "I know I sort of started this whole thing, but you don't have to finish it if you don't want to. I'm sorry I pushed so hard. Maybe it wasn't my place. I was just worried about you. I thought a little adventure was what you needed, but if I was wrong, tell me. I know you think I'm wedding-crazed, and, well, I probably am, but that's not what this was about for me. I don't care if you come home engaged. I don't want you to if it's not the right man. I never cared if you found a husband. I wanted you to find yourself. You've seemed so lost these past few years, ever since—" She stops, swallows, flicks her gaze to the camera, and then clutches Emily's fingers tighter. "I wanted you to see yourself how your father and I see you—perfect just the way you are."

It's everything Emily needs to hear.

And everything she can't bear to.

Because she thought she had found the perfect man. She thought he'd finally come back to her, finally chosen her. For a fleeting moment in the dark she'd felt as if maybe—just maybe—she was enough.

More than enough.

Everything.

Between the cameras, her parents, and the crew, too many eyes are on her—too many, and yet not enough. All she wants to see is one set of deep blue ones.

He'll be here, she thinks, distantly aware of her mom pressing a palm to her forehead and claiming, "She's burning up."

He'll be here.

A cold towel pats her cheeks. Manicured fingers thread through her hair, gently massaging her scalp. She sinks into her mother's arms.

He'll be here, she repeats like a lifeline. *He'll be here.*

A knock eventually sounds.

The world returns to sharp focus.

Emily lunges out of her mother's embrace and sprints past Nina for the door. Cooper is there with a tropical bouquet, his broad chest taking up the entire frame. She throws herself into his arms to get a view over his shoulder. Trish stands behind him with a headset—Trish, a cameraman, and that's it.

No Jake.

Because he's gone.

He's really gone.

"Down, girl," Cooper jokes.

Emily drops to the floor with a *thud*. The second he sees her face, his grin fades. He steps closer. Before he can ask, she bends at the waist and vomits all over his shoes.

CHAPTER TWENTY-SIX

A DARK SLIVER of green breaks up an infinite blue horizon. Land. The airport.

"Finally," Jake mutters and grabs his phone from his pocket. He stares at the upper right corner of the screen.

Come on.

Come on.

Two bars appear. Then three.

Bingo!

He pulls up Sam's flight information. It lands in thirty-seven minutes. Between disembarking and security, it'll be close. He can't leave it to chance. So he tries to find her number in his contacts, then remembers in a moment of perfect epiphany that he blocked it a few weeks ago after she'd sent him those texts.

Shit.

It takes him two minutes to figure out how to undo that setting, and then he sends her six texts in a row. Desperate? Yes. Sufficient? He's not sure. But before he can send a seventh, he closes out of the chat and forces himself to calm down.

A red bubble catches his eye.

Fifteen missed voicemails.

Fifteen missed voicemails in the last two minutes? It's not possible. He opens the app and his heart immediately wrenches sideways.

Sam.

Sam.

Sam.

Sam.

Every missed call is from her number, starting the day after they arrived in London and ending twenty-four hours ago, probably right before she took off from New York. A sinking feeling drips like awful honey through his insides. The weight settles deep in his stomach as he presses play and lifts the phone to his ear. Even the fresh ocean breeze whipping his hair isn't enough to wipe the sudden nausea away. Her voice slices through him like a knife.

"Jake. It's Sam. I need to talk to Emily. No, this isn't some gossipy thing. It's important. Like really, really important. I promised her a long time ago I would never tell you why, so just trust me, okay? I need to talk to her. Bye."

"Hey, asshole. Let me talk to my sister."

"Please, I'm serious. This is important. True answer. Real answer. Real deal? Ugh. Real, whatever the fuck you two used to say to each other. Just listen to me."

"Call me, Jake. CALL ME."

"Are you fucking kidding me? I'm telling you this is important, Jake. And urgent. I need to talk to Emily, and I know she'll want to keep it private. Please don't make me go to the network. Just give her your goddamn phone."

"Look, it's a medical issue, okay? That's all you're getting out of me. But now, maybe, you understand why it might be important. I need to talk to her."

"Did you block me? You fucking blocked me, didn't you. Ugh. I could kill you. KILL YOU. Dammit, Jake. Check your voicemails. Please, please check your voicemails."

"WHAT THE HELL KIND OF SHOW IS THIS? I called the network, Jake. I spoke to someone named Trish. They said they would pass the message on, but I didn't believe one fucking word that bitch said to me. Emily would have called me if they told her. She'd know I'm freaking out. I don't know why I'm still calling you, except I don't know what else to do."

"I know what to do. I'm going to sue. That'll change their minds real quick. I'm going to sue Trish. I'm going to sue the show. I'm going to sue you. That's right. I'm going to sue the whole fucking network if I have to. Denying medical treatment has to be illegal. It has to be. My old roommate is a lawyer. I'm calling her. Did you hear that, Jake? I'M CALLING HER! Tell that to your bosses."

"Apparently, it's not illegal depending on the contract Emily signed, but it's FUCKING DIRTY. I hate you. I really, really do. Pick up your GODDAMN PHONE!"

"I haven't told my parents. Em left me in charge of her affairs and she wouldn't want them to worry, but I'm this close to airing out all your dirty laundry, Jake. THIS CLOSE."

"Okay, going to the parents was a low blow. But don't think I was doing you any favors. Em's story is hers to tell. And much as it pains me not to shove your complete idiocy in your face, I've been quiet for seven years so I can stay quiet for seven more days. Oh, by the way, I confirmed my plane tickets. Your show doesn't know the shitstorm headed its way."

"I'm drunk. And scared. And I need my sister. And—fuck. Am I crying? Shit. Forget this happened. Who am I kidding? You're not listening anyway."

"Fuck you, Jake. FUCK YOUUUUUUU."

"My flight leaves in about an hour, so I wanted to give you one last chance to help me get through to Emily. She needs you right now, Jake. She needed you then, too, she was just too stubborn to admit it. And—god, I want to tell you what's going on. You'll drop everything. I know you. I hate you for what you did to her, but I know you. If you knew the truth, Jake. If you only knew…"

He waits, and waits, and waits for the silence to fill.

The phone beeps.

The message ends.

His hand falls to his lap and his phone slips from his fingers. It drops to the deck of the boat with a *thunk*. He stares ahead, unseeing. When he heard Nick mention a doctor's office, he knew it could be bad, but this? This panic from Sam —cool, collected Sam? Those messages? The urgency in her voice? The fear?

He's gutted.

Completely gutted, as if the past five minutes have physically reached inside his chest and ripped everything out, leaving a trail of blood and gore and debris across the Indian Ocean.

He can't lose Emily again.

He can't.

And if he has to defy God himself, then that's exactly what he'll do.

The second the boat stops, Jake is on his feet. He runs. Down the dock. Along the walkway. Through the terminal until he's forced to stop in the logjam at security. He updates his phone incessantly, waiting for the confirmation that Sam's flight has landed. The second the flight status changes, he calls her.

Straight to voicemail.

Again and again and again.

Then he's running, and calling, and running, and calling, darting through crowds, jumping over suitcases, nearly knocking people over as the door to her gate looms. By the time he gets there, passengers are already unloading.

"Sam!" he calls. "Sam!"

A security guard grabs him by the arm when he tries to run onto the jet bridge.

"Sam!" he shouts again, his voice turning hoarse. "Sam! Sam! Sam!"

An auburn head pops up in line. She finds his eyes, her expression equal parts annoyed and relieved. He's bowled over by how much she looks like Em. The terror he's been keeping at bay crashes over him, leaving him staggering as she makes her way to him. Jake grabs the wall to keep from falling over. He feels as if he's been hit by a truck. He probably looks it too, sweaty and disheveled from his race across the airport. The fact that Sam doesn't even comment as she stops in front of him is a reminder of how gravely serious the situation is. He's never known her not to take the bait.

"What's going on?" he pants.

"It's about fucking time," she sneers and grabs his arm to lead him to a quiet corner away from the gate where no one will overhear. "How much do you know?"

"Nothing," he snaps. "Not a goddamn thing. I told Em I loved her last night. We slept together, and it was the best fucking night of my life. Then I went to my boss first thing this morning to quit the show. I overheard them talking about some call from a doctor's office, then I got all your voicemails, and—" He inhales sharply. "What the hell is going on, Sam? What's wrong with Em? Is she okay? Will she be okay?"

"I hope so." The vulnerability in her response does little to calm his alarm. Sam squints up at him, disbelief ripe in her familiar golden eyes. "She really didn't tell you?"

He shakes his head. "Tell me what?"

"God, I could kill her." Sam groans, then sharpens her gaze on him. "I could kill you. I could just strangle the both of you right now!"

"Sam—"

"I can't tell you, Jake."

"Why not?"

"I can't."

"Come on. You owe me."

"What?" She gapes at him, but he stands firm.

"You. Owe. Me."

"I OWE YOU?"

"Christmas, seven years ago, when you stopped me from leaving that letter outside your house. You lied. Emily didn't know I was there. She didn't tell you to send me away. And if you had let me leave that letter, if you had left it alone, maybe she never would have—maybe we never would have—maybe—"

"You have *no* idea what we were going through. Jake. No idea."

"Then tell me."

"I CAN'T!" she shouts, then takes a deep breath before turning a fierce eye on him. "I promised her I wouldn't. I *promised.* And she's my sister. She's my best friend. My loyalty belongs to her. It always has."

"Then where does that leave us?"

"Well." She shrugs. "I flew nineteen hours to get here, so I'm going to go find my sister, with or without you."

"I was kicked out of the hotel."

She snorts. "Without you, then."

"They're planning to ambush you." He steps in her path to stop her. "Trish, Nina, the crew. They know you'll go in guns blazing, ready to burn the place down. The cameras will be waiting. They want a scene. They thrive off the drama. Don't give it to them."

She pushes past him with a sneer.

"They'll air it," he says.

Sam stops cold.

"They'll air it," he repeats. "To millions of viewers. Don't think they won't. The juicier the reveal, the better. So whatever it is you won't tell me, if you want it to stay private, don't barge in there like a wrecking ball. The only thing you'll destroy is Emily."

"Well, what should I do, then?" she snaps.

Jake steps closer and lowers his voice. "Exactly what I tell you."

emily

"LET ME IN!"

The shout is the first thing in hours to penetrate Emily's stupor.

Sam.

She bolts up in bed, her head pounding, her throat gummy, more dried snot on her cheeks than she cares to admit. She has no idea how long it's been since Cooper left her room. All she remembers is the caring way he wrapped his arms around her and held her hair back as she puked, the cameras in their face, and Nina saying something about food poisoning. He tucked her in, kissed her cheek, then left. She hasn't moved since—until now.

"Sam!"

The name comes out as more of a croak than an actual word. Emily half falls off the bed and stumbles over her feet in her haste to get to the door.

A fist pounds on wood.

"Emily? Emily!" There's more knocking, followed by

unintelligible shouting. Then, "Get off me, you assholes! I want to see my sister. Emily! Em! Let me in!"

She reaches the door and wrenches it open. Sam breaks away from the security guard trying to restrain her and crushes Emily to her chest. For a moment, nothing exists outside those two familiar arms squeezing her half to death. She feels whole for the first time in six weeks, her other half since before birth finally returned. With a sob, Emily pulls her sister closer. Tears start to flow, a mix of elation and devastation, the highest high paired with the lowest low. Sam is the only one in the world who will understand what she's going through right now, but Emily doesn't even know how to begin to explain that she made all the same mistakes all over again.

"Sam, I— He— I can't— I can't breathe—"

She hyperventilates. Her breath comes in wheezing bursts as she trembles against her sister's chest. Sam pulls back and grabs Emily by the cheeks to hold her gaze. Their golden eyes are the same, yet so different. Sam's ooze authority, giving off a commanding air Emily has never been able to master.

"Shh," her sister coos and wipes her tears. "Shh. I know. I *know*, and that's why I'm here."

The insinuation stops Emily cold. She searches Sam's face for a sign, unable to read her expression.

What does she know?

How could she possibly know?

Before Emily can ask, Sam steps to the side to reveal the camera at her back. She grabs Emily by the hand and pulls her deeper into the bungalow. Nina and Phil follow silently behind, moving like shadows in the dark. The blinking red light above the lens is the only indication that they're real. Sam guides her to the couch and they sink to the cushions together with their hands clutched, mirror images of one another.

"I've been trying to reach you for a month," Sam says, turning briefly to the side to glare toward the producer lurking in the background. "These assholes wouldn't connect my call, and then after a three-hour delay and a nineteen-hour flight, they had the audacity to try to lock me in my room until the morning. But this can't wait, Em."

Sam grips her shoulders and looks directly in Emily's eyes. A cold sense of dread washes through her, no longer related to Jake.

"What, Sam? What's going on?"

"You need to call Dr. Hughes."

Emily scrunches her brows. "Dr. Hughes? I don't—"

"Em." Sam cuts her off and digs her fingers into Emily's shoulders. "You need to call Dr. Hughes, now. He'll explain everything."

"I—"

"Here," Sam interrupts again, shoving a cell phone into Emily's empty hand. Emily stares dumbfoundedly at the device. She looks up at Nina, who nods encouragingly, then back to the phone, then to her sister, whose eyes have gone wide with unspoken meaning.

If they let Sam bring a phone, they want her to make this call, and they want her to do it on camera. There's only one problem.

Emily has no idea who the fuck Sam is talking about.

Dr. Hughes?

She stands and turns her back to the camera as she scrolls through the contacts, freezing the moment she finds a listing for *Doctor John Hughes.*

Her heart skips a beat.

For the first time in hours, it flickers with the barest glimmer of hope.

She only knows one John Hughes, and he sure as hell isn't a doctor. He's a director. Jake's favorite director. The very man who decided eight hours in detention was worth a perfect diamond earring.

Idiot, Emily thinks as she presses the button to dial. *You absolute idiot.*

"Hello?" His answer is urgent and quick, as if he's been sitting next to his phone for god only knows how long, desperately waiting for it to ring.

"Hello, Dr. Hughes," she murmurs, hardly even a whisper. "This is Emily Ann Peters. My sister, Sam, said you've been trying to reach me."

"Em." He exhales her name as though it's a prayer. "Thank *fuck* it's you. Don't say anything, okay? Let me do the talking for a minute. I'll explain everything."

"Okay," she mutters softly, then remembers the ruse. "Yes. My birthday is May 24th, 1998."

"Everything I predicted in my note happened," he starts.

Emily sucks in a breath. *Note?*

She cuts her gaze to Nina, who watches eagerly from the couch. A memory flashes of the producer standing by Emily's nightstand that morning, hugging her clipboard protectively to her chest as if hiding something.

That bitch.

She saw her crying and watched her be physically ill for hours, yet said nothing. All because of this, right here. This stupid moment with Sam, and the phone call they somehow knew her sister would demand. All for television drama, as if her real-life feelings meant nothing, as if she meant nothing.

"I told them about us," Jake continues, oblivious to the realization racking through her. "Then I quit the show. I made them agree to let you finish out the season, no harm to your brand, and they had me sign an NDA before escorting me to the airport. But before I left, something else happened. I heard them mention a phone call to a doctor's office, and something about Sam. They wouldn't tell me anything, so I cornered Sam in the airport, but then she wouldn't tell me anything, and... I'm scared, Em. I'm really fucking scared. Are you okay? I mean, are you..."

He releases a long, shaky breath.

Emily closes her eyes and pictures him on a chair, running his fingers roughly through his hair with his spine bent, oozing dejection and stress and fear, all for her.

Because he loves her.

And he didn't run.

And after seven years, he deserves to know the truth.

Except...

Emily glances at Nina again, then at Sam, then at the camera. They're not alone. Far from it. Millions of people will be watching this scene in a few short weeks. Millions of people will hear everything she says. Millions of people will find out the truth.

Who cares?

The thought comes sudden and swift. Emily knits her

brow and swallows, surprised to realize the constant pit of worry in her gut is gone. Because the reason for the big secret was always Jake. *He* was the one she didn't want to find out. *He* was the one the truth would get back to if it got out. *He* was the one she was worried about.

And now she's not.

Because she's everything.

Every. Fucking. Thing.

And for the first time, she truly believes it.

"I—"

"Shh," he cuts her off. "Don't say anything. Sorry, I didn't mean— I wasn't— This isn't about me right now, Em. It's about you, and the secret that is entirely your right to keep. Don't give Nina the satisfaction, or Trish, or any of those assholes. That's not why Sam and I planned this. Tomorrow, you have your final date with Ethan, and then the day after that are the proposals, and then you're done. You'll get an extra week at the resort as a customary gift, but once filming wraps, they won't monitor you anymore. You'll get your phone. You'll get access to the real world. It's just two more days. I convinced Sam it was okay to wait, to give you the time you need, but only on one condition. I'm supposed to tell you that Dr. Laghari called, and you need to call her back as soon as you can. And yes, it's taking all of my willpower not to Google search that name right now, but no, I won't. I'll wait until you're ready to tell me, if you're ready to tell me. Dear god, I hope you'll tell me."

He groans softly into the phone.

She can easily picture the grimace distorting his

handsome features. Guilt pinches her chest, dwarfed only by the wave of fear the sound of that name unleashed.

Dr. Laghari.

Emily curls her fingers into a fist to stop their trembling. Her hand moves unbidden to her stomach and hovers over those three little scars puckering her skin. Her pulse pounds. She finds Sam's eyes again, but this time, she can read her sister's expression perfectly. Dark and draining memories flash as a plug closes her throat, like a hand around her neck.

She forces herself to breathe.

To calm down.

To take a moment before jumping to the worst possible conclusions.

"Thank you, Dr. Hughes," she mutters.

"I booked a room at the airport hotel for the next three days. I'm not going to leave this phone, okay, Em? Call me when filming is over. If you want to. If you can. If you— Dammit. I'm doing it again. Just..." He sighs heavily. "Know that I love you and I'll be waiting. Always."

The phone clicks.

Emily lowers it from her ear.

She turns.

The silence hangs there, full of anticipation. That red light blinks, capturing every quiet beat of her heart. Everyone waits for the storm to hit, for the explosion, for the cinematic reveal.

"I, uh, have a cavity."

It's the first excuse Emily thinks of—and it may as well be a nuclear bomb with the way the entire room bursts into action. Nina falls back against the cushion with a sneer. Phil snickers into the camera with a shake of his head. And Sam, with the dedication of only a true ride-or-die, leaps theatrically from the couch and clutches Emily's arms with a look of utter devastation.

"A cavity!" she cries. "Are you going to be okay? You fuckers!" She rounds on Nina and Phil, her pointed finger as threatening as a knife. "I told you assholes it was something serious! I told you, and you wouldn't listen. Do you hear that? A cavity? Do you know what happens if you don't treat a cavity? It spreads. And spreads. And spreads. She might need a root canal! Oh my god, what if she goes septic? If she dies—"

"Sam." Emily grabs her sister, trying her absolute best to keep it together. "It's okay. I'm fine. It's just a cavity—"

"Just a cavity? Just a cavity!" Sam whirls on Emily. It takes everything within her not to burst into laughter the second she sees the mischievous twinkle in her sister's eyes. "Did you listen to a word I said? Root canals! Sepsis!"

"I'm fine," she cuts in, silently adding, *Shut the hell up before I crack.*

Sam folds her lips into her mouth to hide her grin and stays quiet. Twin telepathy for the win.

"I'm fine," Emily repeats, this time looking over her sister's shoulder toward Nina. The producer's expression is probing. She's aware there's something she missed. "And I'm sorry about this. Sam had a...traumatic experience at the dentist when we were younger. She takes oral hygiene very seriously."

"As one should," Sam says indignantly. "Gum disease is a modern epidemic."

"Ignore her." Emily shoves Sam behind her back and pinches her arm emphatically. "We were ten," she continues.

"Her dentist appointment was the week after Halloween. She had five cavities." Emily pauses dramatically and leans in, lowering her voice. "She had to get a fake tooth."

Sam cries out. "I couldn't show my face in the cafeteria for a month!"

"Anyway." Emily releases a deep breath. "As you can see, my sister is dramatic and I'm absolutely fine. Sorry she got you all worked up over nothing."

"Are you sure you're okay?" Nina peers at Emily in a way that makes her squirm beneath the pressure. Sam was always the better liar.

"Positive."

"Then I guess we're done here." Nina relents. As if a switch is flipped, the scrutiny in her gaze disappears. She's the picture of ease, back to playing her friendly role. "We're just glad you're okay. Right, Phil?"

"Right."

He drops the camera from his shoulder.

The red light blinks off.

Emily's free.

"Come on," Nina says as she stands up. "It's late, and we start early tomorrow. We should all get some sleep. Phil can escort Samantha back to her—"

"Oh," Emily interrupts, keeping her tone neutral. "Does she have to go?"

Nina and Phil exchange a glance.

Emily jumps in quickly. "I haven't seen her in months, since she lives in New York while I'm full-time in Georgia. And after she flew all this way, it would mean so much if I could get a little more time with her. I promise, I'll save all the gossip for the cameras in the morning. The viewers will already know she barged into my room. Can't she stay here? Please?"

"Yeah," Sam adds and bats her eyelashes. "Pretty please?"

Nina looks between them. The moment extends as one second turns to two. She knows this request isn't as innocent as it seems, yet she almost looks intrigued. The producer's dark brown eyes fill with curiosity as she scans Sam up and down. Then she crosses the room and holds out her hand. "Phone."

Emily surrenders the cell phone.

Sam tenses behind her.

The second that phone leaves the room, any hope of calling Dr. Laghari goes with it—or so Sam thinks. But Emily has a plan.

As soon as the door closes, leaving them alone, she turns to her sister. "When is your flight home?"

Sam grins. "Sick of me already?"

"Answer the question."

"Tomorrow afternoon."

Emily scoffs, forgetting the situation for a moment to bask in the pure ridiculousness of flying nineteen hours to the most beautiful place in the world and staying for less time than the flight. Typical workaholic Samantha. But it's so perfect Emily could kiss her.

In fact, she does.

Emily pulls her sister close and smacks a big wet one on her cheek while a laugh spills from her lips.

"What?" Sam asks, confused. "I have an important meeting."

"I'm sure you do." Emily shakes her head. "Can you skip it?"

Sam narrows her eyes. "Why?"

"For a week in paradise."

"Huh?"

Emily grabs her sister's hand and pulls her in front of a mirror. A single face stares back. Auburn hair. Golden eyes. Heart-shaped bone structure. Cheeks covered in freckles. Perfectly identical. Two of the same. Shared since birth. The only difference at the moment is the wicked grin on one, and the sullen grimace on the other.

"Repeat after me," Emily says and Sam sighs. "My name is Emily Ann Peters, and you're not my perfect match."

CHAPTER TWENTY-EIGHT

THE PHONE RINGS and Jake practically flies out of the dinky hotel bed. "Hello? Em? Hello?"

"Mr. Moore? This is the front desk. There's a Miss Samantha Peters here asking for your room number. Do we have your permission to—"

"Yes," he interjects. "Let her up."

Three minutes later there's a knock on the door. Jake flings it open.

"Sam, what—"

He stops cold, tilts his head to the side, and grins.

"You're not Sam."

The topknot, pencil skirt, and makeup might have fooled his colleagues, but Jake knows Emily when he sees her. She's written in his soul. It's a visceral reaction, the way his body heats, his heart races, and his blood rushes to one very specific spot.

Yet instead of throwing herself into his arms, she does the

most Samantha thing imaginable. She puts both her palms to his chest and shoves as hard as she can.

He stumbles back, doubting for a second.

Until she shrieks, "You left a note?"

"Yes...?" He holds his hands up innocently.

She shoves him again. "A note!"

"What else was I supposed to leave? Nothing?"

"No," she snaps and gears up to shove him again, but he dances out of her reach. "You weren't supposed to leave at all!"

"Em."

"Don't *Em* me."

He finds refuge behind a chair and stares at her pointedly. "I had to leave."

"Why?"

"Because, this show is the opportunity of a lifetime for you, and I wasn't going to fuck up your dreams again. I didn't want to force your hand. I explained all this—in the note!"

"Jake."

She sighs. The golden fury in her eyes cools just enough for him to see the hurt and fear beneath it. Everything suddenly becomes clear.

His voice is hoarse when he softly murmurs, "You didn't get it, did you?"

"I think Nina took it."

"Dammit!" He scrubs his hands through his hair as guilt racks through him. "There was a note. I swear, there was a note, Em. I—"

"Shut up."

She takes his hand to silence him and steps closer. A

gentle scrape fills the quiet as she slides her palm over his unshaven cheek. Jake drops his forehead to hers and breathes her in while her nails rake over his scalp. A shiver spills down his spine, extending all the way to his toes.

"Listen to me, Jacob William Henry the Third, and listen good," she murmurs, her gaze boring into his. "The next time you spend the night in my room, you will not, under any circumstance, leave until I am awake. Understood?"

The edge of his lip tugs up. "So you're saying there's a next time?"

"Jake."

"Understood."

"Good."

He smirks. "You're sexy when you're demanding."

"I've been channeling my inner Samantha for too long." She rolls her eyes and steps back, then reaches up to release the tight cinch of her hair. Auburn waves cascade down her back and it's all he can do not to sink his hands into them, especially when she exhales a soft groan. "God, I've been waiting all day to do that. You have no idea how good it feels."

"I know how good it looks," he murmurs, not bothering to hide his arousal as she shakes out her hair and returns to herself. "How'd you and Sam manage to make the switch, anyway?"

"It was easy."

Jake frowns. Fooling their high school English teacher for an hour so Emily could sneak out of school early on her birthday had been easy. Fooling Nina Chen for five minutes, let alone an entire morning, was anything but. "Really?"

"Yeah." Emily shrugs. "After I hung up with you last night,

I told Nina that Dr. Hughes was my dentist and I had a cavity."

He snorts. *Genius.*

"Sam made a big splash, the way Sam does, and it must've left Nina feeling guilty or something, because when I asked if Sam could spend the night in my room, she said yes."

Nina Chen, guilty? Not a chance.

"So I used the time to catch Sam up on the show," Emily continues, unaware of the doubts spinning through his mind. "I warned her about today's date with Ethan, and then prepped her for the proposals tomorrow. When my parents arrived for filming this morning, I was dressed as Sam and Sam was dressed as me. None of the crew seemed to notice, especially once Ethan arrived. She was practically salivating to rip him a new asshole, and I think Nina could sense it because she hardly glanced my way. Come to think of it, I'm actually curious how their date is going. I mean, he's a jerk, but I think I pity anyone who has to face my sister when she's in rare form like that."

Emily trails off with soft laughter and shakes her head.

Everything becomes clear.

Nina wasn't fooled. Far from it. She just saw a better opportunity and took it. Sam's always been the bold one, the loud one, the one everyone is drawn to. She's the perfect leading lady for a show like *The Love Match*, which deals in absolutes, and Nina must've sensed it immediately. A finale with Sam at the helm will be inherently juicier than one led by Emily because Sam doesn't shy away from the drama. She thrives in it. Nina probably noticed the switch right away.

Hell, she might have even predicted it. To her, it was like a golden opportunity falling right into her lap.

But maybe Emily is right, too.

Jake surprises himself with the thought, yet it feels accurate when he thinks back to that final look Nina gave him and the hint of regret in her eyes. Maybe she did feel guilty. Maybe Nina Chen has a heart, after all. A teeny, tiny, barely beating, most-likely-stained-black heart, but a heart just the same. Because letting Sam stay meant letting Emily run here to him.

Jake opens his mouth to say as much, but at the same time, Emily inhales sharply and turns toward the nightstand on the other side of the room. Worry lines pull at her forehead, and his stomach sinks. The reality behind her urgency crashes back in. She's here for much more than a reunion with him—how much more, he has no idea, but even thinking it makes his blood run cold.

"Before we say anything else, I need to use your phone."

He nods, unable to find words.

Emily walks to the bed and lifts the handheld from the receiver. Jake stays frozen on the other side of the room. His heart comes to a halt as her elegant fingers gently tap in the number. The subsequent ring deafens in the quiet. At the gentle *click* of an answer, Emily's shoulders hitch.

He holds his breath.

"Hi, Dr. Laghari? This is Emily Peters. I'm sorry to call on your private line, but my sister said it was urgent so I didn't want to wait for the office to— Yes. Uh-huh. Uh-huh. That's no problem. I'll be back in the United States tomorrow. Yes. Okay. Thank you."

She hangs up.

Bows her back.

Drops her head into her hands.

Jake is there in an instant.

"It's okay," he says, even though he has no idea if that's true. But it has to be. And maybe if he says it enough times it will be. "I'm right here, Em. I'm right here and I'm not going anywhere." He runs his hands up and down her thighs, trying to soothe her as he fights not to fall apart. "It's okay. It's going to be okay."

"Jake."

She sucks in a sharp breath, lifts her head, and...

Smiles.

"I'm fine."

A laugh pours from her lips. Relief and joy and disbelief all blend into one as she takes his fingers and squeezes them with all her might.

"I'm fine," she repeats while her eyes well with tears. She brings his hands to her lips and kisses his knuckles softly, the look in her golden eyes enough to make all the panic rising within him melt away. "There was an issue at the lab. The blood sample I provided before filming got contaminated, so they need me to come in for another draw. Totally routine. They couldn't tell Sam over the phone because of HIPAA. I'm *fine*."

And god, he wants to believe it.

But in the back of his mind, he can't help but scream, *WHAT IS GOING ON?*

She says she's fine.

But blood tests and lab work don't sound fine.

The panic in Sam's voice on those messages didn't sound fine.

The look in Emily's eyes back on that first night and how hard she flinched at the mere mention of New York, that wasn't fine.

And he's not fine.

He won't be—he *can't* be—until he knows the truth.

"Em."

He hates how the light dims in her eyes. "I know, Jake—"

"Please, let me finish," he cuts in and shifts their hands until he's kneeling before her. Jake clasps her fingers, every word he's about to say as sacred as a prayer. "I love you, Em. Whatever is going on, whatever you haven't told me, nothing will change that. And I mean nothing. I've been in love with you since the moment I saw you in the hallway on that first day of school, and I loved you every second that we were apart. And no matter what happens, I'll keep on loving you as long as my fucked-up heart is beating. God knows I've made mistakes. I'll never forgive myself for leaving you the way I did, when you needed me most, and I need you to know that whatever you're about to say, I'll be here. I'm not going anywhere. I'm not leaving you ever again. I'm yours as long as you'll have me. And I'll prove it to you. I'll spend the rest of my life proving it to you if I have to, I—"

"Jake—"

"No, Em." He brings her fingers to his lips, holds her gaze, and breathes this promise into her skin. "I love you. Real answer."

She doesn't say anything.

She doesn't move a muscle.

She runs her gaze over his face, studying every angle as if searching for the truth. Or maybe she's simply memorizing this moment. Maybe she's holding on to these last few seconds of *before*, because he knows without her having to speak that whatever is coming, their lives will never be the same.

She finally swallows.

They lock eyes.

"A week after you left," Emily murmurs, the words dropping like bombs about to blow, "I was diagnosed with cancer."

Kaboom.

emily

THE COLOR DRAINS from Jake's face. His tan cheeks turn ashen and pale before Emily's eyes. He freezes, turning his gaze inward. The cogs in his brain spin visibly on overdrive as the past seven years and that fateful night play over and over in his mind. The wheels come off the track. But while he shuts down, Emily comes alive.

The words tumble out, one after another, like a flood unleashed. She's lost the will to care about the damage left behind.

Because it feels so good.

After seven years of running, seven years of hiding, seven years of worrying it might get out, she's finally free. The truth is staring them both in the face, and all Emily wants to do is meet it head-on.

"The morning after Dr. Copeland called to tell me I wasn't pregnant, I went back to her office for some follow-up tests. It was like any other visit to the gynecologist. She felt around, drew some blood. I didn't think much of it, until she called the next day to order a CT scan. By that point, I'd realized you left. You weren't answering your phone. You weren't responding to texts. Your mom called me in a panic wondering where you were. My dad offered to put a search out on your truck, but I knew where you'd gone. To LA. To film school. I knew it in my bones, same as I knew that Dr. Copeland ordering a CT was bad. I told Sam. She made me tell my parents. The four of us went to the hospital together. But I was alone when Dr. Copeland called to explain that the scan revealed evidence of a germ cell tumor in my left ovary. She said I was lucky. That they found it early. That these things often don't get caught until they reach more advanced stages. If not for the pregnancy tests picking up the increased level of HCG in my blood, it could have been another year or more before they found it. She offered to put us in touch with some specialists in Atlanta, but I needed to get out of Georgia. I wanted to go to New York. I wanted to get away from…you."

Emily pauses to swallow, overwhelmed by the rush of memories. They come in fragments. The stark white spot on the scan. The sound of Dr. Copeland's unnaturally calm voice. The terror rising in her chest. The tears. The screams. Eighteen days passed between Jake leaving in the middle of the night and Emily leaving in the bright light of day, but she remembers them only in flashes, time fluid, her sense of self lost. It was as if she floated in a void untethered from the world. If not for Sam, she might have drifted away entirely.

"My dad had to stay and work," she continues, "but my mom figured out coverage at the flower shop. She took Sam and me to New York. We convinced Sam to start school, but in between classes she came to every appointment she could. I postponed my acceptance to FIT and met with Dr. Laghari instead. She recommended surgery and a round of chemo, so I did both. My mom found me a small apartment to live in while I underwent treatment. She stayed while I recovered, letting her assistant run the shop. By December, I was in remission. A complete success, Dr. Laghari said. I'd have to be monitored for the rest of my life to make sure it didn't come back, but the odds were in my favor. I was thrilled. We all were. It was the good news we needed to get through the holidays. We all went home to celebrate Christmas with my dad, and I was set to return to New York in the new year to finally start school, to get my life back on track. And then…I heard them."

Emily closes her eyes.

Just like that, she's eighteen again, back in her childhood home. She was on the way to the freezer for ice cream when she heard voices coming from the back porch. She didn't mean to pry. She was about to leave, when—

"How are we going to tell the girls?"

She stepped closer.

She pressed her ear to the door.

"We're not," her father said firmly.

"We can't exactly sell the house in secret," her mother replied.

"So we tell them we've been wanting to downsize. We're getting older and it's too much upkeep. We're going to get a small apartment in town."

There was a pause.

"Will it be enough, you think?"

"To get through the next year, yes. And after that, we'll

find a way, Tina. After everything she's been through, we can't take FIT from her, too. And Sam is loving NYU. Do you hear her talk about that place? It's where she needs to be. It's where they both need to be. I'll sell a kidney before I force either of them to come home."

She backed away from the door with her heart in her throat. When she stepped into the living room, Sam was closing the front door with a scowl on her face. They made eye contact like two deer caught in the headlights. Emily didn't know what to say. Sam clearly didn't either. So they said nothing. They sank onto opposite ends of the couch without muttering a word because the second one of them broke, the other would have to do the same. A *Friends* rerun played in the background.

"Weren't you getting us ice cream?" Sam finally asked.

"Oh, right."

It was an unspoken vow of silence.

Emily returned to the kitchen just as her parents came back inside. They froze, clearly wondering what she'd heard. She smiled warmly and feigned ignorance, but inside she broke all over again. Right then and there she knew what she had to do.

"Between the medical bills, the apartment in New York, and tuition for Sam," she explains to Jake, blinking away the memory, "my parents had maxed out their savings. They couldn't pay for FIT without selling the house, and even then, it wouldn't have been enough. Sam would've dropped out of NYU if she heard. I know she would have, so I couldn't tell her. And I couldn't tell my parents. It would have destroyed them to know that I knew. But it was all my fault. So I did what I had to do. I went back to New York with Sam after break. And on what was supposed to be my first day of school, I sat in on a few of my classes, then walked to the admissions office and pulled my acceptance. I moved back to Georgia. I spent the spring working at the flower shop with my mom. I applied to a state school so I could live at home. And I tried to move on. From you. From New York. From cancer. From…everything. And I thought I had, I really did, until I woke up one morning to find my mother on national television airing me out to the whole world as the lonely shell of a person I'd become."

"Em—" Jake croaks, unable to quite find his voice. "Why didn't you— I mean, I would've—"

"I know." She brushes her thumb over his cheek, hating the glassy sheen in his eyes. "That's why I didn't tell you. That's why I didn't tell anyone back home. I made my sister and my parents swear to keep it within the family, because I knew the second it got out, it would get back to you and you'd drop everything. I couldn't live with that, Jake. I didn't want you to be stuck with me in Georgia when it was clear you wanted to be all the way across the country, living your dream."

"Em." He shakes his head. Raw pain pulls at his skin, twisting his features and tightening them. "You're the only thing I ever wanted, the only thing that mattered. And if I'd known— If I'd had any idea—"

"I know you think that, Jake—"

"I know it." He clutches her hands, and his eyes come into sharp focus as they zero in on her with an intensity she's never experienced. "You're the most important thing in my life."

She looks away, unable to stand it. "There's more you don't know."

"I don't care."

"You need to listen, Jake."

She swallows and sits back on the bed, needing a little space to breathe. So far, they've only dabbled in the past—in facts and flashbacks she's had time to accept. They haven't touched upon the fears that keep her up at night, the ones that leave her gasping for air, wondering what might be, or the doubts that make her feel hollow and wanting, as if she's missing some essential piece of herself. Sometimes she wonders if a bit of her soul still lives in those small organs Dr. Laghari cut out. Emily presses her fingers against the scars hiding beneath the fabric of her shirt. The ache is still as real as when she woke up from surgery, healed but no longer whole.

There's a reason she's been alone for seven years, and it's not just because of Jake. It's because every time she gets to this moment right here, panic swallows her voice. It's so much easier to run than to face it—to face the fact that she truly may not be enough. For a partner, yes. But really, for herself.

Jake puts his finger under her chin and gently lifts it until she meets his blue eyes, now warm as a summer's day. There's no worry or hesitation or doubt in his gaze, just love. "I'm listening."

"The surgery," she begins, but her throat closes up and she coughs to fight through it. He shifts his hand to the back of her neck to hold her steady, grounding her and giving her the strength she needs to say the rest. "It was a bilateral oophorectomy, which means they removed both my ovaries, the left one with the tumor but also the right one because they found evidence of precancerous cells. I was able to freeze nineteen eggs beforehand, and I still have my uterus, but—" Her voice hitches and she tries to cover it by licking her lips. He doesn't waver. He doesn't flinch. "But that's not a guarantee. Not all the eggs survive the thaw, and even fewer become embryos, and even then, the implantation might fail. Some women are able to get pregnant using IVF, and some aren't. I won't really know until I try. And if the cancer comes back, which is thankfully less and less likely with every passing year, I may need a hysterectomy. So basically, what I'm trying to say is, well... There's a chance I won't— A chance I won't be able to—"

Her voice fails her.

She finishes the sentence in silence.

There's a chance I won't be able to have kids.

A silent beat passes before a sob rips free of Emily's lips, pulled from somewhere deep inside—the place where she's been shoving all the unknowns for the past seven years, never speaking them aloud until now. In her heart, she's still eighteen years old, grappling with the whiplash of finding out she was pregnant and realizing for the first time how much she wanted to be a mother, only to have that future so viciously and thoroughly wiped away. She never knew how much she wanted to have children of her own until the moment she was told she might never have them. Nineteen frozen eggs aren't nothing. That's more than some people will ever have. And yet those nineteen tiny chances seem too impossibly fragile to withstand the burden of all her hopes and dreams, to bear the weight of them.

It's been easier not to think about it.

It's been easier to focus on work.

It's been easier to forget her personal life exists.

Or it was, until Jake.

In an instant, he's there. He sweeps Emily into his arms and wraps her up tight. She curls into his chest and clutches his shirt, unable to stop the tears from falling from her eyes. He kisses them away, each touch of his lips a silent promise that he's not going anywhere. And it's everything she's been missing for the past seven years. His strength. His conviction. His belief in her. He always had a way of making her feel stronger, more powerful, ready to take on the world.

"We'll figure it out," he whispers fiercely. His mouth moves over her skin, kissing every inch he can touch. Her forehead. Her eyebrow. Her nose. "No matter what happens, we'll figure it out, Em. Together. We'll do IVF. We'll adopt. Hell, we'll rescue some mangy little dog and treat her like our child, dress her up in clothes and shit. I don't care." He pulls back and grips her cheeks, searching her eyes for the faith, the belief, the hope they once held. "As long as we have each other, Em, nothing else matters."

"You say that, Jake, but sometimes I think about that week we spent planning our future, and I remember that look in your eyes. You wanted the baby. You wanted that life. I know you did. And I might not be able to give it to you."

"A life with *you* was what I wanted," he urges, not an ounce of hesitation in his response. "It's all I've ever wanted, and we've wasted enough time already. Seven years, Em. Seven fucking years we've wasted being scared. We were so afraid of what the other person might be giving up, we forgot what we'd be gaining. Each other. I don't want to spend another day of my life without you in it. Be with me. Now. Forever. Just be with me, Em. Please. I want to be the person by your side, through good and bad. I want to celebrate with you. I want to catch your tears. I want the boring days, and I want the extraordinary ones too. I want them all, Em. I want all of you...if you'll have me."

Every ounce of love and trust in her heart quivers on the precipice.

Emily peeks at Jake through her lashes as a shudder works through her. At first, the vulnerability in his gaze confuses her. She's too wrapped up in her own insecurities to hear the unspoken question at the end of his statement. But when it registers, every last bit of her fear drains away. In all her time spent aching to be chosen, she never realized it was all Jake wanted as well. He's been standing on the sideline for six weeks watching her Hollywood love story unfold with thirty other men. Of course he's unsure. Of course he doesn't know her answer. Because she hasn't told him he's everything.

Every. Fucking. Thing.

But she will.

"Jake," Emily murmurs, her voice going soft as she reaches up to grip the fingers cradling her cheeks. "You're the only person I want. You always have been, ever since the first moment I saw you in the hallway at school. I was walking with my sister, nervous to be one of the new girls, surrounded by strangers. I was happy to let Sam bask in the glory of everyone's attention while I hid behind her. Then I looked up, right into a bulbous black lens. You were looking at me. Somehow, I knew you were. And it was like, for the first time in my life, I felt seen—not as the other twin, but as myself. Then your friend muttered something and you dropped the camera with a scowl. The frown on your face was so adorable, I couldn't help but fall right there. I ducked my head as soon as I felt my blush and tried to cover it with a laugh. I was so sure my crush was obvious. But then you didn't talk to me for a week, until I went to your house to deliver those flowers. You remember?"

He nods and a hesitant smile passes over his lips.

Emily powers on. "I could barely speak standing so close to you. And I thought, *God, Em. Get it together.* But you *still* didn't talk to me. So finally, on the night of that football game after an extensive pep talk from Sam, I went up to you. I dropped so many hints, but you didn't seem to notice any of them. And then I asked you about filmmaking, and you asked me about my dreams, and there was this moment when you put your hand on my leg. Your palm was warm. Your fingers felt so large, so sturdy. And you looked at me—I mean, really looked at me, as if you could see exactly who I was even though we'd barely even met. You said, *You're going to do it.* And I believed you. I believed in myself because of you."

Emily pauses to shift on his lap, no longer cradled across his thighs but straddling them. Jake gazes up at her, adoration clear in his bright blue eyes. She hopes her feelings are just as obvious, painted in her gaze like a message only he can read.

"No one else has ever made me feel that way," she says as she gathers his hands in hers and holds them against her heart. "No one on the show. No one back home. No one but you. So if you're willing to face the unknown with me, the good and the bad of what the future might hold, and everything in between, of course I'll have you. I feel lucky to have you—so fucking lucky, Jake, you have no idea. I love you."

He grabs her by the shoulders and crushes their lips together as if he can no longer stand to wait. He kisses her, claims her, devours her in a way that leaves no room for doubt, no room for thought, just feeling. All her uncertainties disappear, burned away by the heat of his touch.

The future will come.

Whatever hardships it might hold, she's no longer afraid, because they have each other. Not due to destiny, or fate, or any other metaphysical ideal she believed in when they were kids. But due to choice. A choice they're making together. A choice they'll keep making, again and again and again, for as long as it takes. Because they're the only answer.

They're the *real* answer.

Sinking into his touch, Emily tumbles back over the cliff, back into the unknown, back into his arms, absolutely certain that this time, and forevermore, Jake will be there to catch her.

"This still doesn't earn you a diamond earring, Dr. Hughes," she teases when he eventually releases her lips to trail a path of kisses down the side of her neck.

Jake grabs her by the waist and rolls over on the bed with a growl. Emily yelps, the sound shifting to an infectious giggle as he guides her smoothly onto the cushions and settles his weight between her legs. She hooks her ankles behind his back to lock him in place, and he looks up with an easy smile on his lips.

"I'll take whatever piece of you I can get."

epilogue

EMILY CURLS her legs under her and snuggles into Jake's chest. They sink into the velvety yellow couch cushion, one of the few things in her apartment that hasn't been wrapped up in preparation for tomorrow. Takeout containers sit empty on a taped-up moving box with the words *Living Room Crap* hastily scrawled across the top, then in smaller, more elegant handwriting, *Glass vase, candles, ceramic shell bowl with filler.* Needless to say, Jake has been less than helpful cleaning out her apartment, but he makes up for it by being a very comfortable pillow.

She drops her head onto his shoulder.

He picks up the remote. "You ready for this?"

"To say goodbye to *The Love Match* for good?" she asks, then meets his questioning gaze with a grin. She's been ready since they left the Maldives three months ago. "Hell yes!"

He mirrors her expression and presses play. Dramatic music swells as everyone's favorite father figure, Keith Holson, walks onto an empty stage. His voice is low, almost hypnotizing as he promises what is sure to be the most shocking finale yet.

"What did Sam tell you before she left?"

"Nothing." Emily shrugs. "She just offered to make the swap one more time—said she felt like she needed to be there. And my apartment was still a complete disaster three days ago, so I figured the extra time to pack would be helpful."

Clips from the season fill the screen. Meeting the guys on the first night. Flying over LA in the helicopter with Ethan. Escaping on horseback into the English countryside with Cooper. Painting beside the water lilies of Giverny. Tasting wine at a vineyard on the outskirts of Rome. Making out with more men than she actually remembers making out with.

Whoops. Sorry, Dad!

Logically, she knows it all happened, but it feels as though it happened to someone else. It's a movie of her own life, a story made glittering and romantic by the haze of Hollywood glamor. None of it feels real, except for the parts that didn't make the screen—her first sight of Jake outside the window, their clandestine meeting in her bathroom, their escape to the crown jewels, their bungee jump, their conversation by the Trevi Fountain, their hands joined beneath the stars as she led him inside her bungalow. Those are the parts she holds tight to her heart, more important than any others because they led her back to the man by her side.

He kisses her temple, as if he can read her mind. "And Sam going there meant I got to come here and act the knight in shining armor to carry you off into the sunset, i.e. your new castle in LA."

"If by *castle*, you mean a two-bedroom apartment I hope we can still afford in six months, then yes."

"A two-bedroom apartment *is* a castle in LA."

"Why are we moving there again?"

"Because you love me," he teases, nipping at her ear. "And Emily Ann Designs is taking over the world, so you offered to house your soon-to-be-broke, out-of-work boyfriend to keep him off the street, especially since he found a lovely apartment in our price range with actual space for an office."

"Oh, see…" She turns to him. "I thought it was because your big indie movie was going to start filming in a month and if I didn't move to LA, I might never see you again."

"Hey," he says, all humor gone. "That will *never* happen."

She bops his nose with a soft smile. "I know."

"Look." He nudges his chin toward the TV. "Here comes Sam."

Emily watches her sister march confidently across the stage to sit on the couch opposite Keith. In truth, she has no idea why Sam offered to take the heat and attend the live finale in her stead, but she's not complaining. The thought of facing the thirty men she's broken up with has given her hives on no less than four different occasions. Besides, Sam lives for this stuff—the drama, the crushing of men's hearts, the attention. Really, her sister should have been the one to be chosen for the show in the first place, but hard as it is to admit, Emily will always be grateful her mother thought of the rhyme *Emily Ann needs a man* first.

Though I'll never say it out loud.

She laughs softly to herself. Jake gives her a questioning

look, but she shakes her head and absently watches the interview. Not even six months ago, she was sitting on this very couch, alone and afraid and in complete denial. Now, her dream business is thriving. Her love life is looking way up. And though her fear is still there, she's not letting it dictate her life anymore.

Emily flew straight to New York from the Maldives for that blood test. Thankfully, it came back normal. But instead of stuffing her health issues in that little box at the back of her mind the way she usually did, she also met with her fertility specialist while she was there. They discussed the status of her nineteen little eggs, next steps when she was ready, and the probabilities of success. Jake was by her side the entire time, holding her hand and helping her through it.

After New York, he went to LA and she returned to Georgia. Jake wanted to move home with her, but Emily wouldn't let him. There were too many people who would see them and know they were back together—news that would inevitably make its way to the gossip magazines while her season was airing. They'd made so many mistakes in the past. She wanted to do things right this time. Despite the distance, he's been there for her—calling, emailing, texting, his presence proving to be the steady, solid support she needs to face the future head-on, whatever it entails. He even helped her find a support group in LA for women facing similar fertility issues. Her first meeting is set for next week, hard as that is to believe.

After months of waiting, her cross-country move is almost here. In another hour and twenty-three minutes, the show will finally be over, which means her life with Jake can officially begin.

"I think she's enjoying this," he mutters as, on screen, backed by swaying palm trees and rolling ocean waves, Sam tells Ethan he's a self-centered asshole who should probably go to therapy to figure out why he derives so much pleasure from deceiving women on national television. Oh, and that, duh, he's not her perfect match and he isn't worth the earwax she picked on her Q-tip before meeting him for their date that morning.

Emily cringes at the visual. *Ew.*

Jake grins. "She's definitely enjoying this."

"She really is a better Emily than I am."

"No, she's just…"

"Sam," they say in unison as the crystal waters of the Maldives slowly fade to reveal Sam on the couch with a shit-eating grin and Ethan now seated beside her with a glare. Keith looks like a kid on Christmas morning as he dives in on the interview.

"So, Emily, Ethan went from being one of your final two choices to complete pond scum seemingly overnight. What changed for you when you arrived in the Maldives?"

"Nothing changed," Sam offers and shines a hundred-watt smile at Keith. Her entire demeanor shifts as she turns to face Ethan and wrinkles her nose derisively, as if he's not even worth the effort of a proper glare. "I just finally learned to see past his bullshit. Oh, sorry. Can I say *bullshit* live on national television? My bad. Let me put it this way. He's a liar and a con who got off on fooling me into believing I was in love. All he cared about was looking good on TV, so he could fool even more women into believing his massive ego is worth stroking. And between you and me—" She turns back to Keith and leans in conspiringly. "That's the only big thing about him."

"Hey, now," Ethan starts.

Keith cuts him off. "And what made you come to this realization?"

"It was the morning he met my family before our date," Sam answers. She widens her eyes and pouts her lips in a sad puppy-dog expression that manages to come off sympathetic yet somehow fierce. Emily knows it well. She spent her teenage years trying to copy it to no avail.

The viewers will eat it up the same way everyone else always has.

"I was sitting there next to my sister while he attempted to charm my parents," Sam continues. "And I had this thought. *I bet he can't even tell us apart.* It was the way his eyes kept sliding over us as he spoke with my father. The way he accidentally messed our names up more than once. I mean, yes, we're twins. But I'd expect my fiancé to be able to tell us apart, instead of staring blankly in our general direction and waiting for me to announce myself. And then he asked my mother about cookies, of all things. She's a horrible baker! Sorry, Mom. And I realized he didn't remember she's a florist. After all of our dates, and all of our conversations, he couldn't even remember this basic fact about my family. In his misogynistic mind, cookies and flowers may as well be the same. And everything clicked. He didn't want *me.* He wanted fame. He wanted fan adoration. He wanted followers. I could see the next three months of my life play out. I could see the two of us here on this stage, me heartbroken while he vied to become the next lead of the show. And I decided I wasn't going to be used by him any longer. Something I think a lot of the women in the audience tonight and watching at home can understand."

Uproarious applause drowns out the sound stage. Emily grins. She can practically see the dollar signs in Nina's and Trish's eyes from wherever they're watching off screen.

"Hey, did you ever hear from Nina?" she asks, turning from the interview to look at Jake.

He shakes his head. "Not since the note."

Emily nods, unsurprised. When they checked out of the airport hotel the morning after her swap with Sam, an anonymous note had been waiting at the front desk for Jake. It read *I'll miss your embarrassingly white ass cheeks, Jackson. It's been fun co-conspiring with you. Tell Emily I said good luck with her "cavity." Call me in six months when this is over. We'll grab a coffee. - Your favorite platypus*

Emily hasn't quite forgiven Nina for what she did in taking Jake's letter, but she doesn't quite blame her either. Hell, maybe she'll join them for that coffee in three months. Holding on to the past never got her anywhere. And besides, they both gained what they wanted in the end. Nina found the star she needed to close the season in Sam, and Emily reclaimed her happily ever after with Jake—no cameras allowed. Well, no cameras except for his, which sits a few feet away on a taped-up box, having already been retired after a long day of catching her mumble profanity while she struggled with the tape dispenser, kicked a roll of bubble wrap, and finally faced her junk drawer. Junk cabinet. Fine— junk closet!

Apparently, these were memories they were going to want to look back on fifty years from now, or so Jake claimed before a look from Emily finally convinced him to turn the dang thing off. Though, in hindsight, he was being rather cute.

Emily snuggles a little deeper into Jake's side as Ethan is led off screen in what might as well be a body bag with how thoroughly Sam has chewed him up and spit him back out.

"One down, one to go," Jake mutters.

The air in the studio shifts as Cooper walks onto the stage. The audience hushes. Sam perks up and licks her lips with an almost yearning twinkle in her eyes. It's an expression Emily has never seen on her sister's face before—soft, almost gooey, as the cowboy hovers on the other side of the stage. His eyes are fiercely focused on her. His expression is inscrutable. There's palpable tension in the air. Even through the television screen, Emily can sense the atmosphere thicken. Then—

The show cuts to a commercial break.

Emily groans.

"Did you..." Jake trails off.

Emily finishes his thought. "Pick up on the intense sexual vibes between Sam and Cooper?"

He nods.

So does she.

They watch the next fifteen minutes in complete silence as the show cuts to a ballgown-clad Sam waiting barefoot in the sand, surrounded by vibrant orchids and lush tropical vegetation, backed by turquoise surf, while Cooper marches toward her in a suit and a cowboy hat. They keep watching as he delivers his speech, then gets down on one knee to present a gleaming diamond ring. They keep watching as Sam stands there and stares at him, the moment extending almost impossibly long. And they keep watching as Sam, to the utter shock of no one in America aside from Emily and Jake, finally gasps *yes* to the complete hunk of man kneeling before her. Suddenly, her sister's decision to go to LA for the live show becomes perfectly clear.

"Did she...?" It's Emily's turn to trail off.

"Get engaged to Cooper on national television?" Jake completes the sentence. "Yes. Yes she did. FUCK!"

He turns off the TV.

It goes black.

Emily starts laughing.

"It's not funny," Jake growls.

That only makes her laugh harder. Soon, Emily is bent over at the waist, clutching her abs to keep them from aching. She sucks in a breath as she tries to stop giggling, but she can't.

Sam.

The man-eater.

Engaged.

"It's not funny," Jake repeats.

"It is," she forces out between laughs.

"No," he growls. "It's not."

"Why not?"

"Because if *that* Emily Ann is engaged, then you, the real Emily Ann, can't be."

"So?"

He glances at her pointedly.

Emily sobers in an instant. "Jake."

"Dammit." His hands thread through his hair as he starts pacing between the boxes scattered across her living room. "I had this whole plan," he says, to himself, to her, to Sam, all the way across the country yet still managing to be a pain in his ass. "The show was going to end. We were going to be free. And I was going to ask if you wanted to watch a movie, but I was really going to show you—"

He breaks off with a snarl.

Emily shifts forward on the couch. "Show me what?"

"Show you—" He stops to take a deep breath, as if suddenly noticing the annoyance in his tone. His expression shifts. The knot in his brow smooths. The tension in his jaw eases. The look in his eyes softens until their blue hue is as clear as a sapphire, sparkling with an inner light. He sighs. "Show you this."

Jake grabs the remote and crouches before her, putting one hand on her leg as he turns the television back on. This time, a photo of them fills the screen. Emily sits with a dollop of whipped cream on her nose while Jake eats it off with the most graceless man-bite ever. Both of them sport wide grins, all innocence and young love and laughter. She recognizes the picture immediately. It's from their second date. It's also the photo Jake posted to his social media to announce to everyone that she was his, so keep off.

"Jake," she whispers, unable to quite find her voice. "What is this?"

"Something I made seven years ago," he says, squeezing her leg. "I kept it on my computer all this time, because even though I ran, I never stopped loving you, Em. And I never stopped holding on to the hope that someday I'd be able to prove it to you. Even when we were apart, you were always with me. But now we're here. Together. And I don't want to waste another nanosecond of time. We've waited long enough."

He presses play.

Emily gasps as her memories flicker across the screen, clips he filmed of her, of them, photos they took together. It's a montage of the happiest ten months of her life. Her hand goes to her lips. Her heart leaps into her throat, pounding with a joy and anticipation unlike any she's ever known. He made this for her when they were two kids staring down an uncertain future, because he was ready to take on the world together.

And he sits before her now with the same promise.

Jake shifts onto one knee. He pulls something from his pocket. A crinkle breaks the silence as the scene fades to black and the words *Will you marry me?* fill the screen. Instead of presenting her with a velvet box, he holds a Ring Pop between his fingers. The sugary hot-pink diamond is completely ridiculous, yet perfect.

"I knew you would never trust me with the design of any piece of jewelry, let alone the one that will hopefully be on your finger for the rest of your life," he says with a grin. "So I thought this might be a good placeholder until an Emily Ann original could be whipped up. Whatever diamond you want. Whatever setting you want. I don't care how much it costs. I'll sell my body if I have to. If recent reviews are anything to go by, I'll make a killing—"

She punches him on the shoulder. "Jake."

"Em."

She arches her brow. "Jake."

"All right, all right." He takes her hand and brings it to his lips. The wry smile fades, replaced with something more uncertain as he swallows. This time when he speaks, his voice is tender and raw. All traces of humor are gone, making it clear the words come straight from his soul. "I spent a lot of time trying to think of the perfect things to say, but that wouldn't be us. That wouldn't be real. And this is, Em. This is the realest moment of my life. And when it comes down to it, I love you. Simple as that. I can't promise never to hurt you again, because I'm sure I'll make mistakes. But I *can* promise I will never leave. I *can* promise I will always fight for you. I *can* promise I will spend the rest of my life doing everything I can to deserve your love. There's nothing I want more than to be worthy of you, Emily Ann Peters, because you are the most incredible woman I've ever met in my life. You see the best in people. You've always seen the best in me. You're so strong, so driven, so passionate. You make me feel like I can do anything, be anything. And no matter what life brings, I can promise you this. I can promise you forever. Because that's how long I'll love you. So..."

He takes a deep breath.

Emily holds hers.

"What do you think? Will you marry me, and make me the happiest man in the—"

"Yes!"

She shrieks and flings herself into his arms. It's the quickest decision she's ever made in her life and the easiest one, too. Jake laughs and pulls her back long enough to slip the Ring Pop over her finger. It snags on her knuckle, but she doesn't care. She grabs him by the cheeks and pulls him in for a kiss, laughing against his lips as he crushes her to his chest. And when he eventually reaches for his camera, she lets him. Because he's right. Their story wasn't made for TV, but it *is* one to remember.

bonus scene

Sign up for Kay's New Release Newsletter to read an exclusive bonus scene between Emily and Jake!

The semi-smutty, super-swoony scene takes place six years after *The Love Rematch* ends. If you'd like to read this extra bit of the story, just visit the following link to sign up :)

https://www.kaymariebooks.com/my-newsletters

Thank you!

The Love Lie is a fake relationship, forced proximity romance telling Sam and Cooper's story! Think *The Unhoneymooners* by Christina Lauren meets *Reckless* by Elsie Silver.

about the author

Bestselling author Kaitlyn Davis writes young adult fantasy
novels under the name Kaitlyn Davis and contemporary
romance novels under the name Kay Marie.

While she's been writing ever since she picked up her first
crayon, she spends more time these days with her "mom" hat
on than her "writer" hat - and she wouldn't have it any other
way! But she does squeeze in as much writing (and reading!)
as she can. Storytelling is a vital part of who she is, and she
can't thank her readers enough for keeping this beautiful
dream of hers alive.

To learn more visit:
www.KayMarieBooks.com

Or follow Kay on social media:
Instagram: @KayMarieBooks
TikTok: @KayMarieBooks
Facebook.com/KayMarieBooks
Twitter.com/DavisKaitlyn

Printed in the USA
CPSIA information can be obtained
at www.ICGtesting.com
LVHW011137051023
758535LV00052B/830